Have you met Barbara Holloway?

KATE WILHELM

CLEAR AND CONVINCING PROOF

MIRA

ISBN 0-7783-2077-4

CLEAR AND CONVINCING PROOF

CLEAR AND CONVINCING PROOF

1

The afternoon that Erica Castle drove into Eugene, Oregon, she was elated, excited at the thought that she would sleep in her own house that night. Weeks earlier an attorney had called to inform her that she had inherited her grandmother's property; she had become a home owner. She had never met her grandmother, had never before been farther west than Indiana, but her mother had talked about the fine old mansion many times in the distant past, and now it was hers, Erica's.

She drove with care, admiring the well-kept houses, the neat lawns and lovely landscaping with flowers everywhere. After grimy industrial Cleveland, everything here looked fresh and scrubbed, sparkling clean. It was an affluent neighborhood, not superrich, but comfortable. No more dingy apartments, inner-city filth, just her own house in a nice neighborhood where flowers bloomed.

Driving slower and slower, she watched the house numbers, then came to a stop, backed up, pulled into a driveway and braked hard, aghast at the spectacle before her. The yard had gone to weeds, knee-high or higher, and a tangle of blackberry brambles was ten feet high. There was trash strewn in the driveway, beer bottles, an oil can, a broken chair... The two-story house had peeling paint and bare wood in places. There was a broken window held together with duct tape, a broken banister on the front porch.

She felt as if for weeks she had been floating, as buoyant as a dandelion seed in a breeze, only to have a giant hand reach out now and crush her back to earth. Moving with leaden legs she got out of her old station wagon and approached the front of the house, forced herself up the three steps to the porch, across it to the door.

It was worse on the inside. The smell was so bad that she gagged and took a step back, then hurried through a hallway to the rear of the house and opened a door. Trash was everywhere, more beer cans, wine bottles, liquor bottles, pizza boxes, junk furniture, piles of newspapers, a foam mat on the floor....

She didn't go upstairs and didn't linger inside the house longer than it took for a hurried glance. Junk. Nothing but junk. Then she stood on the back porch and regarded the rear of the property: more blackberries, more weeds, more trash. The brambles had nearly covered a small garage.

She fought tears and made her clenched fists relax. "All right," she said in a low voice. "So there's no free lunch."

The house could be cleaned up, painted, the yard cleaned and made neat. Then she would sell it. After cashing out her pension, she had eleven thousand dollars. If she had to use part of it to get the house ready for a sale, so be it.

The giant hand that had crushed her was rubbing her nose in the dirt, she thought grimly the following day, when the attorney informed her that there was also a property tax lien of eight thousand dollars. He put her in touch with a Realtor, Mrs. Maryhill, who walked through the house with Erica and pointed out what needed doing before putting the house on the market.

"See those water stains? Needs a roof. And probably the wiring needs an overhaul... Maybe there's dry rot in that bathroom. Hard to tell with so much mold... Three windows need replacing.... That water heater's twenty-five years old, has to be replaced.... All the oak flooring needs to be refinished. What a shame to let it go like that."

Then, on the rear porch, she said, "I'll tell you straight, Ms. Castle. You sell it as is, and maybe you can get fifty thousand, maybe not even that. And it might take months or even years. See, no Realtor is going to want to show it. Put in ten, twelve thousand, bring it up to par with the neighborhood and you can get $150 thousand to $185 for it. It's really a very nice old structure, solid, good wood, but gone to pot now. Depending on how it's finished, how it appears, maybe you'd get up to two hundred. But it's going to take a lot of work first."

Two weeks later Mrs. Maryhill dropped by again. "Just in the neighborhood," she said, looking all around. "My, my, you've been busy, haven't you? You're doing it all yourself?"

"So far. I thought I'd see how much I could manage before I yell for help."

The electricity was on; the kitchen and the downstairs bedroom were scrubbed and usable and just needed repainting; the odors in the house now were of Lysol and bleach, trisodium phosphate, ammonia and Pine Sol. Junk was high in the driveway, with more added daily. The heap looked like a rising volcano of obsidian; some of the trash bags even steamed in the sun.

To Erica's surprise the house she was unearthing was very nice, as Mrs. Maryhill had said earlier. The first floor had four spacious rooms and a small pantry; the upper apartment had four rooms; and the basement was dry with a good concrete floor.

"Eventually," the Realtor said, "you'll have to hire help. If you decide to take out a mortgage, hold off as long as possible. Get the house in the best shape you can before anyone comes to inspect it. Do you plan to get a job?"

"I hadn't given it any thought yet," Erica said. She suspected that Mrs. Maryhill had assessed her financial position quite accurately. No one did the kind of cleaning Erica had been doing if they had a tidy fortune stashed away.

"Well, consider it," Mrs. Maryhill said. "Banks like to think their clients can repay a loan. They're funny that way." She smiled widely. "And something else you might consider," she said, "is doing some volunteer work for the time being. A few hours a week, at least. You'd meet local people who may be willing to give references, you see. You know the rehab clinic over on Country Club Road? That would be a good place for you. Close enough to walk to, but more important, you'd meet a good clientele, some of the patients, doctors, therapists, the sort of people banks adore for references."

"The only thing I'm qualified to do is teach," Erica said. "Fifteen years of experience. But I suppose I could work in a kitchen, something like that."

Mrs. Maryhill shook her head. "No, no. You want to meet people. You have a lovely voice. Volunteer to read to the patients."

All afternoon and into the night Erica considered both suggestions. Regardless of her years of experience, she knew she would not be qualified to teach full-time here. For that she would need Oregon certification, which would take time, and possibly require some classes, and she had no intention of going that route. She was truly burned out, she admitted, but perhaps she could get a temporary certificate and sign up as a substitute. Most school districts had a number of substitutes who worked all hours, even full-time, but without the perks: no medical insurance, no pension, no paid holidays.

Besides, it would be temporary. As soon as she got a loan, and finished fixing up the house, she would sell it. She didn't want a house and a job; she wanted some money for the first time in her life. Sell it, take a long vacation, buy a new car... As she scrubbed away grime accumulated over many years, she came to appreciate the fine woodwork, the lovely cabinets, good cedar-lined closets, lead-glass-fronted bookcases in the living room. Two hundred thousand, she told herself. She could endure anything, even teaching fifth grade, for that kind of payback.

More to the point, she would need an income. First she had to spruce herself up, she decided, fingering her hair, lank and mousy brown. She was forty years old and felt fifty, and suspected she looked it. Start with the hair, she told herself; she could not volunteer for anything, much less apply for a teaching position looking like a charwoman.

The next week she put in her application with the school district and then drove to the Kelso-McIvey Rehabilitation Clinic, which turned out to be four blocks from her house. There was a large parking lot in front of the two-story building, a high hedge and a covered walk from a wide drive. A big van under the cover had a mechanism lowering a patient in a wheelchair.

Erica passed it and entered the building, which was not at all institutional. Baskets held potted plants and more plants in ceramic pots were on the reception desk. A teddy bear leaned against a pot with a basket of peppermints nearby. A pretty, blond young woman at the reception desk greeted her and, on hearing her name, said, "Mrs. Boardman will be free in a minute or two. She's expecting you. You want to sit over there and wait? I'll tell her you're here." She wore a name tag: Annie. She motioned toward a waiting room where a few other people were seated, and then smiled at the patient an attendant was wheeling in.

"Mrs. Daniels! How nice to see you. How's it going? You look wonderful!"

Erica was not kept waiting long. Annie beckoned her and led the way down a brightly lit corridor, chatting as she walked. "Boy, can they use volunteers here. Half the people you see working are volunteers, in fact."

"Well, I won't have a lot of free time," Erica said.

"Ten minutes makes a difference," Annie said. "Here we are."

She tapped on a door, opened it and moved aside for Erica to enter. A tall, lean woman rose from her desk as they entered. She looked to be sixty and was dressed in chinos and a T-shirt. Her hair was gray, straight and very short, almost too severe, but bright blue earrings and a matching necklace softened her appearance, and her smile was warm and friendly as she came around the desk to take Erica's hand.

"Ms. Castle, how do you do? I'm Naomi Boardman. Thanks, Annie. Will you be around for a bit?"

"Until four-thirty. I'll be at the front desk until

Bernie gets back from the dentist. That should be any minute now." She smiled at Erica and left.

Then, seated in two visitors' chairs, Naomi Boardman and Erica talked. It was not a real interview, Erica came to realize very fast. Things had already been decided. Naomi made it clear that they wanted her.

"When I brought it up with Darren—he's our head physical therapist—we agreed that it's a marvelous idea, to have someone read to the patients. They work so hard, harder than any of the staff, and they are exhausted by the end of the day. This would be relaxing, and even comforting, we believe."

The patients varied in age, she said, from young children to octogenarians, suffering the effects of bicycle accidents, strokes, congenital birth defects, fire, brain tumors—all kinds of trauma. Although most of them were outpatients, there was also a fifteen-bed hospital on the upper floor. Sometimes it was filled with a waiting list, other times not. At present, she said, they had eleven patients up there.

Feeling a growing disquietude, Erica asked, "But who would I be reading to? What age group? How many?"

"Well, we won't know that until you begin. Maybe four, maybe ten. All ages. And anything you would find suitable for your fifth grade classes would work fine." She smiled at Erica. "You'll have a lot of latitude. It won't be so much what you read, you see, as the fact that you will be reading to them. And you have such a nice voice."

It was arranged. She would begin on Wednesday, starting at five in the evening. Naomi hesitated over the hour. It was best for the patients because some of them were so fretful by then, restless and exhausted, but it might be hard for Erica. Not at all, Erica assured her. Then Naomi called Annie back and asked her to show Erica the facility. "Welcome to the Kelso-McIvey Rehabilitation Center," Naomi said.

"I've never heard anyone call it that," Annie confided, as she started the tour. "It's just the rehab clinic. Down that way are the therapy rooms. We won't go in while they're being used. This way to the garden. Darren thinks it's a good idea to get people out in the open as much as possible."

Erica saw little of the clinic that day, but later she came to appreciate the many ways the curse of institution had been obliterated. One wall held children's art, colorful, fanciful, honest. Another displayed whimsical figures from Disney or Dr. Suess. Dorothy with her steadfast companions on the yellow brick road. Superheroes. Christopher Robin and Pooh. There was a ceiling-to-floor wall of greeting cards: Valentine's Day, Christmas cards, birthday cards, thank-you cards. There were plants throughout, in baskets, brass planters, hanging from baskets, on wall brackets. The visitors' waiting room had a game table, large-screen television, current magazines, a jigsaw puzzle in progress on a table. She laughed later when she followed arrows from the children's ward to the upper lounge. The arrows began to go this way and that, a drunkard's walk trail, and then climbed a wall, ending abruptly. A splotch on the floor was the start of the arrows from there, more or less steady to the lounge. She learned that Naomi had been the decorator, and it all worked delightfully.

The offices were like offices everywhere with the usual furnishings, but when she viewed the therapy rooms later, she caught in her breath. Medieval torture chambers, she thought, mortify the flesh and save the soul. But here the plan was to save the body. Tables with straps dangling, holding curiously shaped brackets, cups, straps. A device that appeared to be designed to support body parts—legs, arms, torsos. Several treadmills, walkways with rails, one with a contraption that was like a rescue seat she had seen on television hauling a person from a sinking ship. A small swimming pool in a room so hot and humid it was like a steam bath. A mechanism there apparently could lift a patient and lower him or her into the water, then fish the patient out again.

On that first day, she caught glimpses only as she was escorted to the garden, screened on three sides by shrubbery. It was laid out in such a way, Annie explained, that each section of the path was a particular length, a quarter of a mile, a third of a mile, an eighth. The whole thing, if you covered every path, zigzagging around, would be two miles, with a waterfall at one end and steps going up to it on both sides. There was a koi pond up there, with a couple of benches, a nice place to relax and watch the fish.

Apparently it was simply decorative, but that was deceptive, she said; Darren knew that one of the hardest tasks some patients encountered was going up and down steps. Everything had been laid out by Darren, she said, and a landscape company had planted it and maintained it.

"For the most part, you can't see one path from any other one," Annie said. "There could be half a dozen patients out here, and they'd be invisible to one another. All Darren's doing."

She started down one of the paths. "This goes to the back gate, and across an alley from there is where Naomi and her husband live. He's the resident doctor here." She stopped and put her finger to her lips.

A woman's voice came from ahead, somewhere out of sight. "Darren, I *am* trying. I really am."

"I wasn't talking to you, Mrs. Daniels," a man said softly. "You know I wouldn't say something like that to you. I was talking to that lazy leg. It knows I'm speaking to it, and it's just plain lazy. Muscles can get like that, just lay back and pretend they don't have to do a thing. Hey, leg, you can't fool me. I'm on to you. Stop dragging that foot! You hear me, now hustle."

After a moment, he said, "See? It knows I'm on to it. Good job."

Annie touched Erica's arm and turned back toward the door. When they were out of range of the others, she said, "When she came here a couple months ago, she couldn't even move. Now she's up and walking. That's Darren's doing, too."

She sounded boastful, smug even, but when Erica glanced at her, she looked sad and averted her face. "On to the kitchen and lounge," she said briskly. "You'll like the lounge. It's like an old country house parlor."

She was wearing a diamond-studded wedding ring, her pantsuit was expensive, her nails manicured, her blond hair styled beautifully. Erica recalled what she had said, that she would be there until four-thirty. A volunteer? It seemed so. A wealthy volunteer, from all appearances. Mrs. Maryhill had been correct; Erica would meet the right sort of people here.

2

When Annie left, it was a few minutes past four-thirty, and she drove faster than usual, knowing there would be a traffic snarl at the entrance to Coburg Road and the bridge at this time of day. Normally the short trip would take no more than five to eight minutes, but because she was running late already, it took longer. She didn't know why that was, but it seemed to work out that way every time. It was ten minutes before five when she entered the waiting room of the surgical associates, waved to Leslie Tooey at the reception desk and took a chair in the waiting room. Leslie nodded and picked up her phone to tell Dr. McIvey that she had arrived.

That was a bad sign, Annie knew. It meant that he was not with a patient, possibly that he had been waiting for her. He hated to be kept waiting. He sometimes was ready to leave at a quarter to five, sometimes not until after six, or even later, but whenever it was, he wanted her to be there.

Leslie slid open the glass partition and said, "You can go on back now."

Annie forced a smile and walked through the waiting room to the door to the offices, paused for Leslie to release the lock, then walked to the office where her husband was waiting for her to drive him home.

He met her at the door. "I don't want to hear about the traffic," he said. "When will you get it through your head that it gets bad this time of day? Start earlier. Do I have to tie a note around your neck? And take off that stupid name tag."

He strode out as she fumbled with the name tag. She had forgotten she was still wearing it. They left by the rear door.

David McIvey was forty-seven, at the peak of his physical attractiveness. Tall, well-built, with abundant, wavy brown hair, brown eyes and regular features, he impressed strangers who often mistook him for a ski instructor, or a model, or a sportscaster— someone in the public eye. He was also at the peak of his profession—the most sought- after neurosurgeon in town, and the most successful.

"Why did you marry me?" she had demanded one night, two years earlier, the only time they had ever really quarreled. "You don't want a lover, a wife, a companion. What you want is an indentured servant."

"I will not be drawn into an adolescent, fruitless discussion of relationships," he had said, rising from the dinner table. "You have everything a woman could possibly want, and what I need in return is a peaceful, orderly home." He held up his hands; his fingers were long and shapely. "I confront death on a daily basis. That requires absolute concentration, certainty and order, and I cannot be distracted by disorder when I get home. I cannot tolerate absurd, childish outbursts of temper or foolish, female hysteria. Call me rigid, inflexible, unyielding, whatever you like, but you have to give me what I need, and that is simply peace and quiet when I get home."

"You don't even realize how it hurts when you treat me like a slave."

"You know where the box is that holds all the belongings you brought into this house. I won't try to hold you here, or restrain you in any way. You are free to take that box and leave whenever you want to, but if you stay, you will accept that my needs are to be met with whatever grace you can manage."

"And my needs?"

"You have no needs that involve me. We will not discuss this again. You know my schedule."

What had set off the argument that day was the fact that she had been held up at the rehab clinic, helping restrain a teenager who had had a violent reaction to a medication. David had not wanted to hear about it, and had become an ice-man with a coldness that had persisted throughout dinner.

A week after the argument, she had talked to a

lawyer, had shown him the prenuptial agreement she had blithely signed.

"You didn't consult an attorney before you signed it?" the lawyer asked in disgust. He waved away her answer. "Doesn't matter. You signed it and you were of age, and presumably in your right mind. You agreed that if you want out before ten years pass, you will take with you no more than you brought into the marriage. No settlement, no alimony, nothing. On the other hand, he can kick you out at any time if you fail your wifely duties, commit adultery, turn into a drunk or an addict…. Very generously, he agreed that if he's the one to end it, he'll give you severance pay, so to speak—three months' living expenses. Mrs. McIvey, why did you marry the guy?"

"I loved him," she said in a low voice. In a lower voice she added, "I believed he loved me."

It had been more than that, and less, she had come to realize. At twenty-two she had been thrilled to be noticed by the older, brilliant and very rich doctor. And she had been infatuated, blind and deaf to the advice of her parents, Naomi, a few friends. David had been devastated by the divorce his first wife had instituted; she had cleaned him out, he had admitted. His child support payments were astronomical, with access to his two children severely limited. He desperately wanted a decent home life, a companion, a wife. Two months after they met, he and Annie were married.

The lawyer gave her some advice that day. Start a journal, write down the schedule you have to maintain and what happens if you are late. Keep a record of what you do every day for a few weeks, and after that, note any changes. Keep your journal in a safe deposit box, or under lock and key at home.

She listened and later followed his advice, but she didn't get a safe deposit box. It was impossible to imagine David reading her private journal; he neither knew nor cared what she did as long as he was not thrown off his schedule. He wanted his breakfast to be ready at six-thirty, and then to be driven to the office. He could drive but he didn't like to; she had become his chauffeur. She returned to the surgical offices at twelve-thirty to take him home for lunch—which she prepared—and then was back to get him at four-forty-five. What she did the rest of the day he never asked.

But the attraction of a never-ending vacation soon palled. They lived in a condo complex, where it appeared that the other women were professionals who worked, or had small children, or were a good deal older than she and played bridge. David's schedule precluded day-long shopping with lunch outings. She could not take a run up to Portland for the opening of a museum show or art gallery. She could not spend all afternoon playing bridge, which she didn't know how to play to begin with. Invitations from other women in the complex dwindled to nothing within a year. Since a housekeeper-cook came every afternoon to clean and prepare dinner for seven-thirty, she didn't change sheets, dust books, scrub a bathroom, learn new cooking skills. Even Saturdays were rigidly scheduled, at least the mornings were. David jogged on Saturday morning; she took him to the Amazon Trail at eight-thirty and picked him up again exactly one and a half hours later.

They seldom entertained or accepted invitations, although they did go to an occasional concert or play, and once or twice a month they had dinner with his mother.

He could be tender, and even passionate, she also wrote in the journal. His passion during sex had excited her to an extreme. It was the passion and abandon of stories, of dreams, and she thought that was why she had been determined at first to make it work. She had felt certain that that passionate *other* would come to the surface all the time, that he would unfreeze, relax, that his rigidity was caused by fear that she would desert him the way he said Lorraine, his ex-wife, had done. After the second year she had abandoned that hope. Not Jekyll and Hyde, but rather Don Juan in bed and Cotton Mather out of bed. Medicine was his god, the operating room his church, the scalpel his scepter.

What she could do, she had decided, was spend time at the clinic, where she felt comfortable and relaxed, and where the only friends she had in Eugene could be found. In many ways being a volunteer was better than working full-time at a salary that barely paid subsistence wages. She had told Naomi years ago that she planned to work and save for a number of years, and then take time off, travel, see New York, Paris…. Working full-time, she had been able to save nothing.

Gradually she had come to realize that she was changing, not David. She was the indentured servant, she thought, a bonded servant whose reward would come after serving for a certain number of years.

She would be thirty-two when the ten years were up; she would still be young. Think of it as working and putting money aside to fulfill dreams later, or like being imprisoned for a crime you didn't commit, she told herself. You can endure anything for a limited time, if you know when the end will be. She endured and followed his schedule and rarely was late, and she counted the months ahead, the months already passed. She kept a faithful record of her days, which were blameless, virtuous, along with his deeds and words and her accommodation.

And when her servitude ended, she reminded herself now and then, she would make his first wife look like a piker.

3

Three afternoons a week Erica walked to the clinic to read to the patients. Her audience changed from week to week, sometimes from day to day, but those who attended were almost excessively grateful.

Since she arrived so late in the afternoon, she had reflected during the first week, her chances of meeting many people were limited. Accordingly, she began to get there by four-thirty, sometimes earlier. She had met Dr. Boardman, a tall craggy man, with prominent bones, big hands and a kindly, somewhat abstracted manner that suggested he was paying little attention to those around him. A mistake, she had come to realize. He and Naomi were parents to the clinic and he was looked on as a mentor, a guru or confessor, to whom people—staff, as well as patients—took their problems, whether personal or medical. She had met people in the offices, nurses, everyone in the kitchen, a number of volunteers. She saw Annie now and then, but never to talk to her. Although she was apparently there every day, Annie always left at just about the same time that Erica arrived.

Erica made it a point to stop by the reception desk to chat with Bernie Zuckerman often. Bernie was a stout woman, dimply and cheerful, in her forties. Bernie was always the first to know anything happening at the facility, and although she might have been able to keep secrets, it had not yet been demonstrated. Most people at the clinic visited with her habitually, and that was where Erica had met the ones she knew. But she had not met many of the therapists yet. They were usually gone by the time Erica finished reading.

That day, the first of August, Erica stopped at the kitchen, as she always did, to get a glass of ice water and chat a moment with Stephanie Waters. When Bernie introduced her as the cook, Stephanie had said indignantly, "I am not a cook. I am a nutritionist." She was fifty-plus, stately, with burnished copper-colored hair, a figure that was without a curve from shoulders to hips, and she was a dictator in the kitchen.

After leaving the kitchen, while passing a therapy room, Erica heard Darren's low voice from beyond the door that was ajar.

"See, it's like this. You already learned all this

stuff once, and your brain said, that's it, done. Then whap, the part of the brain that knows how you walk got zonked right out of business. We're going to teach some other part to take over its job. Most of your brain, everyone's brain, is just sitting there not doing a thing until there's some learning to do and then lights go on all over the place. Let's watch the video now. See that little fellow crawling around? He's decided it's time to get up and walk. That's hard-wired in, to get up and walk, only the brain doesn't know yet exactly how legs and feet work, or just where they are, or how to keep balance. Watch. There he goes…. Whoops. Wrong move."

Erica hardly dared to breathe, listening. Darren's voice was deep and low, not laughing, but amused and easy.

"Up again, try again… Whoops, down again. He's starting to get frustrated. Don't blame the little guy. That's hard work he's doing, and he keeps falling down. Whoops. Okay, he's making progress. He's learned not to let go of the chair, I see. That's good… Too bad, down but not out… Uh-oh. A temper tantrum. Back to crawling… And up again. He can't help it, he has to get up and learn to walk…."

Darren laughed, and after a brief pause a child laughed, too. "He's got quite a temper, doesn't he?" Darren said. "And a great throwing arm. Up again. What's happening is that his brain is learning all the things that don't work, and trying other things. Ah, he let go of the chair. One, two, three…and down he goes…."

Reluctantly Erica moved on. Bernie had said that Darren had magic in his hands; he knew exactly what the patients needed by feeling them. And magic in his voice, Erica thought, as she made her way to the broad staircase to the second-floor lounge, appreciating the many lessons Darren was giving that child: he was going to work hard; his brain could be reeducated; he had to learn to walk all over again; frustration and even a show of temper would be acceptable. And the most important lesson: he was going to walk again. Darren was a superb teacher, she decided.

In the Boardman residence that afternoon Naomi and Greg Boardman were having a drink with Thomas Kelso. Every week or so he dropped in for a chat, for a drink, just to poke his big nose in, he sometimes said. He was eighty-two, and his nose was indeed very large. It seemed that everything about him had become more and more shrunken except his nose. It was hard to imagine a more wrinkled face and he was stooped and inches shorter than he had been years ago. He had no hair left and wore a yachting cap indoors and out, year round.

He sipped wine and nodded. It was a good claret. "Joyce isn't going to make it," he said. "David will agree tomorrow to pull the plug. No point in his pretending otherwise."

David McIvey's mother had suffered a massive stroke a week before and had drifted in and out of a coma for several days, then she didn't come out of it.

"I'm so sorry, Thomas," Naomi said softly.

"There are worse ways to go," he said.

She suspected he was thinking of his wife, trapped in the ever worsening dementia of Alzheimer's.

"What's going to happen," Thomas said, "is that David's going to push to change our charter as soon as he has Joyce's shares. Next month, six weeks. He won't wait long."

"If we lose the nonprofit status," Greg said after a moment, "we'll lose the volunteers and there isn't enough money to pay new staff for the work they do. Christ, we don't pay the staff we have what they could earn anywhere else. They'll move on and we'll have to drop half our patients."

"I know all that," Thomas said with a scowl.

"I heard a rumor floating around when David and Lorraine divorced, that part of the settlement she accepted was his shares in the clinic," Greg said thoughtfully. "Anything to it?"

"Not just like that. The two kids got the shares with no voting rights until they reach majority. Until then David keeps control. Lorraine won't object to changing the charter. It's money in the bank for the kids," Thomas said bitterly.

Upon his mother's death, David would come into her shares of the clinic. Owning them, and with control of his children's shares, he would control fifty percent of the vote.

The sudden catastrophic stroke and imminent death of Joyce McIvey had shaken Thomas Kelso profoundly, in a way that his own wife's decline had not. He had seen that coming for several years. His grief and mourning had turned into dull acceptance, knowing that his wife was on the spiral that circled downward inexorably, with no hint of when it might end. He set down his glass and leaned forward in his chair. "Greg, I've made an appointment with Sid Blankenship for this coming Thursday. I want you there."

"Why?" Greg asked.

"I intend to change my will," Thomas said. "If you'll agree to it, I'm leaving you my shares of the clinic, and Donna's, too, if that's legal. As you well know, there's no money in it, just a lot of work and responsibility. We wrote our wills years ago, and I don't know if my power of attorney is sufficient to override the provisions in her will. The way it's set up now, her clinic shares will be divided among the kids when she dies. And if they inherit, those three kids will sell out in a minute to the highest bidder, which in this case would be David McIvey. I'll see him drawn and quartered before I'll let control of the clinic fall into David's hands."

"Amen," Greg said softly. "Amen."

After Thomas Kelso left, Greg returned to the clinic. Things to see to, he said vaguely, but Naomi suspected that he wanted time alone wandering about in the garden. She started to prepare dinner, thinking through the implications of Thomas's visit.

If Greg and David both controlled fifty percent of the clinic, it meant that David could not sell out to one of the health organizations, for one thing. And he could not change the charter from nonprofit to profit making. But only if Greg could hold out against him. That was the sticking point, she admitted to herself. Greg had started his practice as a general practitioner, working alone, keeping his own hours. Naomi had been his office manager, bookkeeper, factotum. Early in their marriage she had delivered two stillborn daughters. They had struggled with grief, then had found solace in hard work. She had scolded him: he spent too much time with patients, talked too much with them, and he had too many. A killer schedule, she had thought, but a necessary one at that time. Then things began to change: bureaucracy, Medicaid, Medicare, HMOs, insurance companies, malpractice insurance…. The day his insurance agent told him bluntly that the company would no longer insure doctors in private practice working alone, he had threatened to quit medicine altogether. His colleagues were joining groups, joining HMOs, forming corporations, becoming more and more involved with paperwork, not medicine, and he was in danger of losing his hospital privileges, he had railed. Medicine was becoming just another big business, and if he had wanted to go into business he would have gone after an MBA, not a medical degree.

Then, Thomas Kelso and William McIvey had interviewed him and offered him the resident physician's post, and her the job of personnel manager. Their salaries would be modest, not in the corporate six-figure category, Thomas had said, but the directors took no salary at all, and Greg and Naomi would not have anyone breathing down their necks or second-guessing their every decision.

Greg was the kind of doctor Robert Frost had had in mind. He let the patients talk, never rushed them, listened to whatever they wanted to talk about—medical problems, family problems, work or school, whatever. He explained everything to them. He might sit up half the night with a frightened child or hold the hand of an elderly patient who was suffering, until painkilling medication took effect.

What he seemed incapable of was dealing with mechanistic authoritarians, the law-and-order, rigid types who knew the rules and never strayed from them, and gave no quarter to anyone who did. Like David McIvey.

If David and Greg got into a conflict, and they would, Naomi was not at all certain Greg would hold his ground. She was not certain that he could hold his ground.

Years before, a patient of David's had told her how David had nearly gloated over her X rays, how he had described where he would cut, what he would do. "It was the most terrifying hour of my life," the woman had said. "I don't doubt that he's the brilliant surgeon people say he is, but he's a monster, too. I think he lives to cut people. That gives him pleasure, that and frightening his patients. He knew he was frightening me, and he kept on and on about it. Never a word of comfort. He's a monster."

David was as implacable and unyielding as a gla-
cier, moving steadily forward, crushing anything in
its path, oblivious. And David had made it clear that
the clinic could not survive as a family hobby in the
face of the modern business climate.

If Erica left the clinic promptly at six on those hot
days, she still had a couple of hours of daylight to
work on the outside of the house, which she had
started to paint. She had scraped and brushed flak-
ing paint off, had primed bare spots, and now she was
putting on the final coat. Later in the year, when the
season changed, she would concentrate on the inside,
she had decided, and try to get as much done outside
as possible now. In the mornings she worked on the
west side, out of the sun. In the evenings she moved
the ladder to the east side. Gradually the house was
getting painted. That evening she set up her ladder,
got her brush and paint and climbed up. It was a
two-story house with high eaves, a stretch from as
high on the ladder as she dared to go.

She had not yet hung the paint can on the ladder
when she felt the ladder starting to shift, to tilt. She
dropped the brush and grabbed a gutter for support.
It wouldn't hold her weight, she thought wildly, as
the ladder shifted again. It wouldn't hold her and she
didn't dare let go and start climbing back down.

Then she heard Darren's voice from below. She
recognized the voice instantly from listening to him
at the clinic; the same easy cadence, not laughing,
but not taking the situation very seriously either.

They had not met, but she had seen him with patients, with the interns, talking to Greg Boardman, and she had stopped to listen to him more than once. Looking down she saw his broad face grinning up at her.

"Drop the paint and hold on to the ladder," he said. "I'll keep it steady for you."

"The can's open," she said, hearing the words as inane. "You'll be splashed with paint."

His grin broadened. "Just drop it. Let it go."

She dropped the can and it splashed paint like a geyser. Then she climbed down the ladder as Darren held it steady.

At the bottom, on solid ground again, she looked at him in dismay. "Oh, Lord, I'm sorry! Thank you. I think you saved my life."

He was spattered from his shoes up, with paint on his jeans, his shirt, arms and hands, and some even on his face. He laughed. "Maybe just your neck. You set the ladder over a hole in the ground. Got a hose?"

She shook her head. "Come on around back. You can wash up a little bit at least. I'm Erica Castle."

"The book lady," he said. "I'd offer to shake hands, but it's probably not a good idea. Darren Halvord."

She led the way around the mountain of trash to the back porch, where he hesitated. "I'd better leave the shoes outside," he said. "I'll track up your floor."

He took off his running shoes, then followed her into the house, where she got out towels and a washcloth and pointed him toward the bathroom. "I could wash your clothes," she said, "but I don't have anything you could put on."

"They'll keep until I get home."

When he returned, with a clean face, hands and arms, she held out a glass of iced tea. "It's about all I have to offer. Or some pretty cheap wine."

"This is good," he said, taking the tea, then gazing about the kitchen. About five feet ten or eleven inches tall, he didn't give the impression of being large, but his arms were corded with muscles and his shoulders were very broad. She had thought his eyes were black, but now saw that they were dark blue, with pale lashes, pale eyebrows. His hair was straight, cut short, probably a dark blond, sunbleached. Laugh lines at his eyes looked as if they had been drawn with white ink on a russet background.

"How did you just happen to come by in the nick of time?" she asked, moving to the table to sit down. He sat opposite her and sipped the tea.

"I always come this way or a block or two over. My place is behind that mall on Coburg, four blocks from here. I didn't know you lived in this house. I thought it was vacant, going to ruin."

"Well, it was going to ruin, that's for sure. I inherited it from my grandmother."

She talked about the shape the house had been in when she arrived, about teaching in Cleveland, the trip out. He was easy to talk to, and, she realized, she had been starved for male company. That was a surprise; she had been so tired by bedtime day after day that her thoughts of men had been rare, easily ignored. The few times she thought of Ron, her former fiancé, she had felt only satisfaction of being done with him, done with that endless, go-nowhere engagement. After the first date or two, there had never been any excitement in that relationship. She had never felt the least bit threatened or exhilarated, but rather an unexamined acceptance of her role in his life, one of accommodation to his twice-a-week need for sex. They had been engaged for six years.

"After I start teaching in the fall," she said, "fixing up the house will go faster. I'll hire someone to help out, repair or replace the roof, do a number of things."

"Will you rent out the apartment? It is a separate apartment, isn't it? I noticed the outside stairs."

"It is. That's way down on my list of things to get to. I haven't even started on it yet."

"Can I have a look at the upstairs?" he asked then. "See, I have a three-room apartment over by the mall, and the traffic's getting worse and worse. I suspect that the owner of the building will sell out to a developer for a big box store or something in the coming year. I'll be house hunting then."

"It might be that long before I get things in shape upstairs." She started to say that her plan was to fix up the house and sell it as soon as possible, but she didn't.

"Let's have a look."

It was worse than the downstairs had been when

she'd first arrived. She had cleaned out the refrigerator and left the door open, but had done nothing
else. There were mats on the floor, rags and paper
bags, fast-food boxes, pizza boxes, bottles, broken
chairs and a wobbly table, and the whole place was
horribly dirty. She was ashamed, humiliated to think
that she owned it, more humiliated to think her
mother had lived like this for years, until her death
from a drug overdose.

Darren examined the apartment carefully, then
nodded. They went back down to her kitchen. "Let's
talk rent," he said.

"I told you, that's last on my list."

"Would $750 a month be okay? That's more than
I'm paying now, but it's a lot bigger, closer to work
and not being crowded by a mall."

She poured more tea, got out ice cubes and shook
her head. "Next year maybe."

"I thought we might make a deal," he said, accepting the freshened tea. He sat down again. "I could
start cleaning it up and do some of the other things
that need doing, like hauling away the trash, replacing the glass in those windows. In return I get a free
month's rent, and I get to park my truck in the garage.
And have my son with me some of the time. He's
eleven and part of the reason I need more space."

She stared at him, at a loss.

"I can furnish pretty good references," he said,
and then grinned.

"Oh boy, can you! I just hadn't considered even
trying to rent it yet, not for months and months."

"Okay, think about it and let me know." He drank more of the tea and put the glass down, then stood up. "See you at the clinic."

"No, wait. What am I thinking? Of course, it's a deal. It's just so…so unfair for you. To have to clean up that filth, I mean."

"My department. Don't even think of it. Eventually I'll want a key to the outside door. I'll probably get started over the weekend. You just stay off that ladder, okay? I'll get it painted along the way." He held out his hand. "Deal," he said. "We can get a rental agreement, whatever it takes, later."

They shook hands, and for the first time in her life she fully understood the old expression: to touch a live wire. She knew that he went out to the porch, that he put his shoes on, waved to her and walked out of sight, but she had become immobilized by that touch. Abruptly she sat down and looked at her hand, opened it, closed it hard, opened it.

"Oh, my God," she said under her breath.

4

"What it means," Greg Boardman told Naomi on Thursday night, "is that it's a legal tangle, a nightmare. When the court granted the power of attorney to Thomas, there was another document, a power of acceptance. Since Donna had a will, the court ruled that her intentions were perfectly clear, and the terms of the will had to be satisfied. Her shares will go to their kids when she dies. Thomas said that when they wrote their wills they were still trying to get the kids interested in the clinic, and had hopes that Lawrence, at least, would get involved. It seemed a good idea, I guess, to bequeath them shares. And now that old will is the determining factor in who will control the clinic."

Thomas Kelso's kids were middle-aged, and none

of them, as far as Naomi could tell, gave a damn about the clinic. Lawrence was a molecular biologist at Princeton; the twin daughters were both married to well-to-do businessmen in Los Angeles.

"I thought Thomas had the authority to vote her shares, even to sell them," she said.

"He does. But if he wanted to sell them, he would have to prove it was a real sale with a bona fide buyer. There would have to be an evaluation with a real market value, and then the proceeds of the sale would have to be used for her care, and when she dies, anything left over would go to the kids. He can't sell them to me for a buck." Very bitterly he added, "Thomas is beaten, and he knows it. He's plenty pissed."

"Not just Thomas," she said after a moment. Greg's craggy face was drawn and he looked tired. She knew he had not been sleeping well. His face always revealed his inner self: conflicts, concern, love, whatever emotion was uppermost was as visible to her as if written in script on his features. It was not only that he was close to his sixtieth birthday, she also knew, although that was a factor. Where he could go at his age was problematic. But he cared deeply about the work at the clinic. Everyone who went to work there and stayed cared deeply. Maybe that was a mistake, getting personally involved, caring so much. It was a disturbing thought. She pulled her attention back to what Greg was saying.

"He'll try to get the power of acceptance changed, but it will take time, and if the judge doesn't agree to the change, David McIvey will end up in charge."

* * *

More and more often during the past few years Thomas Kelso had found himself pondering the unanswerable questions that he should have put behind him as a youth. When did life begin and, more important these past months, when did it end? Joyce McIvey had been brain-dead for forty-eight hours when they disconnected her life support; her body had resisted death for another forty-eight hours. When did she die? Brain-dead? Heart-dead? Which was the final death? When? If there was a soul, when did it depart? At the funeral service for Joyce, sitting apart from the family, he had regarded them soberly: David with his pretty little wife on one side of him, his two children on the other, Lorraine, his first wife, at the end of the row. The two wives and the grandchildren had all wept for Joyce, but David had been like a statue among them, untouchable, unmovable, remote.

Thomas had heard the story of how David had signed the order to discontinue life support for his mother, and then had gone straight into surgery. Had his hand trembled, his vision blurred?

Thomas felt he could almost understand David, not entirely, but somewhat. His mother had had a good life and had lived to be eighty with no major health problems. She had been happy most of her life, and her end had been merciful. A fulfilled life. An enviable one. David was merely accepting of the fact of death, and perhaps even grateful that it had been merciful. He was a scientist, a doctor. He understood and accepted death in a way that a layperson could not.

But he should weep for his mother, Thomas added to himself. He should not order her death one minute and draw blood with his scalpel the next.

He did not go to the cemetery, or to David's house after the funeral. Instead, he went home, but his own house seemed oppressive, too silent, too empty. That afternoon the silence and emptiness were more like a vacuum than ever, like a low-pressure area where there was not enough air. The silence was that of holding one's breath, not simply the lack of sound.

He left the house and sat in his car for a minute or two, tracing the pattern of wear on the steering wheel cover. He had worn it down to nothing in spots. Realizing what he was doing, he stopped. The salesman had said nine out of ten Volvos ever sold were still on the road. Twenty years ago? Twenty-two? Now and then he thought he might trade it in on a new model, then he forgot until the next time he noticed that it was old. He shook himself and drove to the clinic.

He parked in Greg's driveway, walked the path to the alley, across it, and into the garden, where he made his way to the waterfall and sat on a bench in the shade, listening to the splashing water, watching the koi swim back and forth effortlessly. There, listening to the music of the water, he let his grief fill his eyes with tears. Grieving for his wife, for Joyce and William McIvey, grieving for the clinic. They had shared a vision, the four of them. Now he was the only one left, and the vision was fading.

He had not yet moved when he heard a girl's voice. "You bastard, you moved the chair farther away!"

"Maybe a little farther," Darren said. "And does your mama know you use such language?"

"Who the fuck do you think taught me?"

Darren laughed. "The deal still goes. You walk to the chair and earn a ride back."

Thomas could see them when they rounded a curve, Darren and a teenage black girl. Sweat was running down her face. She was using two canes, learning how to walk with a prosthetic, an artificial leg from the knee down. They rounded the curve and were heading out of sight again when she began to sway.

"I can't feel it! Darren, I'm falling!" Her voice rose in a wail.

"No, you're not. You're fine." He had his arm around her before she finished speaking, and for a time neither of them moved. "See, what happens is that something in your head wakes up and says, 'Hey, I don't have a foot down there,' and you feel like you're going to fall. What we have to do is convince that something in your head that it's okay, there's a working leg and foot, and it's yours, so get used to it. Ready? Just a few more steps now. Here we go."

Thomas watched them out of sight, then he realized his hands were clenched into tight fists, and he relaxed them and flexed his fingers.

"I'll fight you, David," he said under his breath. "I'll fight you every inch of the way."

* * *

Everything was muted at the clinic that afternoon. A few appointments had been canceled. Some of the therapists and nurses had taken time off for the funeral, and some of the volunteers had excused themselves. Greg and Naomi were gone for the day.

In desperation Bernie had called Erica. "If you can just sit at the reception desk for an hour or so, I'll help out in the kitchen. Stephanie's gone to the funeral."

Due to the reduced staff and cancellations, traffic was light that afternoon. The two interns working under Darren's supervision had their patients as usual, and Winnie Bok, the speech therapist, was on duty. A few others were there with their own flow of patients arriving, leaving. But Erica was not rushed, and she daydreamed that she had trained in physical therapy instead of education, that she now worked full-time here, consulting with Darren, joking with him in the lounge, walking home with him at the end of the day....

She chided herself for indulging in romantic schoolgirl fantasies, but they persisted. In fact, she seldom even saw him. He left the clinic every day before she finished reading, and he didn't walk; he rode a bicycle. She had not seen it the day he saved her life, but she had been too shaken to notice much of anything. Sometimes she could hear him in the upper apartment, and one time she had made dinner for two, only to find that he had already left by the time she went up the stairs to invite him to share it.

It would be different, she told herself, after he moved in. They would be neighbors, and how much closer could neighbors be, separated by a floor, a ceiling? He would drop in for a chat, for a cup of coffee; she would invite him to dinner; they would have long talks. They would find the key, or simply remove the lock on the upper door of the inside stairs.

Bernie returned a little before four-thirty. "They're back," she said. "Stephanie chased me out of the kitchen. She's in a temper."

"Why? What did you do?" Erica got up from the chair and moved aside as Bernie took her usual place.

"Me? Nothing. Stephanie said that Dr. McIvey plans to take over running the clinic. Believe me, if that happens, this place will clear out like the plague swept through."

"Why? What's wrong with him?"

Bernie looked past Erica and smiled. "Hi, Shawn. How's it going?"

A tall youth had entered with a woman, his mother probably, Erica thought. The boy was wearing a neck brace and had his arm in a sling.

"Okay," he said.

Bernie buzzed Tony Kranz and the boy started to walk toward the therapy rooms while his mother went to the waiting room. Tony met the boy halfway down the hall and they walked on together. Tony didn't look very much older than his patient. He was one of the interns who had come for his clinical practice, and to work under the direction of Darren

Halvord. The interns, Erica had learned, worked for peanuts, but they would have paid for the chance to work under Darren for a year or two. After this apprenticeship, they were considered to be prizes by other institutions.

Bernie did not have a chance to answer Erica's question. A couple of patients were arriving for their four-thirty appointments, and others were leaving, some of them stopping by the desk to arrange appointment times or just to chat a moment.

Erica picked up her purse and the book she was reading, *The Canterville Ghost,* and wandered off to the lounge. She had started coming every weekday to read and knew there would be other chances to quiz Bernie, or one of the kitchen aides, a nurse, someone. She had not met Dr. McIvey, had not even caught a glimpse of him, but every time she heard the name David McIvey, or most often, Dr. McIvey, it was with that same tone of dislike, distrust, whatever it was. Yet, Annie had married him, and apparently planned to stay with him. Curious, she thought. It was very curious.

A week later Thomas Kelso advised David that the bylaws of the corporation required a reorganization of the governing board of directors. They met in the directors' office at the clinic immediately after David left his surgical office.

The directors' office was a pleasant room with a leather-covered sofa, good upholstered chairs, a round table with straight chairs and windows that looked out on the garden. In the past, the four directors had sat in the easy chairs, or on the sofa, not at the table, but that day Thomas had left his briefcase, a legal pad, pencils, water glasses and a tape recorder on the table as if to signify that this was not the companionable get-together of old friends who seldom disagreed. He was already at the table, scanning notes he had made over the past day or two when David entered.

After their greeting, which Thomas likened to a meaningless tribal ritual, he got straight to the point. "Since we have no secretary present, I'll tape our meeting. We are required to keep a record of all meetings, you see." He turned on the tape recorder. "Now, our bylaws demand that we have four directors' positions filled at all times. After your father's death, Joyce assumed his function as vice president, along with her own duties as secretary, of course. Those two positions now have to be filled."

David watched him with narrowed eyes. He was tired. He had been in surgery for six hours that day, and he had seen patients in the office as well as in the hospital. He shook his head. "I don't know what Mother did exactly, but whatever it was, it ran her ragged. I don't have that kind of time, as you well know. I'm a working doctor. Hire someone to do whatever she was responsible for."

"I'm afraid we can't do that," Thomas said. "Have you read the bylaws, David?" When he shook his head again, Thomas said, "Well, you should. But I'll tell you now what's in them. We set this up as a nonprofit clinic, of course, and we agreed that the directors would receive no compensation for the work they did relating to it. We can hire people like Greg and Naomi to run it, therapists, nurses, other staff, but we, the shareholders, receive no pay. Only the shareholders can hold office, and, in fact, are required to hold office and fulfill the duties of the office or else relinquish their shares. In that event the relinquished shares shall be evenly divided among the other shareholders."

"That's insane," David said.

"Maybe so. But that's how we set it up, and for fifty-two years that's how it's worked." He pulled out a folder from his briefcase and handed it to David. "The bylaws and our mission statement, our charter," he said. "We kept it as simple as the law allowed. Why don't you look it over? It's short. Won't take you long."

When David started to read, Thomas got up and crossed the room to stand at the window gazing out at the garden. Chrysanthemums were beginning to bloom—bright red, yellow, bronze. End of summer, he thought, that's what chrysanthemums meant. Another season, another year winding down.

When he heard the papers slap down on the table, he turned to regard David, who was scowling fiercely. Thomas knew exactly what was in those bylaws. He and William McIvey had spent a great deal of time on them, and he had reviewed them all thoroughly during the past few days.

"What exactly was Mother responsible for?"

David asked in a tightly controlled voice. No emotion was visible on his handsome face, no anger, no disdain, no disbelief. Nothing.

"As vice president, she was in charge of fund-raising. We have three major campaigns annually, as you probably know. She wrote letters to contributors, donors, escorted them on tours of the facility, a garden tea party every June, an annual auction, things of that sort. As secretary she kept notes at all our meetings and put them in order for the annual audit, as required by law. It wasn't too onerous, but exacting. There are formulas, rules that must be followed."

"Annette could do those things," David said after a moment.

"Not unless she's a shareholder and is elected to office by a majority vote." Thomas returned to the table and sat down.

"David, there's no money in this clinic. In fact, for years we ploughed money back into it from our practices. We never intended to make money with the clinic, and we wrote those bylaws in such a way as to ensure that our mission would remain true to itself if one or more of us became incapacitated, or just wanted out."

"I could assign some of my shares to Annette, let her assume those duties that way. Another husband and wife team. You'd have no grounds to oppose that."

"You would have to give her the shares outright," Thomas said. "No strings attached. And she would have to abide by the bylaws just like everyone else. No, I would not oppose that." He sipped his water, then asked, "Why do you want to stay in, David? This is far removed from your field."

"Exactly," David said. "What I can see here is a surgical facility, neurosurgery, cardiovascular surgery. You have fifteen beds upstairs, and room for twenty more, room to expand, rooms to convert to surgery." He leaned forward, and for the first time ever, Thomas saw a flare of passion in his eyes, heard it in his voice. "Thomas, I'm the best neurosurgeon on the West Coast. We would have people come here from all over the world. A specialist's specialty, dedicated to those two areas. We could do it together, you and I."

Thomas realized how seriously he had misjudged the young surgeon. He had thought David wanted control in order to sell out to one of the health organizations, or to change to a for profit facility. This had not occurred to him, that David had his own compelling vision. Time was on David's side, he thought with a pang. At that moment David looked almost exactly the same as William McIvey had years ago, when he and Thomas first conceived of the idea of the rehabilitation clinic. They had been driven by the plight of their young patients ravaged by polio. After the vaccine came along, they had changed to a general rehabilitation clinic. But he remembered with startling clarity the fierce passion that had seized them both, remembered the determination William McIvey had demonstrated, the not-to-be-denied drive that had compelled them both. Now he was seeing that same determined look on David's face, in his eyes.

David was still talking. "Rehab can happen anywhere. It doesn't need a special clinic. You could rent space in a dozen different buildings tomorrow and be set to go. It's insignificant compared to what surgery demands. That's one thing. The other thing to consider is what you do here and what I propose. You see people in wheelchairs, people on crutches all the time. They don't get special care. They learn to manage without all the trimmings you give them. You tinker with them, a little bit better is good enough, but I go in and fix them. I cure them. That's the big difference."

When Erica finished reading that day she found a group of people in the staff lounge: Greg Boardman, Naomi, Annie, Darren, another therapist, Stephanie… Naomi motioned her in. "We're having a high tea," she said. "Of sorts. Crackers and cheese and punch, at least. Have some."

Her gaiety was forced, and Greg wasn't even pretending this was a party. Stephanie held out a glass to Erica and said, "Now I'm off and running. Feeding time upstairs."

She hurried out and a moment later David McIvey stood in the doorway. "Annette, let's go." He didn't wait for any response, didn't speak to anyone else, turned and left. With hardly a pause, Annie put down the glass she had lifted to her lips, picked up her purse and followed him without a word. Her cheeks flared with color, and she held her head unnaturally high.

Erica, facing Darren, was startled at the expression that crossed his face and vanished. Stricken, furious, but more, he had looked deeply hurt for that brief moment.

5

The week before Labor Day Darren moved into the apartment, and parked his truck in the newly cleared garage. His son, he said, would bring some things over during the Labor Day holiday.

"Usually we go camping or something when I have a couple of days off, but he's excited about having his own room. He wants to pick out the color and paint it himself, hang his posters, make it his room."

Erica straightened up from weeding a flagstone patio outside the kitchen door. Finding it had been another surprise, hidden as it had been under a layer of dirt, weeds and spreading grass. Sometimes she felt that a miracle had taken place: the house was in decent shape, and they were starting to tackle the job of taming the jungle in the yard. It was turning into a real home. She rubbed her back.

"You said he's eleven?" she asked.

"Twelve in February. He has a half brother, who is six, and a creep, according to Todd. They share a room. And there's a half sister, who is ten, and a spoiled brat, again according to Todd. He's looking forward to his own room, his junk left wherever he puts it down."

Erica laughed. "The mess on the floor will be his mess. That's different."

"Right. Anyway, we'll be in and out, around, all weekend." He took a step or two, then paused. "I heard that you asked Bernie to give a copy of the book you've been reading to Glory. That was good of you."

Feeling awkward and even a little embarrassed, Erica said, "Just a cheap paperback, used. Glory mentioned that she would be leaving before we finished *The Canterville Ghost* and she'd never know how it came out. Sort of like following a serial for nine episodes and missing the tenth and final one."

"Yeah. And I bet no one in her house has ever owned a book before. Anyway, that was good of you. We're going to grill salmon tomorrow. Want to come?"

She caught her breath and nodded. "I'd love to. I can make a pretty good potato salad."

"Deal," he said, and moved on around to the side of the house and the stairs to the upper apartment.

Trembling, she returned to her weeding with renewed energy. She could finish before dark, tidy up for a cookout. Later she would make the potato salad; it was better if made a day ahead of time. Maybe a cake. She didn't know if the oven worked; she had not tried it. If it worked, she would bake a cake. She would have to go shopping for ingredients; she knew she had no chocolate, little butter. Cake pans? No matter, the stores were open late. Her thoughts raced, making plans, making a mental list of what to buy. Napkins. Paper plates. Ice cream. They were having a cookout, she, Darren, his child. They were having a cookout on the patio. She was too self-conscious to sing out loud, but under her breath she was singing.

Years before, as a new teacher, she had learned to make a long-range school-year plan, nothing too specific, then a more detailed monthly plan and, finally, a very detailed weekly plan. Year after year the plans had served her well. She laughed to herself when she realized she was still doing it. She was now planning to bake a cake although she had never baked a cake in her life. No matter. She would buy a mix. Even her fifth graders had been able to make cakes with mixes.

Greg and Thomas were in Sid Blankenship's office the Friday after the holiday. Sid was shorter than either of them, and rounder, fifty years old, with a pink face as smooth as an egg. He had gone to work for his father years ago, and when his father retired, he had inherited the office, furnishings and many of the clients, including Thomas Kelso, who to Sid's eyes looked to be a hundred years old or older.

They had just concluded the transfer of Thomas's shares to Greg, which left him out in the cold, Thomas thought morosely. But that was step one.

Sid had filed the petition for a change of the power of acceptance, and they had to wait for the court to get around to it. It was out of their hands, Sid told them.

Now Thomas leaned back in his chair and said, "I keep thinking that what I can't afford to do is wait around very long. David will have his own attorney go over the bylaws and search for loopholes, of course. Sid, are all court orders open to public scrutiny? Is the power of attorney I have open to scrutiny? Is the power of acceptance?"

He was not reassured by the guarded look that came over Sid's face as he considered the questions.

"One more," Thomas said. "Is there anything in the bylaws that would prevent us from forming a nonprofit foundation to ensure a succession of directors without altering our mission statement?"

Sid gazed into space with a thoughtful expression, then said, "Most people assume the power of attorney gives you absolute control, to vote, sell, dispose of, whatever. Likely, David McIvey has assumed that. But you're right, if an attorney goes digging, he'll find the documents. As for the foundation idea, I'd have to do a little research. It might require another petition to the court, but off the top of my head, I think it can be done. It would adhere to the original intent of the founders, but it would probably take a majority vote, Thomas, and you don't have it. Fifty-fifty. Remember? McIvey could simply say no, and that would be it."

"David can't handle the workload and has no intention of trying," Thomas said. "He'll turn a few shares over to his wife and hang the work around her neck. And the minute he does that he won't have fifty percent of the shares to vote."

Sid regarded him soberly for a moment, then said, "I may have limited experience in such matters, but it seems to me that wives generally go along with what their husbands demand unless they're engaged in a custody battle or a messy divorce."

Thomas looked at Greg. "You tell him about Annie."

"Well," Greg said, groping for a starting place, "she's pretty special to us, to Naomi and me, I mean. Almost like a daughter. I feel as if I know her pretty well. She grew up on a dairy farm over at Tillamook, then went to college in Monmouth and got out when she was still only twenty-one. She answered an ad in the newspaper for a job at the clinic. Very shy, a little afraid of Eugene, the biggest city she ever lived in, pretty… She was so innocent, not like most kids her age. Anyway, we gave her the job and let her stay in the guest room at the residence for a couple of months. She loves the clinic, the patients, what we do there. After she got married, she began coming as a volunteer. She's there most days for several hours. I don't think she'd want the clinic to be turned into a surgical center for wealthy clients."

Although Sid thought that was a naive view, one which did not answer the question of whether she would cross her husband, he did not voice this opinion. "Okay," he said. "Let me look into the foundation idea. I think it's a good one if you can get the majority vote for it. And I think the court would agree. The law approves of an orderly succession of directors, maintaining the status quo. Let me get back to you in a week or two. McIvey isn't going to do anything until he consults his own attorney. Then you'll have to have another board meeting to elect Annie McIvey to office. Say she's in by mid-October. You'll have to allow another month for McIvey to consider your proposal before you can insist on a vote. Mid-November. Hang on, Thomas. Everything takes time. That's just the way it is." He put aside his usual caution then and added, "I think you've got him, Thomas. I think you've come up with the way out."

Erica sat in the clinic kitchen with Stephanie one afternoon sipping coffee while Stephanie kept an eye on her prep cooks and the two volunteers.

"So what's with this Dr. McIvey?" Erica asked. "Every time his name comes up it's as if a cold front has passed through."

"That's good," Stephanie said. "That's what it feels like, all right. I'll give you a couple of examples why he's loved by all. A few years ago, five or six maybe, this kid comes in with McIvey's referral for hydrotherapy. She was on the basketball team at the U of O and began having terrible leg pains. Diagnosis—stress fractures, shin splints. Hydrotherapy ordered. And if that didn't work, McIvey was going to operate on her back, a disk problem or something. Anyway, that isn't how it works here. Darren and Greg examine every new patient, take a history, do a complete workup, and if they decide therapy is needed, they decide what kind, schedule it, everything. If they decide they can't help a prospective patient, they say so. Darren said no for that girl. Her mother protested, and he advised her to get a second opinion. Well, McIvey hit the ceiling. He said Greg was a medical hack who couldn't make it in private practice, a know-nothing who should be turned out to pasture, God alone knows what all. And he called Darren a voodoo doctor, a shaman, an ignorant, superstitious laying-on-of-hands fraud who should practice in a tent at revivals or something."

Her face was flushed at the memory, and her eyes were flashing with anger. "The mother took her kid up to Portland, to the Health and Science University Hospital, and got another opinion. It turned out the girl had a tumor that was causing pressure on her spine. A doc up there operated, and a few months later she was playing basketball again. McIvey knew it was Darren's call. He's the one who knows what will or won't work. Greg backs him up every time, but it's Darren's call."

"Wow," Erica said. "McIvey made a bad diagnosis

and got mad because they knew it? I thought people got second opinions pretty often."

Stephanie nodded. "I guess he didn't make the original diagnosis. First the coach said shin splints and sidelined the kid. A GP said shin splints and got some X rays and tests to confirm it. McIvey just went along with the diagnosis, didn't bother to order more tests or look further. Darren said she'd had shin splints, but being out of action for six weeks or longer had let them heal. They weren't causing pain anymore. And neither was a disk problem. No physical therapy would help her. Most doctors welcome a second opinion, but God doesn't. And McIvey thinks he's God."

"You said a couple of examples. What else?"

"It isn't quite as dramatic, I guess, but telling. After that, a few months maybe, McIvey came over one day and wanted to go through the personnel records. Naomi said no. She called Greg and he said no and called Dr. Kelso. Dr. Kelso came right over and told McIvey that the records were not open to the public, that only the directors had the right to examine them. McIvey said the only records he wanted were Darren's, that he didn't believe he was qualified to treat patients, and he wanted to check his background, his training and references, before he referred another patient to the clinic. Dr. Kelso made him stay out in the waiting room while he and Naomi collected some of the file and took it to him. McIvey said he wanted the whole file and Dr. Kelso said he had given him all he was entitled to see. Of course,

Darren's education, training, all of it is impeccable. He's recognized as the best physical therapist in the Northwest, maybe on the whole West Coast. They say he has magic in his hands. They can tell him more than a dozen X rays. Anyway, McIvey was furious. See, he was out to get Darren. Still is, I suspect. The day he gets control here, Greg, Naomi and Darren will all be out before the sun goes down."

Erica finished her coffee, then said, "But he still sends patients here, doesn't he?"

"Sure. He knows this is the best facility for hundreds of miles, maybe all the way to Los Angeles."

"I don't understand any of this," Erica said. "Why would he try to drive out the best therapist *and* get control? Be second-rate or something."

"That's the stickler," Stephanie said, nodding. "No one here understands it. But that's how she blows. I've got to get back to work."

It was a glorious late summer, Erica thought when she left Stephanie to walk for a few minutes in the garden. Dahlias, zinnias, marigolds, chrysanthemums…too many flowers to name were riotous, defying the calendar. Back in Cleveland there would have been a frost by then, but here in Eugene, it was a golden time of color everywhere. Working in her own yard one day, she had asked Darren when to expect the first frost. He had laughed and said Thanksgiving, or Christmas, or maybe not at all this year. Of course, she had thought he was kidding, but it was the end of September and flowers were still in bloom.

She had made friends with Darren's son, Todd, who had been shy and silent at first, but she had known hundreds of boys his age over the years and had known not to push. Still more child than adolescent, with sun-bleached hair and high color on his cheeks, he had the grace and directness of a child, but responded like a serious young adult to a serious adult who treated him with respect. She was very respectful with him.

When he offered to show her his collection, she had rejoiced. His collection had turned out to be an assortment of posters. He had painted his room forest green with cream trim, and on the walls he had mounted his posters: lava fields, high mountain lakes, totem poles. She had been puzzled until he said, "We collect things, Dad and me. This year it was totem poles. I take pictures and we get them made into posters. Last year it was volcanoes. I think we'll do trees next summer. You know, the biggest, the oldest, like that. I'm supposed to do the research."

She had decided his Christmas present from her would be a bonsai tree.

Walking in the garden that golden afternoon, she thought briefly about Dr. McIvey, but decided he could not cast a very long shadow. He would be crazy to get rid of his best therapist and the two people who made the clinic work. He was too busy with his own practice to meddle. Then it was time to go to the upper lounge and read to her patients. She smiled as she realized what her phrasing had been: *her patients*.

6

"Bernie, what's going on around here?" Erica and Bernie were having coffee in the staff lounge. "And don't tell me it's nothing. Greg looks ill and Naomi is snapping like a turtle. What's up?"

"I wish to God I knew," Bernie said after a brief hesitation. She helped herself to leftover Halloween candy. "Something is. All at once Annie's a shareholder and Dr. McIvey is spending time going through the personnel files while Naomi stews and paces. Teri—you know Teri Crusak in the office?— she said that McIvey demanded the keys to the locked files, all the personnel records, and Naomi said to give them to him."

"I didn't even know there were locked files," Erica said.

"Yeah, there are. Confidential stuff about the staff. Not me. I've got no secrets. But others." She shook her head. "Anyway, whatever's in there, he's got now." She lowered her voice. "Stephanie said she wishes he'd eat something here. She'd season it with arsenic."

Erica remembered something else Stephanie had said, that McIvey was out to get Darren, that he had tried to get his personnel records a few years back and had not been allowed access. Now he had them, or could easily get them.

Keeping her voice as low as Bernie's, she said, "Stephanie thinks he's targeted Darren. Do you?"

"Sure. And now that Annie's going to be around even more, doing some of the stuff McIvey's mother did, it's like he's stoking the fire."

Annie and Darren? Erica lifted her cup, then put it down again. Annie and Darren. She had seen his expression that one time, the hurt and anger.

"Nothing to it," Bernie continued, "but you put kindling on a spark and fan it a little, lo and behold! you get a blaze. Maybe he's counting on something like that, to use as an excuse to get Darren out. Or else he's just plain stupid, and I don't think anyone ever accused David McIvey of stupidity."

"Were they...? I mean before she got married, were they going out?"

"How it was," Bernie said, "she came here when she was still just a kid, and he treated her like a kid for about a year. But she was sort of in a hero-worshiping phase, and he was the hero. Gradually he seemed to notice that she wasn't just a kid. He backed off. He thought he was too old for her. He's what, about thirty-eight now? I think that's right. Anyway, we were all watching to see how long it would take for her to get through to him. About a year, a little more. Well, McIvey came along and spotted her and said, I want that, and what David McIvey wants, David McIvey gets. Like David and Bathsheba. You know the story?"

Erica nodded. Her lips felt stiff, her mouth dry. She took a sip of coffee, then said, "I can't believe there's anything going on now."

"But she'll be around a lot more, not stuck back in the office. Old Mrs. McIvey was here all hours when it was fund-raising time, showing people around, having talks with Darren." She shrugged. "We'll see."

That afternoon Annie dropped in on Naomi in her office. "Are you busy? Can we talk?"

Naomi closed a folder on her desk and stood up. "Let's go to the house. No one will disturb us there. And I could use a cup of coffee."

They walked out together. It was a cold, sunny day, with thin cirrus clouds streaking the sky in the west. Annie stopped to sniff the air. "It's going to rain. Back home I used to go out to the bay and watch the sky move in. I thought of it as the sky eating the ocean, moving in to eat the land. The first gale of the season was always exciting. I never got over that excitement when the first gale blew in. Our lower pasture flooded every year," she added. A sharp memory surfaced and she saw herself as a little girl, her hair wild in the wind, saw how the cattle—black-and-white like picture-book cows—all turned to smell the ocean, the approaching storm front. She shook herself. "Not quite the same here, but I like the first storms of the season."

They entered the house through the back door into the kitchen, and while Naomi was busy with the coffee, Annie wandered about the room, as if checking to make certain it was how she remembered from when she had lived there. The same silly salt and pepper shakers—Jack Sprat and his plump wife; the same African violets in bloom on a windowsill—they were never out of bloom, it seemed; the same yellow vase with fresh flowers...

As Naomi waited for Annie to begin, she got out mugs, sugar and half-and-half. Annie always used enough cream to turn her coffee nearly white.

Annie had come to a stop at the back door where she stood gazing out at the herb garden: rosemary, thyme, silvery-green sage, feathery fennel and dill, dark-purple basil, bright-green basil... It was like an illustration from a book about medieval convent gardens. Annie could imagine the cloaked and hooded figures out there with cutting baskets. The coffee was ready. She turned back to the room, to the table where Naomi had already taken a chair and was pouring.

Annie liked the fragrance of coffee more than the taste, she thought, as she took a seat opposite Naomi.

Then without preamble she said, "Why did David give me five shares?"

"He didn't tell you?"

"He said it was a formality."

Naomi nodded. "In a sense it is, I suppose, but there's more to it than that. As a member of the board of governors, you certainly have a right to know the issues." She told her most of it, leaving out only the part about Donna Kelso's will and how her death before a court decision was handed down would change the equation. "So it was fifty percent versus fifty percent in favor of, or opposed to, a nonprofit foundation. Eventually he'll try to find a way to force a vote for a change of mission, to turn the clinic into a surgical facility. That's what he really wants."

"But he gave up some of his voting power by giving me shares," Annie said.

"He had to give up shares or take on a workload that he couldn't possibly handle. He had no choice."

"There's something else," Annie said after a moment. "He said to be sure to ask you how Mrs. Kelso is doing. Why? What does that mean?"

Naomi drew in a breath. He knew, she thought. He was letting them know he was aware of Donna Kelso's will. His attorney might have tricks of his own to use to string out everything until the matter was settled by the death of Donna Kelso. And until then he would use Annie to maintain the impasse the equality had created.

Hesitantly, uncertain for the first time, she told Annie about the terms of Donna Kelso's will.

"He'll win," Annie said when Naomi became silent. "He'll have the McIvey Surgical Institute." She tasted her coffee, put it down again. "It isn't even for the money," she said. "He really doesn't care about money." Abruptly she stood up. "Thanks, Naomi. I have to go. See you tomorrow."

Naomi watched her rush away, then continued to sit at the table thinking she had never hated anyone in her life the way she hated David McIvey. She had seen Annie change from a happy, laughter-loving child into a woman with shadows in her eyes, with a strained expression when her husband's name was mentioned and an almost total withdrawal into some other space when he was present. David McIvey had marked her. And he would drive Greg out without a moment's hesitation, destroy Darren, destroy the clinic. All in a day's work, inconsequential. Collateral damage, she thought bitterly. That's what he would bring about on his march to where he was driven to go.

She agreed with Annie—it was not for the money. As a surgeon he was making a lot of money already, and apparently spending little. No yacht, no private plane, no palatial mansion. He didn't collect art. Annie had said the condo was almost sterile, and neither of them wore expensive jewelry, except for her wedding ring. What was driving him was more compelling than money. Power? In the operating room he was a god, power enough. She stood up and took the coffee mugs to the sink where she poured out Annie's coffee, rinsed both mugs. She picked up a wooden spoon from the counter, then became still again, looking out the back window, over the herb garden, past the screening hedge, to the upper floor of the clinic.

"God wants a larger domain," she said under her breath. "He wants people to come from all over the world to seek the healing touch of his magic wand, the scalpel, to pay homage…." She heard a snapping sound and looked down in surprise at her hands. She had broken the spoon handle in two.

The anticipated storm moved in that evening with gusting winds and driving rain. Annie stood at a window in the living room of the condo watching the fir trees dance in the rain. When David came into the room after changing his clothes, she said, without turning to look at him, "I'm going to vote for the foundation."

"Annette, don't be a fool," David said. "You will vote exactly the way I tell you to. That's a given."

She shook her head. "I think the foundation is a good idea, the continuity is important." She turned to face him. He was not even looking at her, but at the mail.

"The court will not agree to such a change when one board member is incompetent and another, with majority shares, is opposed," he said, opening an envelope. "That isn't how the system works. There's no point in delaying the inevitable."

"You could have a surgical clinic somewhere else," she said. "You could build it to suit yourself, do it that way." He didn't ask her how she had learned about the surgical clinic. He had not told her, and he didn't care who had any more than he cared what she thought about it. He never asked her anything.

"I already have a facility." He threw the mail down on the coffee table. "My father built it with every intention of leaving it to me, and I intend to use it. I played second fiddle to that clinic all my life, and now I'm moving into the first fiddler's chair. Period."

For a moment his face was transformed by fury like that of a thwarted child, or a wronged youth, neglected and vengeful. The expression was fleeting, and once again his expression became as unreadable as that of a Greek statue. "Annette, listen carefully because I won't repeat this. Greg and Naomi will be out of there in three months, and Darren sooner than that. How they leave is still open. With the unanimous highest recommendations of the board of governors, or with a serious reservation included in a report by a major shareholder? Greg is incompetent, and Naomi has no training in bookkeeping or anything else as far as I can tell. And Darren has a criminal record. He's an ex-con, a drug addict who, I am afraid, has reverted to his old habit."

She stared at him, then started to walk across the room, toward the hall and the foyer.

"Where are you going? Dinner is just about ready."

"I don't know where I'm going. Out."

* * *

Annie had been driving aimlessly for hours when she pulled in and stopped at the parking lot of the clinic, although she had no intention of running to Naomi and Greg, or of entering the building. The rain was so hard that the windshield wipers had not been able to keep the glass clear enough to continue driving.

When the rain eased, and it probably would in another hour or two, fog would form, she thought. The earth, buildings, pavement, trees, all still warm from summer's heat, chilled by the first real rain of the season brought dense fogs here in the valley. She was thinking again of her father's milk cows, placidly grazing as water crept up into the lower pasture, until Molly Bee, the matriarch of the herd, started to move in a leisurely way toward higher ground, and all the others left off cropping grass to follow her. "Who elected her queen of the cattle?" Annie had asked her father a very long time ago, almost too distant a time to recall. "I think she's self-appointed," her father had said. "But no one questions her authority."

She would give the shares to someone else, she thought suddenly, and shook her head even as the thought formed. David never made idle threats. He would smear Darren, Greg and Naomi, and in the end he would still have the clinic. She didn't doubt that for a second. He would have the clinic. Her cell phone rang and she ignored it just as she had before. It would be David ordering her to come back home.

Even if she gave the shares to Naomi and Greg, it wouldn't stop David....

They both knew what was happening. If they couldn't save the clinic, they could protect themselves one way or another, or retire. Greg was old enough to retire, or go to a small town and practice medicine.

Then she thought, what if Darren leaves first? She knew he had been offered a position in one of the biggest rehabilitation centers in Los Angeles. Or he could go to Seattle. Or Portland. He could go almost anywhere, make better money, still do the work he loved and had been born to do.... If he handed in his resignation now, he would leave with excellent references, no smear, no blot on his record.

She didn't know whether he would accept that idea, and chances were good that he wouldn't, but he had to have the choice. He had to know what was going on. Leave now, or stay and be forced out later, and possibly be destroyed professionally... He had to know. She called his number on her cell phone.

When Darren agreed to meet her, she quickly said, "No. I'll come to your place. Where do you live now?"

The storm had made Erica restless, unable to concentrate on a book, or the television, or anything else. What if the shingles blew off, or the new roof leaked, or a tree blew down? She heard the car in the driveway and went to a front window to see who was coming this late. She knew that Darren was home.

She always knew if he was in the apartment. When she saw Annie leave the car, look at the house uncertainly, then go around to the outside stairs, she burned with resentment, with an ache that started some place she had no name for.

"We have the next board meeting on Thursday," Annie said. "I'll try to stall, but I'll probably have to vote. Think about it, Darren. He's going to win, one way or the other. He will. He always does. He's…he's like the storm, unstoppable until he gets his way."

"We'll find something to do," Darren said. "Greg, Dr. Kelso, I…we're pretty formidable, too, you know. We'll think of something."

"Is it true, what he said? Drugs, prison?"

"It's true. One day, over a double chocolate malted milk, I'll tell you about it. Now you go on home. And thanks, Annie."

"Oh, God! I haven't had a chocolate malted milk in years. Not since…"

Erica was in the kitchen when she heard the car leave. Darren was pacing back and forth, back and forth. Neither of them slept much that night. Darren paced and Erica listened to his footsteps while the rain beat on the house.

David was in bed when Annie got home a little after ten-thirty. David always went to bed at ten-thirty.

7

The low pressure front came in waves. The rain eased, fog formed and was very heavy in the morning. Then the sun came out and burned away the fog and brought up steam from roofs and pavement. A few hours later a new wave of rain rolled in and the sequence began again. Annie loved it. The front carried the smell of the ocean inland.

At lunch on Monday Annie toyed with her salad. David ate his with a good appetite. Neither of them had mentioned again the discussion about her vote. He had said, "Period." That meant no more discussion, no compromise; the matter was settled.

David was saying, "I need those studies before two o'clock tomorrow. You'll have to leave as soon as you drop me at Greg's house in the morning. I'll have Naomi take me to the hospital."

She nodded. It often happened that patients from an outlying area, Pleasant Hill, or Cottage Grove, someplace closer to Eugene than to Portland, were sent to the University Hospital in Portland for a diagnosis. If surgery was decided upon, they frequently opted to have it done in Eugene, where it was less of a burden on family members and patients alike. It also often happened that the Portland hospital failed to send the required lab results or X-ray studies to the doctor in Eugene. Several times each year Annie drove to Portland herself to collect them.

"It's going to be foggy again, and probably raining," David said. "We'll get an early start. I'll sign Dwyer out at seven-thirty."

He had to see his patient at the clinic, sign him out, leave follow-up orders with the nurse and then be at the hospital to make his own rounds by eight.

Annie nodded again. She was looking forward to the drive to Portland; she needed time alone to think. She felt as if her brain had been on strike for days, and no matter how resolutely she started, she kept stopping in frustration, unable to reach any decision.

When Erica arrived at the clinic that afternoon, she saw Annie outside one of the therapy rooms. Annie looked up guiltily, then motioned her closer to the door, holding her finger to her lips.

A woman was saying in a harsh furious voice, "I'm paralyzed, goddamn it! Don't give me any of that crap!"

"I know you are," Darren said calmly. "And you're mad as hell and don't intend to take it any longer, so get out of the way, world. Right? Well, see, I'm pretty sore myself. You're too young, for one thing. It isn't fair. Lightning bolt stroke and zap, you can't move. But we accepted you as a patient, and we don't take anyone unless we can help. We're going to help you, and you're going to work harder than you thought you could."

"Oh, Jesus! Just tell me what I'm supposed to when I can't do a fucking thing!"

"First thing every day will be hydrotherapy. Nice warm water, and you wear angel wings. It's really a flotation device. You couldn't sink or flip over if you tried. And Tony will put you through a series of exercises. That's to regain muscle tone, strength building, in the nearest thing to weightlessness we can come up with. You'll see. After that a little snack, and then Chris will guide you through an imaging session, meditation, self-hypnosis, whatever you decide to call it. That's hard, but it works. Lunch next, and in the afternoon I'll help you parachute jump." He laughed, a low rumbling sound. "We omit the plane and chute, there's just the harness. That's to bear your weight. And underfoot a moving walkway, to remind your legs how to work."

He paused a moment, then said, "You can see that you have a busy schedule lined up. After all that you might want to listen to our Rikki read. Most folks upstairs do. Her name's Erica but some of the kids started calling her Rikki—you know, like Rikki-Tikki-Tavi—and I guess we mostly all do now."

Erica gave Annie a startled look; Annie raised her eyebrows and nodded.

"And if at any time during the day you feel like screaming," Darren said, "do it. Or if you need a little something, say a margarita or a slug of gin, say so. Not that we can give you a liquid painkiller, but a magic pill or something will have the same effect." His voice dropped lower, and no longer sounded amused or playful when he said, "Connie, we're going to make you walk again, and use your hand and arm, and control your body. We are. Any other questions?"

One of the other therapy room doors opened, and Annie looked at her watch in dismay. "I've got to go. See you around, Rikki." She ran.

Erica continued on down the corridor toward the reception desk to check in with Bernie, thinking Rikki. She had never had a nickname before. They must talk about her, or maybe about her reading, which they seemed to think was helpful. They probably knew she was practically destitute, that Darren was her tenant. What else? What else was there, actually?

The clinic opened at eight each weekday morning, but Bernie arrived fifteen or twenty minutes early to check in staff and be ready for the first patients, some of whom were convinced that they had to show up at least ten minutes before their appointments. That Tuesday morning Bernie was surprised when Erica hurried in by way of the front door at a quarter to eight.

"I'm going to be late, and I parked in the van spot," Erica said. "On my way to Santa Clara Elementary. Will you see that Tim Dwyer gets this? He said he's going home today." She put a book on the desk and hurried back out.

Bernie glanced at it and smiled—one of the Harry Potter books—and then put it under the counter. Others were arriving, some stopped at the desk, some just waved. The first patient of the day came in, and she sent him and his wife to the waiting room. Another busy day had started.

Carlos Hermosa pulled into the gravel spot provided for his truck, leaving just enough room for a car to pass in the narrow alley. Rain or shine, he thought, getting out, and today it was rain and fog, rain and fog. But the bird feeders needed filling, the pump at the waterfall needed to be checked, slug bait had to be put down. The first rains brought out slugs and snails in hordes, and they woke up hungry. The cyclamen were starting to bloom, and he knew from experience that the evil critters would head for them straightaway. And, he reminded himself, he had to check the supports for the dahlias. Heavy blooms like they had, soaked now, would pull the plants right over if he didn't see to them. He was humming under his breath, ignoring the rain as he prepared two pails to take into the garden with his implements, birdseed, slug bait.

The gate was open, but that just meant that Dr. Boardman had already gone in. Either he or Carlos unlocked the gate every morning. Carlos went into the garden and to the first bird feeder, manipulated by a cord and pulley, up high enough for the folks upstairs to look out and watch the birds. And the birds were real gluttons. He never had found out how much was too much for them. They ate whatever he put out.

At twenty minutes past eight, rounding a curve in the path, he came to a stop, then dropped his pails and ran to a man lying on the path. "Madre, Madre," Carlos whispered, crossing himself.

He backed up a step, and another, then turned and ran to the clinic. Inside the door he pulled off his rain hat and hurried down the corridor, dripping water, toward Dr. Boardman's office.

Darren and one of the young interns met him in the corridor and Darren said, "Carlos? What's wrong? Are you sick?"

"Dr. Boardman," he said. "I have to see Dr. Boardman."

"He hasn't come in yet," Darren said. "What's the matter with you?"

"There's a dead man in the garden," Carlos said in a hushed voice.

"What the hell…?" Darren muttered. "Show us."

Carlos led the way to the path where the dead man was lying with rain streaming off his face.

"Jesus," Tony Kranz whispered, gazing at David McIvey. There was no need to touch him, to feel for a pulse, no need to try to do anything for him. His sightless eyes were wide-open, his skin as white as marble.

What had started as a normal busy day became much, much busier.

8

That evening Naomi, Greg and Thomas sat in the living room of the residence and talked.

"It's been a madhouse all day," Greg said, handing Thomas a glass of claret. "They didn't even remove the body until four this afternoon. And they'll be back tomorrow with more questions."

Thomas nodded. And the next day and the next, he thought, right up until they made an arrest, probably. "Tell me about it," he said. His wrinkled face became so creased when he frowned that he looked inhuman, and he was frowning ferociously.

"McIvey came by this morning to make sure Naomi could drive him to the office," Greg said, "and to get the key to the gate. He was going to sign a patient out. Annie dropped him off at seven-thirty, then left to go up to Portland to collect some X rays. Someone was waiting for him, or followed him, or he surprised someone who was already in the garden for God knows what reason. Anyway, he was shot in the heart at close range. The police kept asking exactly what time he arrived, what time he left, and I told them seven-thirty, then they wanted to know how I could be certain. God, you answer a question and they start pounding on the answer. The police wanted to know about the keys, who has one, when we lock up, when we open up. God knows how many keys are floating around. I don't. You have one, we do, Carlos. Joyce had one. Who else? I don't know."

"Darren has one," Naomi said. "He told them he doesn't know where it is, but he did have one."

Greg nodded, then said, "So he left the house here, sometime around seven-thirty. That's about all I know directly." He shook his head and went on, "The rest is what they call hearsay. You wouldn't believe the rumors that have made the rounds today."

"I probably would," Thomas said. "Let's have them."

"Right. A patient says she heard what might have been a shot. She was in a wheelchair near her window waiting for breakfast, and she looked out and saw a dwarf in a shiny black cape and hood."

"So are the police looking for a dwarf?" Thomas asked with a touch of sarcasm.

"Who knows what they think, what they're looking for? Carlos found the body sometime after eight.

He doesn't know exactly what time it was. And Carlos said McIvey had been dragged off the main path out of sight. The police haven't confirmed it, but if Carlos said so, I believe it. He'd notice something like that."

"A powerful dwarf," Thomas said. "Go on. What else?"

"Darren said he passed the open gate and saw an umbrella blowing around in the wind. He left his bike and walked in, closed the umbrella and leaned it against the building out of the rain. He didn't see anyone and didn't see the body. He thought the umbrella was mine." He drew in a breath. "It was McIvey's. Anyway, Darren got here before eight, but he doesn't know how much before. Who pays attention like that?"

He got up to pour more wine. Thomas shook his head when Greg started to refill his glass. He never drank more than one glass of wine when he had to drive. He knew that at his age, if he was involved in any infraction of the law while he was driving, he might lose his license. He took no chances.

Naomi leaned forward in her chair and said indignantly, "The police searched the entire clinic and garden. They had someone in the pond, had blocked off the alley to search there, and even here, the residence and garden. I don't even know what else. They're looking for a gun, or for a shiny black cape or something. They intercepted Annie when she got to the hospital in Portland. An officer stayed with her when she picked up the X rays, and then drove her

back to Eugene. They didn't tell her anything, just
that there had been an accident. What a nightmare
that trip home must have been for her! And they got
her to open the trunk of her car and the glove box
for them to have a look inside." Naomi's voice was
tight with anger.

"Where is she now?" Thomas asked.

"Upstairs in the guest room resting. She can't
stay alone in that condominium tonight. I took her
over to get a few things. A detective went with us and
put tape on the doors, sealed them." She ran her
hand through her hair, a gesture she used when upset.
By now her hair looked like a straw bale that had
come loose from a binding wire, standing out in all
directions. "They acted as if they suspect her!"

Thomas waved that away. "Well, they do. They
always suspect the surviving spouse in a homicide.
But, Greg, Naomi, if they decide she couldn't have
moved him, if indeed he was moved, you know
they'll suspect both of you, me maybe. We all will
benefit from this untimely death, I'm afraid. Not as
much as the widow, certainly, but enough. And we
have to decide how much to tell them of the hassle
we've been going through. I hope the subject hasn't
already been raised."

Greg snorted with derision. "They asked the
group first, then when they questioned us separately.
'Do you know of any enemies he had, anyone who
might have wanted to harm him?' Not a soul in that
lounge stirred, except maybe to shake their heads.
Nope, we don't know anything like that."

Thomas regarded Greg for a moment, then he said, "I suggest we keep it that way. If they want to know about the only board meeting David attended, I believe Annie can provide the tape for them to listen to. I explained their duties to the three new shareholders—David, Annie and you—and then I proposed that we consider creating a foundation. We adjourned without further discussion." His gaze was unwavering. "Is that your recollection of our meeting, Greg?"

The tape would not reveal the flush of rage that had colored David's face, or his tight-lipped silence, his curt nod…. "That's how it was," Greg said.

In the upstairs guest room Annie lay on the bed staring dry-eyed at the ceiling, remembering how happy she had been living in this room, in this house years before. How safe she had felt. She could not recapture any of those feelings; the girl she had been was out of reach, so distant she seemed dreamlike.

Tomorrow she would have to go home, she thought dismally. The detective who questioned her had said that it was part of the routine to look over the victim's papers, check his computer; he might have received a threatening letter, something of that sort, without mentioning it for fear of alarming her. With near panic she thought of her diary, several diaries by now. She would have to put them away before the police saw them. But she wouldn't have to face the police alone. Her mother would come to stay with her for a while, she had said on the phone, help her through this terrible time. She would be there by ten; by then Annie and the detectives would be there.

She was glad that her mother was coming. They would go out for lunch or for dinner. They might eat at six or not until nine. They could go shopping together and pay no attention to the clock. She would never keep a real schedule again as long as she lived.

She was free, Annie thought in wonder. Her servitude had ended.

Erica drove straight to the clinic from school that afternoon. She was stopped at the entrance to the staff parking lot, where a uniformed officer asked for ID, checked her against a list, then called someone on a cell phone. The lot was full of police cars, the alley blocked off with crime tape, and some television vans parked as close as they could get. The officer waved her on.

Inside the entrance to the clinic she was stopped again, this time by a plainclothes detective.

"Ms. Castle? I'm Detective Mike Clarkson. I'd like to ask you a few questions," he said.

"It's true, then?" she said. "Someone shot Dr. McIvey? I heard it on the news on the car radio."

"It's true," he said. "We're using this office." He escorted her to Naomi's office.

"Why me?"

He was middle-aged and polite, but straightforward to a fault. He didn't wait for her to sit down before he started. "We're asking everyone who was in the clinic between seven-thirty and eight this morning. That's not your usual routine, I understand. Why were you here?" He flipped open a notebook.

She moistened her lips, startled by his brusqueness. "I usually come in the evening, around four-thirty, to read to the patients upstairs. One of them, Tim Dwyer, told me yesterday that he would be leaving today. I knew he would be gone before I got here. I dropped off a book for him, so he could finish it at home."

"Okay. Tell me about it, what you did, where you parked, everything you recall."

"There's nothing to recall," she said. "I parked out front under the overhang, where the medic vans usually stop. It was raining and I knew I'd only be a minute, long enough to run in, leave the book and go back. No van would be by that early." She stopped and took a breath. "Anyway, that's what I did. I came in and gave the book to Bernie at the reception desk, and I left again and went to Santa Clara Elementary School. I was afraid I'd be late because of the rain and fog. I was in a hurry."

There were a few more questions. She had seen Dr. McIvey a few times, but had never met him. She didn't know any reason anyone would have wanted to harm him. She had not seen anything out of the ordinary that morning, no strange cars, or strangers. She had not heard anything that might have been a gunshot. She pointed out that she wouldn't have known if a car was strange or not, since she was never at the clinic at that hour normally. He took her name, address and phone number, then snapped his notebook closed and stood up. Interview over.

She hurried to the lounge, where, as she had expected, people were clustered at the windows, trying to see what the police were doing now, and talking in low voices. The stop-and-start rain had started again.

People moved slightly to let her edge in, and she heard the various rumors that were flying throughout the clinic.

"Haven't moved him yet, just left him out in the rain all day."

"They put a tarp over him."

"And a tent all along the path."

"Mrs. Johnson said it was a dwarf dressed in black. Now she's saying it was a demon sent to collect his soul."

"Carlos is beside himself. They're destroying his garden. He says McIvey interrupted someone trying to steal the koi."

"Those koi are worth a thousand dollars."

"Darren made them move all their cars and everything around to the back. Poor Dr. Boardman was in a dither and Darren just took over. They were scaring patients and visitors away."

"Naomi and Greg have Annie under lock and key."

"They were after drugs. Come in, grab a bunch of drugs and get out before many people were up and about."

"A gang that robs pharmacies and doctors' offices, looking for drugs."

"You ever try moving a dead weight like he was?

Believe me, a woman couldn't have done it unless she was built like a wrestler."

Erica pulled her coat more tightly about herself, chilled, when men with a gurney entered the garden and headed up the path toward the tarp that had been put over the body of David McIvey. A hush settled over the observers.

That night the fog moved in again, and Erica felt so cold she shook. The fog did that; it crept in and got to you no matter how tight the house was. She took a hot bath, then turned off the lights and stood gazing out a window at the fog-dimmed lights across the way, like earth-bound glowing clouds without definition. She could hear Darren's footsteps, back and forth, back and forth. Or maybe she didn't hear him, she thought. Maybe she sensed him moving back and forth, the way mothers were said to sense when their infants woke up, long before they heard them. She began to shiver again and went to bed where she lay awake a long time, listening to Darren's footsteps.

Across town on Crest Drive, Lorraine McIvey stood at her windows gazing out at the fog. Hers was a beautiful house, with a lot of Port-Orford cedar and a cathedral ceiling in the living room, and one wall that was almost entirely glass, overlooking all of Eugene when the weather was clear. She had liked that when she and David bought the house. "It's spread out at our feet," she had said and they both had laughed.

"You shouldn't have come tonight," she said over her shoulder to Pier Longos. "It's too dangerous driving in that kind of fog."

"Had to come," he said. "To comfort you in your bereavement, and all that. How are the kids taking it?"

She shrugged and turned to face him. She was a tall, graceful woman with lustrous auburn hair that, to her annoyance, had started to show some gray. She kept it touched up. At forty-four she was still handsome, almost as slender as she had been at twenty, although she had to work at that, also.

"They'll survive," she said. In fact, neither her daughter, Caitlin, nor her son, Aaron, had displayed grief at their father's death, although both had been curious and even morbidly interested in the fact of his murder. It was not surprising that they were as indifferent about him, his death, as he had always been about them, everything about them. Aaron had asked if they would be broke now. Aaron was seventeen.

Caitlin had said, "I warn you, if you marry Pretty Boy Pier, I'll leave." She was fifteen.

Pier was good-looking, Lorraine thought absently, but not as good-looking as he thought he was. He had curly black hair, black eyes with long lashes, a wonderful athletic body, great cheekbones. And he was a bad artist, although enough people bought his paintings to keep his ego aloft even if he never had a cent to show for his efforts. She had no intention of marrying him.

"You should have taken him up on his offer last week," Pier commented. "Too late we grow smart, something like that. No?" He swished the remains of a martini around in his glass, then downed the last of it and lazily stood up and ambled to the sideboard to pour another.

"Pier, shut up." It never had bothered her in the past for him to come in, mix martinis, help himself to whatever he wanted in her refrigerator. In fact, it had amused her to think that David, her ex, was paying the freight for her freeloading lover. That night it annoyed her, and Aaron's question repeated in her head: Are we going to be broke now? She didn't know the answer.

"You could always say you accepted his offer and had a handshake agreement until proper papers could be drawn up," Pier said. "Your word against a dead man's word."

Her annoyance turned to icy rage. "I'd like you to leave now," she said coldly. "I have a headache."

"Oh, spare me," he said. "I haven't said anything you wouldn't have thought of in time. What's wrong with my suggestion?"

"Just get out of here," she said and swept past him, up to the next level of the house and into her room, where she pushed the lock in the door.

But it was true, she admitted a few minutes later, after she heard his car leave with a squeal of tires on the driveway. She would have thought of it, perhaps acted on it. She returned to the lower level of the house and started straightening up in the living room, too restless to go to bed or to sit still.

On Wednesday David had called and asked her to meet him in town. He had named a restaurant. She had said no, she was tied up, but he could come to the house on Thursday between one and three, when the children would be in school and the housekeeper gone for the day. To her astonishment, he had agreed. David had rarely let another person set the agenda.

Expecting him to make a case for reduced alimony or child support payments, she had been surprised again when he made an offer to buy back the shares in the clinic that he had turned over to Aaron and Caitlin.

At the time of their divorce, she had had her attorney investigate the clinic. He had told her that as a clinic it was worthless, that without the donations and grants it would sink, but that the physical building and the land were worth at least two million. As a long-term investment for her children, it was worth going after. That afternoon, less than a week ago, she had told David no.

"You'll turn around and sell it, and we'll have a few thousand dollars while you make a mint."

"We can add a provision that if it's sold you will receive ten percent of my share of the proceeds," he had said. "Twenty-five thousand now, and ten percent if we ever sell."

He had thought of it, she had realized that day, and he had come prepared to up the ante. But why?

That was still the nagging question. He never did anything that wasn't first and foremost for his own benefit. What he had said in answer to her question of why had been at least part of the truth, she thought. Old man Kelso would soon own fifty percent of the clinic, and David could not bear to play second fiddle to a senile old man. He wanted equality. She believed that wholeheartedly, but she also believed there was more. But what it was she could not fathom.

"Think about it," David had said, "and let's talk again in a few weeks."

And now he was gone, the deal rejected, and the pretty little trophy wife would get the pie. No more alimony, no more generous child support. There was a trust fund for the education of the children, but nothing else for her. The day they signed the divorce papers, David had made a point of telling her he had changed his will. There would be something for the children, of course, but considering the amount in their education fund, their bequests would be modest, he had said.

He had come into whatever his mother had left, and he made a lot of money himself. His estate would be considerable, and all of it would pass on to the pretty new wife whether or not he had changed the will again. There were no siblings, no other close relatives. It would be hers.

Unless the pretty little thing had pulled the trigger herself, Lorraine thought suddenly, and she stopped moving aimlessly about the room. God knew the dear little thing would have had cause, she thought, remembering the many times she had wished David dead, wished she had a gun, wished for a fatal accident.

It was strange how she had loved him so passionately, blindly, in a storybook kind of way without reservation, and how that blind, all-encompassing love had turned into hatred just as passionate, just as all-encompassing. It had taken nearly five years for it to happen, she remembered, but when the switch came, it was absolute. The new wife had been married to him for almost five years.

She sat down on the sofa to think.

9

The only thing that Barbara Holloway really disliked about being a criminal lawyer was the fact that she had to wear panty hose and skirts for court appearances. Her father had advised her early on that some judges would take it out on her clients if they thought she was improperly dressed for court. At least at Martin's Restaurant she could dress as she pleased, usually in blue jeans and a sweat shirt in the winter. The clients who dropped in were dressed pretty much the same way and did not object. Twice a week either Barbara or her associate Shelley McGinnis held open office in the restaurant where Martin provided space and all the coffee, tea or soft drinks anyone could want. Many of the drop-in clients were eligible for Legal Aid services, but they

CLEAR AND CONVINCING PROOF   97

were hesitant to take advantage of that office, fearful of the bureaucracy, or reluctant to talk to real strangers about their problems, or too bewildered by the paperwork involved. Here, with good coffee at hand, they seemed to feel free to confide in Barbara. Often they offered to pay, sometimes ten dollars, or twenty-five; one even offered to mortgage her house and come up with a thousand dollars in time. Barbara had shaken her head and scolded the woman for putting her house at risk. She accepted the smaller sums and issued receipts, aware that pride was involved.

That Friday she was reassuring her last client of the day. "I'll talk to him, Mrs. Juarez. Of course, he can't have you arrested and you won't go to jail."

"You tell him it's the flea in the house that draws the blood," Mrs. Juarez said.

Her employer, a small shopkeeper, had accused her of stealing twenty-seven dollars from the till. She had worked there for nine years, and his sixteen-year-old son had just started working in the shop. The flea in the house, Barbara thought, and nodded at her client. "I'll mention that."

After she walked to the door with Mrs. Juarez and hung the Closed sign, she headed for the kitchen, where Martin and his wife Binnie were prepping for the dinner crush. The restaurant was small, consisting of half a dozen booths and half a dozen tables. Within an hour it would be packed, although at the moment she was the only person in sight. She met Martin coming through the swinging door as she approached it.

"Hey, full house today, wasn't it?" he said, as he went to her table to collect the tray with a carafe and coffee mugs.

Barbara never thought of herself as short until she stood next to Martin, who towered over her. His white beret glowed against his black face and hair. He couldn't wear a chef's hat, he had explained, because the door frame kept knocking it off as he went in and out of the kitchen.

"I got some new wine from Chile," Martin said. "New supplier. Want to try some?"

"No, thanks. Martin, what's going on here? Shelley said no one will tell her anything. For weeks she's had absolutely no one with a problem, and today I had four. Last week it was five. Have they turned against her? And if so, why?"

Martin laughed. It was a low rumbling sound that seemed to start somewhere down around his knees. By the time it emerged, it shook his frame and was like a receding train heard from afar, with just its vibrations left in the air.

He backed into the kitchen with the tray and she followed, then stood by the door. Martin and Binnie didn't like outsiders in their kitchen. Binnie looked up from the counter where she was rolling piecrust. Her crusts were the best this side of heaven.

"They just want to look at her these days," Martin said. "They don't want to butt in on anyone as happy as she is with their problems."

Binnie wiped her hands and began signing. Barbara could catch a little of it, but not much. Martin laughed again, then said, "Binnie says they want to see if it's true that when she walks, her feet don't even touch the ground."

Barbara snorted in exasperation. "Pass the word that I'll have her do most of the work on their problems. If they won't prick that bubble, I will." Actually her four clients that day had brought in minor problems that would not take much real work; a letter or two, a little research, laying down the law with the shopkeeper who didn't know his own son. If he had wanted to press charges, take it to trial, he would have done something about it already. What he had done was demand the twenty-seven dollars, with the threat of jail, and Mrs. Juarez had been terrified.

"I'll let them know," Martin said gravely. "Barbara, the whip-wielding, merciless dominatrix, has spoken. Sure you won't try some of that wine? The pinot gris is pretty good."

"Can't," she said. "One more appointment today." She glanced at her watch. "In fact, I've got to scoot, like five minutes ago."

She was smiling when she started to drive. Her father called Shelley the little pink-and-gold fairy princess. These days Shelley in love, madly in love, gloriously in love, and equally loved back, was as radiant as a glow worm. Barbara really couldn't blame people for wanting to look at her, to bask in that glow.

Then her thoughts turned to the meeting she was going to be late for.

She had read about the murder of Dr. David

McIvey back in November, and the follow-up stories about the rehabilitation clinic his father had started with a partner, but since the initial stories, as far as she knew there had been nothing else. Certainly no arrest, unless it had happened that day. Early that morning Sid Blankenship had called to ask her to attend a meeting at the clinic. We need advice, he had said. Well, he was a corporate attorney, not a criminal attorney, and he probably knew as much about criminal law as she knew about corporate law, which was damn little, she had to admit. When she suggested that her office might be a more appropriate place to talk, he had said that quite a few people were involved. It might seem like an invasion. Besides, they couldn't all leave the clinic at the same time.

Traffic on Seventh was heavy. Although it was mid-January, Christmas lights were still glittering here and there, and the wet streets and traffic lights along with them made the streets a kaleidoscope of color. When she turned onto the Jefferson Street bridge, traffic stopped. From there on it was stop, go, stop, go. Friday evening traffic, people heading home to Springfield, up to the many new subdivisions north of Eugene, heading for the Interstate. Five o'clock on a Friday night was not a good time to call a meeting, Barbara decided, irritated. It had been a long day, hours in court, a quick lunch and change of clothes, hours at Martin's, and now this.

She was ten minutes late. A heavyset woman at the reception desk stood up when Barbara introduced herself. "I'm to take you straight back," the woman said. Barbara followed her through a wide corridor to a closed door. The woman opened the door, said, "Ms. Holloway's here," and then left again.

Sid came forward and shook her hand. "Thanks for coming," he said. His quick glance had taken in her jeans and boots, she knew, but his face was as smooth as glass, revealing not a bit of what he thought of her inappropriate garb.

She had known Sid for many years. Her father once said that in a close community like Eugene all the attorneys sharpened one another's knives, because if you're going to be stabbed in the back, you want a clean cut.

Sid quickly introduced the others in the room: Dr. Kelso, Dr. and Mrs. Boardman, Annie McIvey and Darren Halvord. Barbara admitted to herself that if they had come to her office, it would have been a tight fit; not impossible, but they would not have been able to spread out the way they could here. The Boardmans seated themselves on a very nice green, leather-covered sofa; Annie McIvey sat rigidly upright on a straight chair; Darren Halvord chose a flowered upholstered chair; and Dr. Kelso and Sid pulled out chairs at a round conference table for themselves, and one for her. The table was made of fine old cherry wood with a rich glowing finish. Although the room itself was handsome, comfortable, no one in it looked at ease.

"I also thank you for coming here," Dr. Kelso said, apparently in charge; he had a folder in front of him.

Barbara thought he looked like a mummified monkey with sharp eyes, and his voice was raspy, the way some old people's voices seemed to get, as if rust had invaded.

"Before we begin," Dr. Kelso said, "Sid has assured us that a consultation such as this, before we have retained you, is held in confidence. Is that so?"

She nodded. "It is."

"Good. Miss Holloway, we find that we are being skewered by a two-pronged fork. At a glance they may appear to be two separate issues, but they are not. They are one and the same. The first is the destiny of the clinic itself, and the second is the murder of David McIvey. Neither can be discussed without involving the other." Very briefly he outlined the mission statement of the clinic, the makeup of the current board of directors and the determination that David McIvey had expressed about the future of the clinic.

"So David was going to apply pressure to make this a surgical facility, and we, the rest of the governing board, wanted to proceed with setting up a nonprofit foundation to continue our mission." He cast his sharp-eyed glance at the others in the room, none of whom had made a sound as he spoke.

"The second problem, the other tine of the fork," he said then, "is the murder. Frankly, Miss Holloway, I don't give a damn who killed David McIvey, and I'm sure that many others will echo that sentiment."

Barbara glanced at Annie McIvey, but she was impassive, not protesting, not agreeing. She looked tired and frightened.

"However," Dr. Kelso said, "for reasons I don't understand, the investigating officers seem to have fixed on Darren Halvord and Annie McIvey as collaborators, conspirators, killer and accessory."

Barbara looked again at Annie McIvey, who was so stiff she appeared frozen in place. Darren Halvord seemed absorbed in studying his shoes.

When Dr. Kelso paused, Barbara said, "Normally, anyone accused of a crime consults an attorney in person, not through a committee. I'm afraid I don't understand."

"Of course," Dr. Kelso said. "You see, probate court is holding David McIvey's estate until the facts of his death are determined. If Annie is charged with murder, or being an accessory to murder, she cannot collect his estate, including his shares in the clinic. In that case it will all pass on to David's children by a previous marriage. And Lorraine, the former wife, no doubt will vote to sell their shares to an HMO or something. There is no possibility that she would go along with setting up a foundation that will bring no income. Since Annie has no money, the board voted to hire an attorney on her behalf and be responsible for the charges."

"And Mr. Halvord?" Barbara asked. He had not been mentioned as a board member or share holder.

"By sifting through their questions, comparing notes, discussing possible meanings, we have come to believe that they will charge him along with Annie with conspiring to do murder, and then concealing the crime, getting rid of the gun and possibly a raincoat or poncho or some such garment. David's body, apparently, was moved, and she could not have done that."

For the first time Darren Halvord spoke up. "I told them that if I'm charged with anything, I can get my own attorney." His voice was deep and low, the words almost a drawl; he sounded not exactly bored, but indifferent, perhaps.

"But," Dr. Kelso said, "we decided that one attorney to represent both of them, in the interests of the clinic, would be more cost efficient. Instead of two sets of investigators, litigators, one would do nicely. And, Miss Holloway, Sid here said that you were the best there is in these parts." He shrugged. "If Darren hired someone less competent who failed to clear him, then Annie would be at risk, and the clinic would be, too. We prefer to do it this way."

Barbara studied him: so old, and so wise, and totally selfish where the clinic was concerned. She wondered if Annie McIvey and Darren Halvord heard the same message that she did in everything he said. He was concerned about safeguarding the clinic; they were secondary.

"All right," she said. "But with the clear understanding that I will represent the interests of Mrs. McIvey and Mr. Halvord. I will keep them informed along the way, but not a committee. Nor will I answer to a committee for any procedure or activity that I deem necessary to do my duty to them."

Without hesitation Dr. Kelso nodded, and Annie visibly relaxed. On the sofa Dr. Boardman and his wife exchanged a quick glance that seemed to be of relief and Darren stopped inspecting his shoes and regarded her with interest instead. Whether Annie knew that her fate was not uppermost in Kelso's mind, Barbara couldn't tell, but, she thought, Darren Halvord had known.

Dr. Kelso opened the folder on the table and Sid cleared his throat, but before either could say anything, Barbara turned to Annie McIvey. "Is it your wish that I should represent you in this matter?"

"Oh, yes."

"And yours?" Barbara asked Darren Halvord.

He nodded. "Yes."

Then she turned back to Dr. Kelso and Sid. "All right. We have a lot of details to work out, and I have a lot of questions. Also, I'll want to talk to each of you individually, probably at some length. I'd like to set up appointments before we break up here. And I want assurance that I'll have the cooperation of others here at the clinic."

No one voiced any objection to the fact that she had taken over the meeting. Dr. Kelso simply pushed the folder closer to Sid and then leaned back in his chair.

But Barbara was not yet finished with Annie and Darren. She asked the young woman first. "Why do you think they will accuse you?"

"Monday morning they practically told me they would. They said that from what Darren had told them, I was in over my head and I might as well just tell them the details. They said it would go easier for me if I told the truth, things like that."

"Okay. I know the routine." Barbara looked at Darren, who nodded.

"Pretty much the same line. They had us in separate rooms, with a guy going back and forth, whispering to the detective who was asking questions, acting as if one of us was confessing or something."

Barbara tried not to show her anger at that kind of questioning—the prisoner's gambit. Make each suspect believe the other one was talking, confessing, turning state's evidence to get a lighter sentence, maybe a suspended sentence on a lesser charge. She nodded at Darren, who nodded back and shrugged. He knew about that, too, she thought. She was looking forward to interviewing him in private, she realized. If she was reading him right, he knew things that a simple physical therapist generally did not know. She turned her attention back to Sid.

"What we've assembled," he said, "are copies of various documents that we hope will assist you in understanding the issues at stake here. Mrs. Kelso's will, the articles of incorporation, the petitions to the court, the terms of David McIvey's will, things of that sort. Also, we added the names and addresses of everyone who was on duty the morning of the murder, the groundskeeper, as well as patients...."

Barbara put the folder in her briefcase: weekend reading. "Good. Thank you. Now, just briefly, fill me in on the morning he was discovered dead. The newspaper articles were pretty sketchy, and it was two months ago."

Their report was almost as sketchy as the newspaper's had been. She didn't pursue it. "Okay. Why are the police concentrating on people connected to the clinic? Why not an intruder, a burglar, someone like that?"

Greg Boardman answered. "Some years back vandals got in and did a lot of damage to the garden, uprooted plants, dumped stuff in the pond, messed things up generally. Afterward we put a padlock on the gate, the only outside entrance there is. I lock up when I leave the clinic every day, around six usually in the winter, and I'm most often the one who unlocks it in the morning. The door from the clinic to the garden is locked at night, and unlocked at seven-thirty in the morning. I gave David the gate key the morning of the murder, and presumably he opened it."

Barbara nodded. She knew well why the police had homed in on Annie; the surviving spouse was always the first suspect. She wanted to ask Darren why they had singled him out, but she decided that such a question, along with many others, should be asked and answered in private. She arranged with Naomi Boardman to have a tour of the garden the following day—Saturday—and set up appointments with the others. Sid hesitated a moment, then agreed to talk to her on Monday, in her office, after his suggestion that she could come to his office was rejected out of hand.

"Anything else?" she asked then.

"Yes," Dr. Kelso said. He had been quiet and watchful, listening intently to everything. "If they decide it was a collaborative murder, what is the usual procedure? Will they arrest both Annie and Darren at the same time, try them together?"

"Possibly," Barbara said. "But understand that I don't have any real information at this point. I don't know what evidence they have gathered. Did anyone see you two conspiring? Overhear a conspiracy? See one of you pass a gun to the other?" At each question Annie shook her head vigorously. Darren was shaking his head also. "Well, if it's inconclusive, in their minds, I mean, what they likely will do is charge the one they think they can get a conviction for with murder one, and charge the other with being an accessory. Murder one seldom allows release on bail, but the accessory may be granted it. They could go for one trial for both, or first one, then the other. In either event it could be many months before a trial actually takes place. I'm afraid you're in for a long punishing ordeal," she added sympathetically to Annie and Darren both.

"And from here on out, you absolutely should not answer any questions unless I'm with you, or my associate is. The police may pretend shock, or try to make you feel guilty over wanting your attorney, but it's a charade. It won't mean anything. Insist, no questions without your attorney present." Although, she added to herself, it was a little late for that bit of advice.

10

That Friday evening, Erica did not linger at the clinic after reading. She had not worked that day, and although she certainly could use the money, she had been happy to have the day off. It was Todd's weekend with his father, and she had invited them to dinner. She knew about the meeting going on in the directors' room; everyone knew about it. She might have time to prepare most of the meal before Darren got home, have it ready for him when he arrived cold and tired.

Over the holidays, when both Todd and she had been out of school for two weeks, he had spent several days in her half of the house waiting for Darren to get home from work. One day she had taken him shopping, and in a Goodwill store they had found a bread machine for ten dollars. That afternoon they learned to bake bread. Another day they had gone to the pound for a kitten. Darren had objected: Todd couldn't have a pet when he was gone most of the time.

"We'll go in halves," Erica had said. "Half his, half mine. When Todd's at his mother's house, I'll keep the kitten here. I've always wanted one, too. Half a kitten is better than no kitten."

"Which half is mine?" Todd had asked.

"We'll flip a coin. Tails gets the kitty litter box. Heads gets the eating end." They had all laughed. She ended up with the litter box and most of the feeding, but that was all right. That Friday she had been home when Todd arrived from school, and he had come straight to her door, looking for his end of the kitten. He was still there playing with the kitten when she got back.

It would be a simple meal: fish, spaghetti, bread, salad and brownies for dessert. She had memorized the recipe earlier and shopped for the ingredients that morning. As she got busy at the stove, Todd played with the kitten, dragging a string for it to pounce upon.

"Rikki," he said, "what happens if you're born on February twenty-ninth? I mean, how do you count birthdays? One every four years? I wish I was born on the twenty-ninth."

She laughed. "I don't think it works like that. Maybe you celebrate on the twenty-eighth instead of waiting."

"My birthday is on the twenty-sixth." He yanked the string hard and the kitten fell on its face. Laughing, he picked it up and stroked it. "I should have named him Clumsy," he said. He had named it Napoleon and they all called it Nappy. Then, still petting the kitten, keeping his gaze on it, he said, "When I'm twelve Mom said I could choose where I want to live. But she said that if Dad's in trouble, I might have to wait."

Erica stirred onion and garlic in olive oil. "I wouldn't worry about it if I were you. There's an old saying, don't borrow trouble. It means don't worry about all the things that could possibly go wrong. In a few weeks I'm sure everything will be fine, and you'll get to make your choice." Todd began to pull the string for the kitten again. She took his silence to mean, What do you know? Or, You don't understand. She added tomatoes and peppers to the skillet.

"Do you know how to play hearts?" she asked then. "I thought maybe we could play cards after we eat."

"Sure," he said. "I know how to play bridge, too. Dad taught me."

She bit her lip. She would have to learn how to play bridge. Someone at the clinic had mentioned that Darren belonged to a bridge club, and she had not given it another thought. But she would learn. Forget hearts, she told herself, and out loud she said, "Or we could play Clue or Monopoly."

Swiftly Todd said, "Monopoly."

She nodded. Of course not Clue. Dr. McIvey in the garden with a gun? She shivered and added mushrooms to the skillet.

When Darren came in, flushed from the cold, he stopped at the door to take off his jacket and boots, then stood for a moment sniffing. "Wow!" he said softly. "Just wow! A feast!"

"Garlic, onions, homemade bread. I ask you, how can you go wrong with that?" Erica said. "Five minutes."

Dinner was a success. Darren and Todd discussed and discarded plans for a shelter for the bonsai, a ten-inch tall weeping cherry that was said to be twelve years old. Erica had gasped at the price tag, then bought it anyway. According to Todd, who had become the authority, it had to be outside, but protected from hard rains and hot sun. And slugs and snails, he had added. In the summer the roots had to be kept cool. The shallow dish that housed the tree would heat up too much and bake the roots.

A little before ten Todd said there was a show he wanted to see. Darren had gone broke minutes before and Erica was very nearly broke; they declared Todd the winner and gathered up the game. Todd collected his belongings and left while Darren was putting on his boots.

As soon as Erica heard Todd going up the outside stairs, she said, "Darren, he needs to talk to you."

Darren stopped lacing his boot and looked up at her. He was tired, she thought, under a strain and trying not to show it, but here, away from patients, away from the clinic, the strain showed in worry lines, a guarded expression. The dancing lights in his eyes had dimmed. "He thinks you're in trouble," she said, "and he's worried."

"What did he say?" Darren asked.

She repeated Todd's words, then said, "I imagine the police have questioned his mother, and he knows it. Maybe they asked him questions. They've been asking everyone questions, of course. He knows there's trouble and he needs to hear from you how serious it is. There's nothing you can tell him that's worse than what he can imagine for himself."

He bent over his boot again and finished tying the laces. Then he stood up and regarded her for a moment. He reached for his jacket and slipped it on. "Sometimes there are things you can't tell your eleven-year-old kid," he said.

She shook her head. "If it's something he'll learn anyway sooner or later, it would be better to tell him now. It's better to tell children as much of the truth as they can handle. It can be devastating to them to hear vicious half-truths and lies from others."

All of Darren's movements had seemed in slow motion—tying his bootlaces, standing up, putting on his jacket. In the same deliberative, deceptively slow motion he reached out and grasped her shoulders and drew her closer, then kissed her forehead. He released her, stepped back, turned and opened the door.

"Thank you, Rikki. Just thanks." He left.

In a dreamlike way she crossed her arms and

placed her hands on her own shoulders where his had
been, then stood with her eyes closed as a shudder
rippled through her, and another....

Promptly at ten on Saturday morning Barbara
rang the doorbell at Greg and Naomi Boardman's
house. It was a cold morning, and the newspaper and
TV weather forecast agreed that an inch or two of
snow would move in later that day. Barbara did not
believe it. It never snowed when they said it would.
Snow in the valley came by night, by stealth, unan-
nounced, always a surprise to forecasters and a de-
light to children.

Naomi opened the door and ushered her inside.
"It's freezing out there," she said. "Come in by the
fire. Do you want coffee? I just made it."

"I'd love some," Barbara said, following Naomi
into a comfortable room where a fire was blazing. The
house was almost too warm, but it felt good. The
drive had not been long enough for her car heater to
take the chill off. The room they entered was cluttered
from the floor up: a bold black-and-beige rug in a
geometric pattern, with scatter rugs on top of it in
bright colors; red cushions on a tan sofa; vases of
flowers, a potted plant on one table; books and magazines here and there; a bowl of candy on an end
table; the coffee carafe and cups on a table, where it
looked as if candles had been pushed aside to make
room.

Naomi was wearing jeans and a heavy dark-red
sweater, and suede ankle boots. She was also wear-

ing dangling parrot earrings. She started to hand Barbara a cup of coffee, frowned at the coffee table by the sofa and put the cup down again in order to clear a space. Then, with both of them seated on the sofa, she said, "Now, do you ask questions or do I just talk?"

Barbara laughed. "Both. I need to fill in exactly what happened the morning Dr. McIvey was shot. And I'll need to fill in a lot of background for everyone here. Let's begin with the morning of the shooting."

"Well, that morning Annie dropped him off at seven-thirty, and she left. Greg let him in and gave him the key to the gate, and a few minutes after he went out, I came down. I went out to get the car out of the garage to be ready to drive him to his office, and then I sat at the table in the kitchen and had coffee and read the newspaper. I thought it was strange that he didn't come back for his ride, but just assumed he had been held up with his patient or something. I didn't give it much thought at all, to tell the truth. I really wanted to make some breakfast, but I didn't want to be interrupted in the middle of it. Then Carlos came to tell Greg that David had been shot."

"Did Carlos say he had been shot?"

"I don't think so. He said he was dead."

She admitted that she had waited until she knew McIvey had left the house to come downstairs. By then Greg had made coffee and had taken his to the study to watch the news.

"I was annoyed," she said. "I thought it was an imposition for him to ask me to drive him to work. He could have called a cab. I almost said no, that it would be inconvenient, but then I thought, why cause a scene or add to the tension we were all under? I just said fine and let it go at that."

Barbara asked questions and she answered readily. Annie had told her the day before the shooting that she had to go to Portland and would not be working at the clinic the next day, and yes, others probably heard her. And they knew that the patient was to be sent home, of course, and that meant that McIvey would have to sign him out and leave follow-up orders.

"You didn't like Dr. McIvey, did you?" Barbara asked when Naomi paused.

"I hardly knew him. But I don't think anyone really liked him, at least as far as I could tell. He was not a likable person. He was cold, brusque and impatient with lesser mortals, which everyone else was as far as he was concerned. So, no, I didn't like him, but I had no reason to dislike him personally. I didn't like what he wanted to do with the clinic."

"Why is Mrs. McIvey living here with you and your husband?" Barbara asked.

For the first time Naomi hesitated. Then she said, "Annie's mother stayed with her for three weeks after David's death, but she had to go back home, and Annie couldn't stay in that condo alone. It's up in the south hills," she added, as if that explained why.

"Many people live alone. Why couldn't she?"

Naomi stood up and crossed the room to bring the carafe and refill their cups. When she sat down again she said in a low voice, "If they charge her, it will all come out in court, won't it? Whatever the police dig up, I mean."

"Yes."

"She has no money," Naomi said. "He kept her on a niggardly allowance, and she had the illusion of having money when she had little access to it. Every month he put a check in a joint account, and she had use of a credit card, but it had a modest dollar cap, and she didn't know that. When she tried to use it the month following his death, the credit card was rejected, and his estate is being held until there is a resolution concerning his death. She has her old job back, the same work she was doing as a volunteer for nearly five years. It pays very little. Eventually she will want her own place, but for now, she's staying here." She said this in a defiant manner, as if challenging Barbara to question it further. "He humiliated her repeatedly when he was living, and he humiliated her even more after he died."

Barbara nodded. It appeared, she thought then, that Naomi did have a reason to dislike David McIvey personally.

"How long have you known her?" Barbara asked.

Naomi told her how Annie had answered their newspaper ad, and had taken her first job out of school at the clinic. "She was innocent in a way. I don't mean virginal precisely, I don't know about that, but inexperienced. She was exactly how I always imagined my own daughters would be at that age," she said, and sighed deeply, then explained about her two stillborn babies. "Anyway, when David McIvey set his sights on her, she had no defenses. She was completely infatuated with him, or with the idea of what she thought he was, I guess."

Not long after that Barbara said, "I hate to ask you to go out in such cold weather, but could you show me the way to the clinic from here, where McIvey was shot, where his body was dragged?"

They bundled up and went through a hall to a bright yellow-and-blue kitchen to the back door and outside. The herb garden was winter-dormant, sleeping under a thick mulch, with a bit of greenery, or more often a gray-green planting of something or other standing in defiance of the weather. Barbara, not a gardener, thought it was dismal.

They passed through the back gate, across a narrow alley, to the gate to the clinic garden, and onto a well-packed path of bark mulch.

"When we came here," Naomi said, "I mean Greg and me, all this was lawn with a few trees and bushes. Darren said it should be laid out as an archipelago of islands, each one planted in tiers so that the illusion was of privacy, to encourage the patients to walk. Many of them are self-conscious and awkward, reluctant to be seen struggling. Anyway, Darren planned the layout, and Carlos and his employer planned the tiers and what should be planted, how to maintain it, all that. So we have islands of flowers and shrubs with a mazelike series of paths winding in and out. See, they're miniature terraced gardens. When they're in full foliage they're five feet tall, six feet, some even higher. Some of the vines are like walls, screening one section from another."

Barbara agreed that it was very clever, well thought out and scrupulously maintained. Even in the winter landscape there was a feeling of privacy about the garden, and there were clumps of green plants, low, spreading conifers, as well as broad-leaved evergreen plants, some draping over the edges of the stairlike risers. Heather was in bloom: dusky pink, lavender, white.

They had gone twenty-five or thirty feet along the path, with the clinic building on the right, the garden on the left, when Naomi stopped. A path branched off between two of the planted islands.

"They say this is where he was shot," Naomi said in a low voice. "And he was dragged up that path to the curve."

"Do you mind?" Barbara said, and started to walk up the path. Naomi hesitated a moment, then joined her. "How far up?" Barbara asked.

On one side the island was eight or nine feet wide, the other side was a foot or two wider. The path they were on joined another, and Naomi stopped where the two came together.

"Here," she said. "He wasn't pulled onto the other path."

Barbara looked up and down the path they had

come to; it curved out of sight in both directions. The one they had just come on went straight to the clinic building, but who would have been out walking on that rainy, foggy morning? "Okay," she said. "Let's get in out of the cold. I have an appointment with your husband at two, so I'll take off now and come back later."

They walked back to the residence where Naomi entered by the back door, and Barbara walked around to the front driveway and her car. An appointment with Greg Boardman at two, and lunch with Bailey Novell now.

Bailey was the only private detective she had ever worked with and the only one her father trusted. They both knew he was the best in the business. He had grumbled, "Jeez, Barbara, Saturday? You've got to be kidding."

"Nope. Tell you what, I'll sweeten the pot and buy you some lunch. Someplace without a basketball game full blast on the television."

They agreed on a seafood restaurant near the sprawling mall a few blocks from the clinic. Seafood, Barbara thought in resignation; he would order lobster or crab, whichever was more expensive.

She was already seated at a window table when Bailey slouched into the restaurant. She gasped when she saw him. He was wearing an outercoat that fell below his knees and seemed to be made of some kind of shaggy mammoth hair. The garment was gray, shapeless, intended for someone inches taller and pounds heavier than Bailey. He had on a matching cap.

"My God," she said when he drew near. "Where did you get that?"

"Like it?" He stroked the hideous fur. "Hannah wanted to go to Portland, hit some of the after-Christmas sales, and I spotted this in an outdoor place. Just what I need, and half price. Do I look like a Sherpa guide?"

She shook her head. "You look like a yak. Take it off and hide it."

Complacently he took it off, folded it and laid it on a chair, then seated himself. Bailey always looked as if whatever he was wearing had come from Goodwill rejects, and today, since it was a Saturday and, at least in theory, he was not working, it appeared that he had put on the worst of the worst. A worn and faded plaid shirt, thin at the elbows, frayed at the cuffs, and corduroy trousers that had been laundered so often they were almost as shiny smooth as satin.

He ordered the seafood platter and a beer for right now. She ordered clam chowder. Then, with his beer in place, he said, "What's up? I thought you'd be taking life easy for a few months. You turning into a workaholic or something?"

"Something," she said. "It's the David McIvey murder. Remember it? Back in November he was shot at a clinic on Country Club Road."

"Vaguely," he said. "I wasn't paying much attention. Client?" Bailey always said that he liked to know who would pick up the tab before he ordered food or drink; he also liked to know there was a paying client before he stirred himself. He knew all about the impoverished clients who came to Barbara in Martin's Restaurant.

"A committee's worth," she said. She told him about the meeting. "So it looks as if the police are narrowing it down to Darren Halvord and Annette McIvey, the widow. There may be something going on between them. I want to know for sure. And I believe Halvord has a history. He'll probably tell me something about it, but I want an outside version as well. Also, the scoop on what the police are up to."

She gave him a copy of the list of people at the clinic, staff, volunteers, Kelso... "I underlined the ones I want you to start with," she said. "The patient Dorothy Johnson saw a demon in a black shiny cape." He gave her a mean look and she shrugged. "Just reporting."

He was scanning the list when their food arrived. "Halvord and Erica Castle live in the same place. Anything there?"

"I don't know. She is listed as first-floor apartment and he's second floor. It may be nothing more than that, but find out. She was there that morning."

She eyed his platter, heaped with a mountain of food. Bailey was deceptive. He looked like a middle-aged bookkeeper or middle school social studies teacher, or something equally benign, but he was sinewy, and he could outeat and outdrink people twice his size. She realized she was thinking of Annie McIvey and the problem of moving a body as large as David McIvey's had been. Was Annie one of those sinewy people with surprising strength?

She finished her chowder while Bailey still had food on his platter. "Just thinking out loud," she said. "You don't have to make a sound, just think for me. Could a woman who is about five foot three, 115 pounds, drag a body that weighs 175 about eight feet?"

"Depends," he said with his mouth full.

"Sorry I asked. Eat your crab."

When he had eaten every bite, finished his beer and wiped his lips, he said, "What I mean is, it depends on how he was moved as much as on how big she is. Head first? Lift the torso and move him? Probably not. Feet first? Grab his ankles, or even one ankle and drag him along, probably. By one hand or arm, maybe. And it depends on the surface of wherever he's being dragged. Waxed floor, probability goes up. On a rug on the waxed floor, way up. Rough ground, it goes down. See? You know how he was moved?"

"Nope. That's your job. Now I've got to run. The police have been on this for weeks. We have a lot of catching up to do."

"Okeydokey. Got an idea. Get the old man to lie down and see how far Shelley can drag him."

"It has to be outside in the rain on a bark mulch path," she said, waving her credit card to catch the eye of their waiter.

"You see a problem with little details like that?" Bailey asked, as he put his ghastly coat back on. At her look he said, "Just wait until later today and the snow begins to pile up, you'll wish you had a coat exactly like this."

"It isn't going to snow. It never snows when they predict it."

She returned to the clinic and met with Greg Boardman who gave her a tour, introduced the staff and volunteers who were on Saturday duty and then talked with her in his office. Most of it was simply corroboration of what Naomi had already told her. And a few more details about David McIvey. Then he talked about Darren Halvord.

"He's the best physical therapist I've ever met," he said. "He has a gift for it." He told her about the basketball player who had had a tumor. "David would have operated," he said, "and it would have been a terrible mistake. He never forgave Darren for being right." He leaned back in his chair. "David and Darren," he said. "Both with magic hands. David was a superb surgeon, no one will dispute that, but the magic stopped at the wrists. He had no empathy, no sympathy for his patients, no understanding that a person is more than a bad artery or a ruptured disk, a code on an insurance form. He was an outstanding technician, and inhuman. Darren treats the whole person. He's attuned to the whole patient, and they respond in ways that sometime seem miraculous. David called him a witch doctor, a shaman. I think he had it just about right."

That night Barbara had a date with Will Thaxton, whom she had known for more than twenty years, ever since they had attended the same high school. They had gone their separate ways and only recently had become reacquainted and started to date. After a leisurely dinner in a very nice restaurant that she didn't like as much as he did, they planned to drop in on three different brew pubs where jazz groups were playing. He knew every jazz group in town, and most of the ones who passed through on tour.

"This kid is the new Miles Davis," he said as they left the restaurant. "You'll see."

She sniffed the air suspiciously. The temperature had risen, and the air was moister. They went to the first of the pubs and danced and listened to music, and drank a little. When they left, she sniffed the air again. "It's going to snow," she said.

"In your dreams. On to the Barrel."

They danced some more and she agreed that the new kid might become as good as Miles Davis, and he argued that he was already that good. It was midnight when they left, and there was half an inch of snow on the ground, and more falling in huge lazy flakes.

"Home," she said, laughing delightedly at the snow. "Isn't it beautiful!"

Slipping and sliding, they got to his BMW, and he drove her home, a slow, slippery drive. At her door, he said, "Of course, I can't navigate that Willamette Street hill."

She nodded. "You'd be insane to try."

So he went in with her, and they watched the snow fall for a time before they went to bed.

11

She roused when Will got up, then turned over and went back to sleep. The next time she woke up, it was to the smell of coffee, and that proved irresistible. Pulling on her robe she hurried to the window, but to her disappointment, the snow was already melting, dripping off trees, turning to slush on the street. Another Oregon blizzard, she thought in disgust.

Her apartment was small: two bedrooms, one used as an office, a living room-dining space-kitchen in one large area where the kitchen could be screened off from the rest, but never was. Propped against the wall were two Monet prints that she had ordered from the Metropolitan Museum and had framed, but had not got around to hanging. The living room had bookcases stuffed full to overflowing, a good reading chair and lamp, a television, a good CD player and a stack of CDs, a couch that looked more comfortable than it was and one cloisonné candy dish that was usually empty because she thought of candy at night, not when she was shopping. It was sufficient, she had decided, and made no further attempt at interior decorating. There wasn't room for anything else, she told herself. In fact, the very nice gifts that her father and friends gave her for Christmas or her birthday—a Waterford vase, crystal goblets, a jade-and-silver clock—she usually boxed up and put away, for safekeeping, she always told herself. It was a lie. She didn't want to bother dusting them.

The apartment was fine for one person, crowded with two, and she was neither surprised nor disappointed when she went to the dining area and found a note propped against the coffee carafe on the table. "Logs to split, elusive loopholes to pry open, chickens to feed. I'll call later in the week. You're a sweet sleeper. W." Smiling at the note, she sat down with the newspaper and coffee, contented.

No demands, no recrimination, no arguments about work, no questions, a perfect relationship, she sometimes thought. They went out on what she thought of as date-type things—movies now and then, theater, concerts. They danced, dined, listened to music, went to bed and then split. Sometimes she mocked his clients, but never as much as he did. He was a corporate lawyer, shoulder deep, he claimed, in trusts, wills, deeds, partnerships and articles of incorporation, all lucrative, some of it shady but not illegal, because, he also claimed, he was an expert at loopholes. He hadn't had a client end up in jail yet, which was more than she could say. Her response had been that at least she took her clients seriously, and he was playing games. He had readily agreed.

"But," he had added, "the games I play have made me fairly affluent. In ten years I expect to be rather rich, and in twenty years filthy rich. And as long as a third of your clients come via Martin's Restaurant, no matter how seriously you take their problems, you'll still be wondering if you can afford a new car from one year to the next."

She thought he was modest about how much money he made. In her eyes he was already rich and she had absolutely no qualms about letting him wine and dine her. He was subsidizing some of her penniless clients.

She realized that she was not tracking a word of what she was reading in the newspaper and put it aside to consider the rest of the day, the following weeks, how much unfinished business she had to attend to, or have Shelley attend to. Meanwhile she had to go over the clinic business once more in order to have it clear in her mind when she told her father about it at dinner that night. She felt almost as if she had been on vacation, and it was time to get back to work. It was a good feeling.

That evening, watching her father work his miracles with a handful of vegetables and a piece of lamb, she told him about the case. She didn't get far because he began scowling fiercely, and since he often saw a snag in the water long before she did, she paused for his comment.

"Why the devil did you take on a new murder case this soon?" he said. "You need some downtime. A bit of a rest. Are you even through wrapping up the details for the Feldman case?"

He might have gone on, but she said, "Dad," in a way that was not going to be an entreaty, but was rather a warning. "And just what the devil are you doing with that lamb?" she demanded, standing to get a better look.

"I'm skewering it." Lamb, red peppers, mushrooms, onions, eggplant pieces still dripping from a marinade...

"Oh." She sat down again and, sipping a good pinot noir, finished telling him what little she knew about the McIvey affair. "Anyway, as far as I can tell, to know David McIvey was to wish him dead. If there were mourners at his funeral, they must have been paid by the hour."

Frank nodded. "It's a mess," he said. "Too many motives. And they run the gamut—passion, greed, zealotry. Even for a decent cause it can still be zealotry—possibly revenge." He shook his head. "Too many possible killers. Any idea why the cops chose Halvord and the widow?"

"Nope. I sicced Bailey onto it." Then she said, "One of the patients at a window saw a dwarf in a shiny black cape, or else a demon out to snatch the soul before it could escape."

Frank groaned. "Just what you need, a dose of the paranormal."

"Actually she could have seen someone. From a second-floor window, looking almost straight down, you might see a normal person, foreshortened, take on a curious shape. I need to look out that window to tell just what she might have seen. And I need a tall-ish man, about your size, to lie down and see how far Shelley can drag him in the rain over a bark mulch path."

"You're out of your mind," Frank said coldly. "Why don't you go see if those fool cats are on the dinette table and if they are, chase them and set it."

She chased Thing One and Thing Two off the table where they had been sitting like bookends gazing out. They stalked from the room with a grand show of indignation, tried to get sympathy from Frank, who told them to beat it, and then went to the sliding glass door to continue gazing out. It was dark and impossible for them to see anything, but they put up a good front.

"They're waiting for the snow to come back," Frank said when Barbara returned for plates. "They were out there rolling in it, lapping it up, playing like kids." They were monster kids, great golden coon cats who weighed in at twenty-plus pounds each.

The McIvey case was not mentioned again until after the meal was consumed, the kitchen cleaned up and a doggie bag of extras prepared for her to heat in the microwave sometime. He usually made enough for her to have another meal at home, and she was grateful. She divided food into two categories: the meals she prepared for herself, ersatz food, and real food such as Frank made. She preferred the real stuff, she had to admit, but it was beyond her ability to produce it. Their Sunday night dinners, while not a ritual set in concrete, were regular, and did not cause a twinge of guilt on her part; Frank liked to cook, and she liked to eat.

Then, getting ready to leave, she said, "Dr. Kelso and Sid Blankenship are coming by at nine in the morning. Want to sit in on it?"

He said he certainly would like to do that.

She appreciated that he, after practicing criminal law for fifty years, knew a great deal more than she did, and he was extremely helpful when it came to citing cases and recalling obscure rulings. Also, he knew every judge in the state, and could wrest secrets from rocks.

And after his own practice of fifty years, it was now one of his greatest pleasures to watch her work. His daughter, Frank knew, was a better lawyer than he ever had been. For the past few years he had been trying to retire, he sometimes said, but he still dropped in daily at his own prestigious law firm, where he was a senior partner, and where criminal cases were no longer accepted. And he was an occasional associate of Barbara's in her criminal cases. He was very grateful for that.

He had what amounted to a superstitious fear, he once admitted to himself, that anyone who stopped doing the work he was destined for had lost the will to live. And he had not been able to take on a case involving life-and-death issues following the death of his wife nearly nine years earlier. Then Barbara had brought him back, even as he had brought her back to practice law after she had left in anger and disgust with a system she saw as corrupt. They had saved each other, he acknowledged silently. He was not certain she understood that yet, but she would one day, he knew.

Before nine the following morning Barbara had an attorney-client agreement at hand and she had consulted with Shelley about the coming week. Frank had come early, he said to make coffee. Maria Velazques, the office secretary, or Shelley, or Frank always tried to get to the coffeemaker before Barbara did. Promptly at nine Sid Blankenship and Dr. Kelso arrived.

Barbara led them into her office and introduced Frank. As they removed their heavy coats, Sid looked over the room appraisingly, with apparent approval. As well he should approve, Barbara thought. Her father and Shelley's father had furnished it, from the rich burgundy pile carpeting to the fine brocade-covered chairs, the luxurious sofa, inlaid coffee table, her desk and visitors' chairs. Kelso appeared not to notice anything. He kept his white cap on and sank down onto the sofa as if tired. He and Sid both turned down the offer of coffee.

As soon as they were seated, Sid read through the agreement, and said, "Fine, fine." He handed it to Dr.

Kelso, who signed it without glancing at the contents. "I'll get the other signatures and get it back to you later today," Sid said. "Now, where do you want to start?"

"Let me see if I have the details of the clinic arrangement correct," Barbara said. "As it stands now, Dr. Boardman owns twenty-five percent of the shares outright, Dr. Kelso controls the voting rights of another twenty-five percent and Annie McIvey owns five percent outright. Why haven't you petitioned the court for permission to set up the foundation?"

Sid nodded. "That's how it stands. However, on the advice of her civil law attorney, Mrs. McIvey has declined to join in such a petition." He was still holding the lawyer-client agreement. He tapped it and added, "This may be the instrument to reduce her anxiety and permit her to sign. But even if she does, it could take months for a final decision to be passed down. Appraisals, audits, background checks... It all takes time."

"And we might not have that time," Dr. Kelso said in his rasping voice. "My wife is dying. She could go today, tomorrow, in six months, perhaps not for a year. But she is dying, and if she dies before we have a foundation in place it might never happen. Make Annie understand, Miss Holloway. She will be protected, her interests will be protected under that agreement and the clinic will survive as a foundation, but only if she agrees to take a stand with us. We can't wait for a formal accusation to be made, a trial, two trials. And if she's found guilty, or pleads guilty to a lesser offense, David's children will get his shares, and his ex-wife will sell to the highest bidder on their behalf. That's what this is all about, Miss Holloway."

She shook her head, regarding him. "No, Dr. Kelso. That is not what this is about. I have been hired to defend Mrs. McIvey if she is charged with murder or being an accessory to murder. That is what I intend to do."

Matter-of-factly Frank said, "Dr. Kelso, no probate court will release an estate as long as the cause of death of the deceased is an issue. Also, if a court takes under advisement the transition from a non-profit corporation to a foundation, as you propose, all assets would likely be frozen for a time until the audits and such are conducted. The court might well take a dim view of the nonprofit corporation spending its meager resources to defend two suspects in a murder case, the outcome of which might well influence the decision. I believe Mrs. McIvey's attorney has given her sound advice."

Sid nodded slightly, as if to say, just what I told him. His smooth face did not change its Humpty-Dumpty bland expression, but Dr. Kelso's face, already like corduroy, seemed to shrivel even more and a deep-maroon tinge appeared on the folded and refolded skin of his cheeks. His sporty cap was more incongruous than ever against his aged face. He turned his sharp gaze from Frank, leaned back and closed his eyes.

"I was home, probably still in bed when it happened," he said. "Greg called and told me, and after the police left, I went to the residence and we talked. And that's all I know about the murder." He looked at Barbara then. "Is there anything else?"

"Not today. Later, after I know more, I'll want to talk to you again."

He nodded and pushed himself up from the sofa. "Not too much later," he said as he put on his overcoat. "When you're young," he said, "you think you have so much time, too much time, time for everything. Then you don't. God's little joke."

Barbara walked out with them and returned with the coffee tray. "What do you think?" she asked Frank, pouring for both of them.

"I think he'll cooperate with you just as long as he thinks it's in his interest to do so."

"And his interest isn't quite the same as Annie McIvey's and Darren Halvord's," she said.

"Exactly."

"He may be the last person in America who still says Miss instead of Ms.," she said. "Holding on to the past or something."

Annie arrived just as Shelley was ready to leave to go to Martin's Restaurant. Standing side by side in the reception room, they could have passed for sisters, with the same build, similar blond hair, similar good bones and features, but Shelley was afloat in her bubble of happiness, and Annie was mired in gloom. And that did make a difference, Barbara thought, waving Shelley out.

"Do you want coffee? A Coke?" Barbara asked Annie, motioning toward her office.

"A Coke maybe."

"Coming right up," Maria said, rising from her desk. "I'll make a fresh pot of coffee, too," she said, then smiled at Barbara, as if forgiving her for the terrible coffee she generally made.

"Hold the calls," Barbara said, ignoring the slight dig, "unless it's Dad or Bailey."

In her office, Barbara gestured toward the sofa and comfortable chairs by the round table with its lovely inlaid semiprecious stones. "Let's sit over there and just talk," she said. She sat down and put her feet up on the table. "See, get comfortable."

Annie smiled faintly and sat on the sofa, not as stiff and rigid as she had been in the directors' room, but not relaxed either.

"How it works," Barbara said, "is that the cops investigate, and if they think you're a prime suspect, they'll question everyone who knows you, ever knew you, or just thinks they might know you. They'll dig up secrets you didn't even know you had, and come up with a lot of things that are true, as well as other things that aren't. I want to get that same kind of information, but from you directly, not from outsiders." She grinned. "A defense attorney hates it when she learns along with the jury that her client was a serial killer back in middle school."

This time Annie's smile was wider and lasted fractionally longer.

"That's a good place to start," Barbara said. "Back when you were a kid. You lived on the coast?"

"Tillamook. On a dairy farm." She stopped, and when Barbara simply nodded, she began to talk about her parents' farm, and then about the bay, the annual flooding, fishing….

Maria brought in a tray with a Coke and coffee and quietly left again. Annie talked on, about college at Monmouth, a boyfriend or two, going to Corvallis with others to dance or do a pub crawl through the minibreweries or see a movie, coming to Eugene to look for a job.

"Naomi hired me. She said they would train me." She ducked her head. "For whatever reason, she took a liking to me, personally, I mean. She wanted to help me. When I told her I was living in a motel, because I didn't have moving-in money—I wouldn't ask my folks. They'd already done so much for me. You know, first and last month, a deposit—Naomi said that wouldn't do. And she invited me to live in the residence for a while."

She was talking freely when she described working in the clinic, which she had loved. "I fell madly in love with Darren," she said, and shook her head. "The older man girls dream of. It never occurred to me that everyone falls in love with him. He takes it in stride if he notices at all. It took a long time for him to notice me in particular, but then we began going out."

"Were you lovers?"

"No. It never got that far. He was being careful,

I think, because I was a lot younger than he was, and he had been married and divorced, and has a son. Then David came along."

And then, Barbara thought, Annie began to spin a fairy tale. Swept off her feet. A perfect marriage. Lovely house with a housekeeper-cook. A family retreat at Sun River, where there were horses, mountain trails to hike, a heated pool. Plays, concerts. Freedom to do volunteer work at the clinic. Beautiful clothes.

She had become rigid again, except for her hands which seemed to have an existence of their own, twisting and clutching each other almost spasmodically, relaxing, only to start again. She appeared oblivious that her hands were belying her words.

Barbara heard her out without interruption, and when Annie fell silent again, she asked, "Is that the picture others will paint of your marriage?"

"No one outside a marriage can really know what goes on inside it," Annie said.

"That's true," Barbara said, "but think how it will appear if four or five others under oath tell a radically different story, and you, also under oath, stick to your version. A jury might go with the greater number."

"I read that you don't have to testify at your trial," Annie said defiantly. "I won't take the stand."

"At your trial," Barbara said, nodding. "Again, true. But, Annie, I'm thinking of Darren Halvord's trial now. You may be called as a material witness. Not only that, but a hostile material witness, and that means the prosecution can ask leading questions, of the sort where you end up damned if you answer and damned if you don't. If you refuse to answer, you can be held for contempt of court, and if it is decided that you lied, you can be held for perjury. It's a no-win situation. The questions no doubt will include things like when was the last time you had a serious argument with your husband? What are the terms of the prenuptial agreement you signed before your marriage to him? When was the last time you met Darren Halvord outside the clinic?"

Annie had gone pale as Barbara spoke, then blanched even more, until it looked as if she might faint. Shots in the dark, Barbara thought sadly, but they had struck home. Not unkindly she said, "Annie, we must not have an adversarial relationship. If we do, I would advise you to get a different defense attorney right away, because you have to be able to trust whoever defends you, and that means you have to be truthful, so that between you and your attorney you can determine the best defense possible."

Annie swished slivers of ice around in her glass and did not look up. In a low voice she said, "There was an agreement. That's why I saw a lawyer a few years ago, to see if it was valid."

Almost in a monotone she began to tell the other side of the perfect marriage. Then she said, "I decided to stick it out because I could work at the clinic, and I was getting training in so many different ways. I had no skills at all before, just a liberal arts education. And we had good sex. David was a wonderful lover. It was just his demanding schedule that I hated. He was a brilliant surgeon—everyone says so—but he was a bad driver, too impatient with other drivers, and he got tense when he drove, so I did it all. I took him to the hospital, met him for lunch, picked him up at the end of the day. Just a busy schedule. He needed to be in control, and since he couldn't control others on the road, he opted out of dealing with them at all."

She drained her glass, then kept her gaze on it when she said, "It's so complicated. When we made love, he made me feel like a princess, or a goddess. I thought he couldn't be like that if he didn't love me. At those times he lost control, his body and mine, no rational mind in charge…." Her voice dropped lower and the words came more slowly, as if she had never thought through this before, and now found it strange, bewildering even. "I kept thinking that he would get over such rigidity in the rest of his life, the way he did in bed. But after…after we made love, he would send me away. Funny, such passion, and then he wanted to sleep alone. The next day it was as if it hadn't happened. I think he was afraid. Losing control like that alarmed him somehow. In his bed, in his arms, I was so sure he loved me." She shook herself and looked up at Barbara then. "I suggested once that we see a counselor, you know, a marriage counselor. He was furious. He said if I needed help, to go get it, but he certainly had no such need."

"Did you talk to someone?"

She shook her head. "I would have gone with him, but not alone. We didn't fight, not like you meant. We had an argument a few nights before he was killed. I was restless because of the storm, the first storm of the season. And I was homesick. We argued about the clinic. He wanted to make it into a surgical facility, and I wanted to go along with the foundation plan. It was just an argument, but like I said, I was restless. I've always loved the first storms out on the coast. Anyway, I didn't want to eat dinner and I went out and drove around, parked here and there to watch the trees in the wind. Then I went home, about nine or nine-thirty. We made up and went to bed."

Liar, liar, your pants are on fire, Barbara thought, but she didn't press it. Later they would come back to it, probably more than once.

"And about Darren?" she asked. "Will the prosecution bring out witnesses who saw you two together outside the clinic, or even inside, as far as that goes?"

"I wasn't seeing Darren, or anyone else," Annie said hotly. "I was so virtuous Caesar would have been proud to claim me. No one can say we were seeing each other. Even if I had been willing, and I wasn't, there wasn't anything between us. I had companionship and friendship at the clinic and did meaningful work there, and sex with David was more than enough. I was not looking for an adventure outside of my marriage. Besides, Darren never would have gone out with a married woman."

"Okay," Barbara said. "What about the morning of the murder? Exactly what did you do?"

Annie drew in a long breath. "I've gone over this so many times it's starting to sound rehearsed," she said. "I drove David to the residence at about seven-thirty. He got out and I left. Up Delta Highway to the Beltline, over to I-5 and up to Portland. I didn't stop anywhere along the way. It was slow going because of the rain and fog, and the traffic was heavy. At the hospital up there, I went straight to the reception desk where I was to pick up the X rays. When I said my name, a detective came over and introduced himself. Detective Cary Rizzo. He said there had been an accident, and he would drive me home. He claimed that he didn't know more than that. His orders were to drive me to the clinic. When we got there, another detective came out and asked if he could look inside the glove box and the trunk. I said yes, and he did. Then we went to Naomi's office and they told me what had happened."

"You didn't get out of the car at all, at the residence or in Portland, anywhere along the way?"

"No. It was raining hard all the way up, and I went straight to the parking garage at the hospital. I got there at ten minutes before ten, and we got back here at twenty minutes before one. We didn't stop along the way that time, either. It was just a slow traffic day." She drew in another long breath. "They kept at it, did I stop at one of the rest areas, or in Salem for coffee, or to use a rest room? I didn't."

"All right," Barbara said. "Let's call it a day. It's

been hard for you, I know, and I'm afraid it won't get easier. Will you be at the clinic tomorrow? I want you to meet another associate, who just happens to be my father. He'll be working with Shelley and me on this."

Annie said she would be there.

Barbara went to her desk after Annie left. She had to make a few notes before Darren Halvord arrived, and she wished that she had allowed more time between the two talks. How much truth, how many lies had Annie told? And if she had turned up bone-dry on such a rainy day, what evidence had the police collected that tied her to David McIvey's death?

12

Darren Halvord was ten minutes late and mildly apologetic about it. "I try to be prompt," he said, taking off a heavy jacket, "but sometimes things pile up. Today they piled up. Sorry." His broad face had bright patches of red from the cold.

"No problem," she said. She made her usual offer of coffee, tea, Coke, and he shook his head. Then, instead of moving to the easy seating arrangement at the round table, she went behind her desk and sat down. Her instincts told her to keep this at a very professional business level; if he relaxed any more than he already was he would be a puddle on the floor. He tossed his jacket on one of the clients' chairs and sat in the other.

"Before we get to McIvey's murder," he said, "I want to tell you a little story. Okay?"

"Shoot."

He grinned. "Right. Down in California, Simi Valley area, there was this nice little nuclear family. Dad, Mom, a boy and a girl. Dad worked for the police department, pretty high up, one of those jobs where no matter who's running things, the job is safe. You know how that goes. Change of administration, out with the old crew, in with the new, through the revolving door. Only some of the people don't have to go out. Mom worked for the city government, too. Another cushy sort of job that was safe, with the records department. No real money worries, good health all around, the all-American family. The problem was with the boy. He had a mouth. And he had eyes and read newspapers, had ears and listened to tales told out of school. All in all he was getting an education that was not in the textbooks. One lesson he learned early was not to ask the dad questions. Dad had a way of answering with the back of his hand. Okay. The kid ran with the wrong crowd and when he was thirteen his crowd got busted for drug dealing and using. He along with others. When his case came up, it appeared that behind the curtain a deal had been struck. Some of the gang went here, some went there. Our kid went to a privately run rehabilitation camp. They called it a ranch. A prison for juvenile delinquents. He was sentenced to seven years, from the age of fourteen until he was twenty-one."

His voice was low and easy; Barbara could not detect any bitterness. He might have been talking about a movie he had seen a very long time ago.

"The kid was having a bit of trouble with withdrawal, and finally he had to go to the infirmary. He was a pretty sick kid, actually. The doctor, Henry Ernst, took care of him and kept him for a few days, or maybe weeks. Later on the kid couldn't really remember how long it was before he was up and working in the infirmary, scrubbing things down, general work like that. It was mandatory that all the guests at the ranch would have classes, calisthenics and work."

Speaking dreamily he described living in the detention camp: drugs, fights, rapes, gangs, classes that no one paid attention to or took seriously, busywork....

"The kid had been there for nearly a year, still working in the infirmary for Doc Ernst when he was there, usually once a week unless there was an emergency, and responsible for keeping the classrooms clean, getting high when his mom sent him a few dollars, planning on the high of his life when he got out. Then a real fight broke out. The guards carried a couple of guys into the infirmary, bleeding from knife wounds, and another kid who was screaming in pain. The guards were doing the best they could to stop the bleeding until Doc Ernst could get there, but the one kid kept screaming, and a guard yelled for someone to shut him up. Our boy went over to him and began feeling him. He wasn't bleeding like the other two, but he was in agony. And our boy felt something strange, as if his hands weren't his, and were doing things he couldn't understand or control.

He grabbed the kid's shoulder and wrenched it in a curious way, and the kid moaned and passed out. Our boy was really scared that he had killed him, but when Doc Ernst came and took over, he said that the screaming kid had had a dislocated shoulder that our boy had set back in place where it belonged."

Darren paused, gazing at Barbara with an intensity that she found disconcerting. Then he said, "I don't know what I did. I didn't know then what I was doing. But I knew that was the thing to do. My hands knew that. Something happened to me that day. I was addicted when I went in, and for the whole first year I was addicted and hurting when I couldn't get a fix. After that day I wasn't an addict. I haven't wanted anything since then. I finished high school and three years of college, and when I was twenty-one I got out, got my bachelor's degree, and enrolled in a four-year physical therapy course."

When he paused, Barbara held up her hand, then pushed her chair back and stood up. "Intermission. I want coffee even if you don't. And you should meet my colleague before she takes off."

Darren stood up and pulled a paper from his jacket pocket. "This is the agreement. Annie signed it but I haven't yet. You can get out now, no harm done. I said from the start that I could get my own attorney if I need one. You see, I know exactly what the D.A. will make of my background. Tough town, tough kid, tough gangs, ex-con, pusher and user... Hang him." He tossed the agreement down on her desk.

"Did I say I wanted out?" Barbara asked. "I thought I said I wanted coffee. Do you want some?"

For a moment neither of them moved, then he nodded slightly. "Yes. I would like coffee."

He met Shelley, and by the time she floated out, he was smiling the same way that everyone smiled in her presence these days. Barbara told Maria to take off, and Darren carried the coffee tray back to her office. This time they sat at the round table, Darren on the sofa, Barbara in a comfortable chair. She did not put her feet on the table.

"So to bring you up to date…" Darren said when they were seated again. He told her how he had finished his training, clinical work for the last year, and then had started applying for an internship for the following year. And no one had accepted him. He got a job at a Buick dealership, detailing used cars, preparing them for resale, and kept applying in ever widening circles. Then Kelso had replied and set a date for an interview.

His academic and clinical references were beyond reproach, the highest, but his personal record made it a difficult decision, Dr. Kelso had told him frankly after the initial interview. However, since they were a closed corporation, their files were not open for scrutiny, except for the requirements of the position, and they would give him a try. He interned for a year, and they hired him full-time afterward.

"Dr. Kelso saved my life," he said. "I was as low as a guy can get, and there didn't seem to be an out for me. Then he opened the door again. I doubt that he realized how important it was to me. What he saw was a good therapist who came cheap."

"It was his decision?"

"Basically, it was. His wife was already showing signs of Alzheimer's, drifting out of conversations, forgetting things. And David McIvey's father was getting tired and didn't much care who came in as long as someone did. He wanted more time to fish and relax, and he had earned it. His wife had her hands full with fund-raisers, things of that sort, not with anything to do with the medical end. Dr. Kelso was practically running the whole thing by then."

During his internship, lonesome, broke all the time, he had met Judy, who had split with her boyfriend a month or so earlier. They had spent a weekend camping out at the coast, and she had ended up pregnant. "We got married," he said. "She lived with her parents afterward, and they hated me for ruining their daughter. Can't say I blamed them much. Anyway, the boyfriend came home and one day Judy asked me if I would mind terribly if Eric and she got back together as soon as the baby was born. What could I say? We'd had one weekend together. So the night Todd was born, her lover Eric was there with us." He grinned. "We scandalized the midwife. Two months later we divorced, and the next day she married Eric. They're very happy together."

"Okay. What about you and Annie? Is there anything going on there?"

"No. And there never was. I took her out a few

times, on a bike ride, to a movie, a concert once. Something might have developed in time—we'll never know. But nothing happened then, and nothing's happened since she got married."

"No private meetings that someone might have seen?"

"No." He hesitated, then said, "Actually we met once, just a few nights before David McIvey was killed. She called and said she had to tell me something. I told her my address and she came over. She stayed maybe fifteen minutes, twenty at the most, then left."

He knew, Barbara thought then. He knew as well as she did how damning that visit would appear. A fight with her husband, out driving in the rain, call the old boyfriend, pay a call…

"You might as well fill in the rest," she said. "Why that night? What was so important? What time was it?"

"Look, Barbara, I mean this. There wasn't anything going on between us, that night or in the past. We care about each other, but as friends."

"So give me the details."

He filled in the details, then said. "He was blackmailing her not to go along with the vote for the foundation. The meeting and vote were coming up in a week. She warned me. That's it." Leaning forward he said, "He couldn't have hurt me no matter what he put in my personnel file. I've built a reputation at the clinic. I can go anywhere in the country and do all right because I'm recognized as one of the best physical therapists around. It's a great clinic. We're helping people who wouldn't be treated otherwise. No money, no insurance, no help. And it would be a crime to see it fold. But the clinic isn't my life, not the way it is for Dr. Kelso, or even for Greg. Financially, speaking of the bottom line now, I'd be better off going somewhere else. His threat was empty."

She studied him for a time. He wasn't boasting in the usual sense, she decided; he was merely stating a fact. He was one of the best in his field. "Did you tell the police about her visit?"

"No. And neither did she. We know how it would look. It was the night the first big storm came in, foggy and rainy. No one could have seen her, and we'll leave it at that."

"Someone in your apartment building might have noticed her."

"It's a private residence with an upstairs apartment, outside steps."

"Where did she call from?"

"I don't know. It was about nine-thirty, closer to ten maybe. She said she was over by the clinic and—" He stopped suddenly, then said, "Oh. She must have used her cell phone. The police will know."

Barbara nodded. "They know, and they know you both lied about it." She looked at her watch; it was twenty minutes after six, and she was getting hungry. "Briefly, tell me about the morning of the murder."

"Yeah, briefly," he said in dull tone, as if his mind

were busy adding up the score and finding himself on a losing side. "I was on my bike. I always ride the bike to work, and all around town. I passed the gate and saw an open umbrella. I got off the bike and leaned it against the fence, and went into the garden to close the umbrella and put it under cover. Then I got back on the bike and rode around to the staff parking lot where I locked it up and went inside. I got there before eight, but I don't know how much before. And I don't know what time I left my place. Sometime after eight Carlos came running in and said there was a dead man. I went out with him and Tony Kranz, and we saw McIvey. I made sure he was dead, that he couldn't be helped. I told Carlos to go tell Greg and to have Greg call the police. And I told Tony to go inside and stay by the door and not let anyone out that way. I looked around the garden a little, but it was pointless. You can't see in a straight line anywhere for more than a few feet. A dozen people could have been lurking out of sight. So I went inside to get warm and to dry off and wait for the police."

"What were you wearing when you arrived that morning?"

"A yellow rain suit with a snug hood over a thermal jacket. Black gloves and boots. Helmet. I know. They were looking for a dwarf in something shiny and black."

"Or a demon," Barbara said.

"Yeah. A demon. Another thing, though. The cops took my bike, boots and gloves. They released the bike after three weeks. Without a pedal. I had to get a new one."

"Oh, boy," she muttered, thinking hard. Impounded as evidence? They must have found blood, or something equally damning. "That's enough for now," she said rising, then stretching. "It's been a long day. Are you going to sign the agreement?"

"Do you still want me as a client?"

She studied him for a moment, then said, "That's a curious way to put it. I might ask if you want me as your attorney. But do I want you as a client? Has a patient ever asked you that? Do you still want me as a patient?"

He nodded. "Yes. And if I can help that person, then I do want him or her as a patient. That's what it's all about."

"And you know ahead of time whether you can help?"

"Yes. Otherwise I say no, and recommend something other than physical therapy."

"Understand that I'm not that certain. I'll do my best, give it my best shot, and I hope I can help, but I can't be so certain. It must be a good feeling, that kind of certainty."

"It is." He pulled on his jacket, then turned to the desk. "I'll sign our agreement now and be on my way." He signed it, and they walked out through the reception room to the outside door which she unlocked. He paused there and said, "I've learned over the years to answer questions my patients don't ask. The answer to your question is no. I didn't kill David

McIvey, and I didn't conspire with anyone else to kill him. And I'm not sorry he's dead."

Unaccountably she felt a rush of anger. "You know why I never ask? If my client says no, I have no way of knowing if it's a lie or the truth. And if the answer is yes, it puts us both in an untenable position since I am a sworn officer of the court. Knowing a client is guilty narrows the course of possible actions drastically. I never ask."

"One other thing to mull over along with the problem of my veracity," he said. "I won't plea-bargain. With my record, pleading guilty to anything from jaywalking to shoplifting to a bit of accidental manslaughter would put me away for the next twenty years."

Her anger subsided as fast as it had flared. Curiously she asked, "Did the police go into something like that when they questioned you?"

"Sure. Even suggested a scenario. We met on the path, had an argument, he pushed me or something and I shot him in self-defense. No sale. They were trying to account for the fact that he was shot at very close range, and there's no way they can see us getting that close together unless there was a face-to-face confrontation."

"Did they tell you that?"

He shook his head. "Sometimes you can infer a lot by what isn't said." He shrugged. "Of course, I could be dead wrong about their reasoning."

"But you'd bet money that you're not," she said, opening the door.

"Yes, I would."

He walked out and she closed the door and locked it, then returned to her office and sat behind her desk, thinking. Darren Halvord was complex, for one thing, she told herself. Highly intuitive, perceptive, street-smart in the ways of the police and their investigation. And cocksure of himself, she added, and wondered if that was what had brought on her surge of anger. He knew as well as she did that if he took a plea bargain he would do hard time. He knew that if he was charged, a plea bargain would be offered. Why wasn't he biting his fingernails? Or fidgeting in his chair, or doing something that indicated worry or fear?

Then she wondered if the scenario he said the detective had suggested had been voiced or even hinted at, or if it was his way of telling her what had happened that morning in November.

13

On Friday Frank met Barbara in the parking lot behind her building. She had been to Martin's, no doubt, doing her weekly stint there. Her jeans and boots were a giveaway. Sometimes he thought he'd give a pretty penny to know what it was that indebted Martin and his wife Binnie to the point of idolatry where Barbara was concerned, but he suspected that he would never find out. He had hinted a time or two that he was curious, and she, ever quick to decipher any clue however faint, had not noticed. That suggested that she had pulled a fast one, but there it rested. He waited for her and they went up together to her office on the second floor.

Bailey was standing by Maria's desk, scribbling furiously when they entered.

"Lard!" Bailey said, his pen poised over the notebook. "She uses *lard?* That's hog fat. Hannah would never use hog fat."

"Then she can't make empanadas," Maria said. Her mama's empanadas were sinful and irresistible. Dismissing him, she smiled at Frank and Barbara, and hit the phone button for Shelley's office. "They're here," she said. She ripped off a page from her notepad and handed it to Barbara—four calls. "I'll make fresh coffee. Anything else?"

"Nope. Take off when you wrap up the cooking lesson. See you on Monday," Barbara said, passing her on the way to her own office with Frank close behind and Bailey trailing after.

Over her shoulder Barbara said to Bailey, "And, no, you don't look like Columbo. You look like a flasher."

He was wearing a shabby tan raincoat.

A few minutes later, the four of them gathered around the inlaid table, Bailey nursing a Jack Daniel's, the others with coffee in hand. Barbara said, "Okay, anything, Bailey?"

He shrugged. "Skin-deep at this point. Alibis. Kelso, home in bed. He goes in and out three, four times a day, no one pays much attention. Just another old black car in the rain that morning. Who'd notice? Boardmans. The doc in his study from seven-thirty until Carlos showed up at twenty minutes after eight. Long time to watch the news, but there it is. Mrs. Boardman got the car out, then read the paper and drank coffee. Both alone until Carlos got there.

Annie McIvey dropped McIvey off and headed to
Portland. Alone. No one has showed up yet who noticed a big silver Mercedes on the road. Halvord left
his place at twenty minutes before eight. His landlady saw him wheel his bike out and take off. He got
to the clinic in time for the cook to have him take coffee to the lounge. She says about ten to eight or a
minute or so earlier. Alan rode his bike that route and
the times check out okay. Halvord's in the clear, if
Castle's story holds up. She's a schoolteacher, in the
area since last summer, no axes to grind or anything
like that."

"Darren Halvord's the only one in the clear," Barbara said, "and apparently the only one who turned
up with blood on his shoe. How about Castle, what's
her connection with the clinic?"

He shook his head. "One of the volunteers. She
reads to the patients every afternoon from five until
a little after five-thirty."

He glanced at his notebook, then said, "Halvord's
record. I have what the personnel file had. You know
about his record?"

"What he told me. Drugs, correction facility until
he was twenty-one."

"You want me to go deeper?"

"You bet I do." Then, frowning, she asked, "How
about McIvey's associates in the medical offices?"

"Nada. But like I said, this is skin-deep. There are
four—were four of them sharing office space. They
get to the hospital around seven-thirty or so to check

on patients, then to surgery, or back to the office to see patients there. No absentees that morning, no one late. No reason to want him dead, to all appearances. And I doubt any of them knew about the arrangement with the entrance from the garden. No reason any of them should have known. If they have patients at the clinic, they pay their calls by way of the front entrance and leave that way." He tapped the old duffel bag that he called his junior detective kit. "What I have is in the report, but that's the gist."

"The first Mrs. McIvey?" Barbara asked after a moment.

"More reason to keep him alive and kicking than to see him laid out," Bailey said. "Alimony stopped the day he bit it. I can check more on her."

Absently Barbara shook her head. "No point. Bailey, if you shoot someone standing up at close range like that, how does he fall? Straight back? Crumple down? Stagger a little, then fall?"

He looked from her to Frank, then back. "Jeez, I don't even know what he was shot with. Peashooter or elephant gun? Makes a difference, you know."

"Let's assume a handgun, not too big."

He sighed theatrically. "Okay. Say a .32. He might grab at his heart and stagger a little. Might even have tried to grab the shooter. A .38? Probably jerk back a little. Reflex. Then fall. Maybe straight back, maybe not. Bigger caliber? Back with the impact, maybe twist around a little. See, Barbara, it's guesswork. Tell me the kind of gun and we'll go on from there." He swished the remaining bourbon around in his glass, then drank it all.

"Do you know what he was wearing?" she asked, ignoring his aggrieved tone.

"No," he said, then stood up holding his glass toward her. She nodded and he went to the bar for a refill.

"You're thinking about the blood, aren't you?" Frank said. "I am, too."

Shelley looked from one to the other. "How did Darren Halvord get enough blood on his boot to take back to his bicycle pedal?" she asked in a low tone.

"Exactly," Barbara said. "McIvey was shot right after seven-thirty. Darren Halvord got there about fifteen to eighteen minutes later. It was pouring down rain, and even if blood did spill where McIvey was shot, wouldn't it have been washed into the bark mulch too much for him to pick up enough to take back to the pedal?"

"It might have pooled in his raincoat, assuming he was wearing one," Frank said. "Then it could have spilled a bit when he was moved and the mover didn't notice since everything was so wet. He walks through it. Takes it back to the conspiracy theory."

Shelley looked sickened and Barbara nodded.

"Anything else for me?" Bailey asked after a moment. When Barbara said just more of the same, he stood up, finished his drink and put on his disreputable raincoat. "You know what I think?" he said heading toward the door. "I think that when they collar your two clients, you're going to earn every penny they pay you. See you guys." He left.

Frank did not say a word, but he thought that Bailey had it just about right.

14

The following Monday Barbara and Shelley were in the directors' room with the Boardmans, Dr. Kelso, Darren and Annie. Shelley had gone to Martin's Restaurant at one, but by two, when no one had come by, she had been too discouraged to stay and had returned to the office in time to catch Barbara on her way out.

Now they were both at the round table; the others were in the more comfortable seats and on the sofa. Shelley had her notepad out. "I thought it best to have present today the directors as well as the two people I've been retained to defend," Barbara said. "I have just a couple of questions. Dr. Kelso, why did you transfer your shares of the clinic to Dr. Boardman when you did?"

Every time she saw him, he appeared older than the last time. He looked more shriveled than a human could get and still be mobile. He looked as if he belonged in a sarcophagus.

He blinked at the question, then said, "Because Joyce McIvey had a stroke and died a week later. I could do the same thing at any time, and I wanted to see this settled before that time comes."

Barbara turned to Greg Boardman. "You've stated that David McIvey arrived at your house at seventhirty the morning he was killed. Can you be certain of that?"

"I'm certain, but proving it is something else altogether," he said after a moment. "How could I prove it?"

"Just tell me again exactly what you did, what he did that morning," Barbara said.

"He rang the doorbell and I opened the door, picked up the newspaper and stepped aside so he could enter. I saw that Annie was backing out already. I had the key to the gate on the side table by the door, and I picked it up and handed it to David. We walked through the house to the kitchen. We said good morning and rotten day, something like that, but no more than that. I think I mentioned that the electronic lock on the clinic door was released at seven-thirty, so it would be open. He left by the back door. I closed it and went over to the counter to make coffee." He paused. When Barbara didn't comment, he went on. "I waited for the coffee, poured a cup and went into the study to turn on the television and watch the morning news. I was still in there when Carlos came."

"Okay," Barbara said. "But how do you know for certain that it was seven-thirty?"

"That's when he said he'd be there, and David was compulsive about being on time, and having everyone else be on time."

On a straight chair at the side of the sofa, Annie ducked her head.

"Anyway, I was keeping an eye on the clock, and I know it was seven-thirty," Greg Boardman said.

"How long was he in the house?"

"Maybe a minute."

"Do you usually spend nearly an hour watching the morning news?"

He looked surprised, then shook his head. "I never do. I simply didn't want to run into David again. I was waiting him out."

Barbara looked at Naomi Boardman. "Can you confirm that?"

"Of course. We were both watching the clock. I knew David wanted to be at the hospital by eight, and that meant he would be prompt. It would take him ten or fifteen minutes at the clinic to check his patient out and sign the follow-up orders, and then ten minutes to get to the hospital. That's why I got the car out to be ready to drive him over. He came at exactly seven-thirty."

Barbara nodded. "The patient at the clinic, Mrs. Johnson, said she got out of bed, used the bathroom, washed her face and turned on the television at seven-thirty. She had just gotten herself settled when she heard what might have been a shot, and she turned her chair in order to see out the window. That's when she saw someone. Either a dwarf in a black cape or a demon. But the point is she could have seen something, and she could have heard a shot. Her line of sight would have provided a view of about six or seven feet of the path where McIvey was shot."

"I don't think she ever claimed he was wearing a cape," Darren said. "I saw her later that morning, and she said it was a carapace. That's why it had to be a demon. A shiny black carapace."

Bailey's report stated that by the time he had reached Dorothy Johnson, she had firmed up her story considerably, and stated with emphasis that she had seen a demon, all shiny and black, with a great big head. There had been no mention of a dwarf or a carapace.

"You wouldn't call her as a witness," Annie said. "She's... Well, she believes in demons, goblins, fairies, who knows what all?"

"Okay," Barbara said. "Even if we leave her testimony out, if Dr. and Mrs. Boardman stick to their timetable, there's no way to put Darren on the scene at the right time. His landlady, Erica Castle, saw him leaving the garage on his bike at twenty minutes before eight. And Stephanie Waters saw him enter the clinic at about ten or twelve minutes before eight. In fact, she gave him the urn of coffee to take to the lounge for her. That would be about the time it would take to ride a bike over, to spot the umbrella, go close it and then go on around to park and enter the clinic. And what would David McIvey have been doing out in the rain all that time?"

"Where does that leave me?" Annie whispered.

"I don't know for certain. When the detective asked if they could look in the trunk and the glove box, exactly what did you do?"

"I said yes. The detective who drove me down from Portland had the key in his hand, and he gave it to the other one. He opened the trunk and the glove box, and I went inside the clinic."

"Did he return the key to you at that time?"

"No. Someone gave it to me later, after they questioned me."

"And while you were being questioned, no doubt, they were going over your car with a fine-tooth comb looking for trace evidence. Bark mulch on the accelerator, a sign of moisture on your floor or anything else that could have been incriminating. Even if you had managed to change your clothes, or swathed yourself in a long waterproof coat and then got rid of it, there's always something. Also," she added, "they've questioned your family and various others about a gun. Did you ever own one?"

Annie shook her head. "Neither did David."

"So that's been another problem for them. Apparently they searched everywhere they could think of looking for a gun and came up with nothing." Naomi was nodding vigorously. "So they don't know where it came from or where it went," Barbara said. "And there's the problem of moving a body of that size. The way he was lifted and moved required some strength. They might say yes, you could do that, and know the defense would be just as positive that no, you couldn't. They may be speculating a lot, but they need hard evidence, what they consider to be clear and convincing proof, to present a case to the grand jury, and they don't have it."

Dr. Kelso had been following all this closely, frowning in concentration. "Where does that leave things?" he asked then, his voice so raspy, it was like a low growl.

"I'm not at all sure," Barbara said. "I don't know what leads they may be following up on. Ballistics for certain, trying to trace the gun. DNA if traces of blood were found on Darren's shoes and gloves. That always takes a good deal of time. The labs are backed up for months. Maybe they're just hoping for a break, for someone to come forward with a useful tidbit."

"I mean with probate," Dr. Kelso said sharply. "Will they release the estate?"

"Again, I don't know. If the police still claim that Annie is a prime suspect, the answer is no."

"How long is it going to take them?" Dr. Kelso asked.

"I don't know. Sometimes no arrest is made for a year, two years. Sometimes within days of a crime. I'm not privy to their plans or their investigation."

Dr. Kelso glared at her for a moment, then sank back against his chair in an attitude of defeat.

"He'll win," Annie said in a dull voice. "David always won, and he'll win again."

"Well, I've told you what I can," Barbara said. "I imagine the police are looking into his associates, possible arguments he may have had with someone we know nothing about, even a passerby who might have followed him into the garden with the intention of robbing him."

It was interesting, she thought, how differently they listened to this. Dr. Kelso might have gone deaf for all the signs he gave, but both Greg and Naomi looked hopeful, and Annie looked as if she had seen a glimmer of light in a very dark place. Darren looked skeptical.

"Meanwhile," she said, "there's very little I can do at this point. The police are waiting for a stroke of luck, a break, forensic evidence, something, and my hands are tied until I find out what leads they are following."

After she and Shelley were in her car in the front parking lot, she asked, "Well, what do you think?"

"I think a giant carapaced cockroach killed him." Barbara laughed. "And?"

"I'd bet there's nothing going on between Darren and Annie."

"Me, too. Just wanted a second opinion."

"In fact," Shelley said judiciously, "I'd also bet he's a lot more interested in you than in her."

"Shelley, let's face the truth here. When you're

with me, no man gives me a second glance. That's just the way it is."

This time Shelley laughed. "He didn't even notice that I was there."

"That's because you're so obviously taken." Shelley radiated happiness and love like a neon sign, Barbara thought, as she started to drive.

"Where are you going?" Shelley asked when Barbara turned the corner and started around the clinic grounds.

"I thought I'd drive by Darren Halvord's apartment, see for myself how far it is, how long it would take to ride from there to the clinic. Bailey had Alan do it on his bike, but while we're so close, I might as well satisfy my curiosity. We'll just start at the end, not the beginning. Want to start timing it about here."

They passed the drive into the staff parking lot, went another ten feet or so and turned into the alley. The residence was on a trapezoidal piece of ground, narrow at one end, widening as they went. They passed an area covered with gravel, where the gardener's truck could park within a few feet to the gate of the clinic garden on the right. Barbara stopped. "Give him time to go in and close the umbrella, come back out. Thirty seconds? About that probably." She started to drive again. The alley was narrow, fifteen feet, the length of a city block. At the end she turned again and, driving very slowly at the speed she thought a bicycle might do, drove the four blocks to Erica Castle's house and stopped at the curb as a green SUV pulled into the driveway. There was a Realtor's logo on the door.

"Four minutes," Shelley said.

Barbara nodded. "Let's wait for her company to leave." She thought a moment, then added, "In fact, maybe I'll have a chat with the lady. Wait here." She left her car and walked up the sidewalk to the end of the driveway where she waited for the Realtor to come out again. It took only a few minutes.

She waved to the driver, a round-faced woman with black curly hair and a wide smile. "Hi," Barbara said when the SUV stopped and the woman rolled down her window. "Is the house going on the market?"

"Are you looking for a house like that?"

"Not me. A friend. She likes this neighborhood and I've been keeping an eye out for her."

"Oh. Let me give you my card, to pass on if you will. No, this one isn't for sale, I'm sorry to say, but I know about others in the area." She handed her card to Barbara.

"Mrs. Maryhill? I'll tell my friend. But this one would be ideal. I thought, seeing your logo, that maybe we were in luck."

"Hasn't she done wonders with it? If you've been keeping an eye out, you must have seen the transformation, what a wreck it was before. It's like a miracle, if you ask me. Last summer she would have snapped up an offer, she couldn't wait to sell it, but now that it's fixed up so nice, she's changed her mind. But do tell your friend that I have others listed in the area."

"I will. Thanks." She moved back and Mrs. Maryhill rolled up her window and pulled out of the driveway, headed down the street.

"Well?" Shelley asked when Barbara returned to her own car.

"Not sure. She wanted to sell last summer when the house was a wreck, according to the real estate lady, but now she doesn't want to sell. Let's go meet her. What's her name? Castle. Erica Castle."

She started the car and drove the rest of the way to the drive that Mrs. Maryhill had just left. An old station wagon was parked at the side of the house.

The door of the house opened and a woman stepped out, hugging her arms about her against the cold. "Annie?" she called.

"And that must be Darren's alibi," Barbara said. "Erica Castle." She got out and waved to Erica. "Hi, I'm Barbara Holloway, with my associate Shelley McGinnis. Got a minute?"

"Of course. Come on in." Erica backed up and stood in the open doorway to wait for them.

"Erica Castle," she said when they entered the house and she'd shut the door. "For a minute there I thought it was Annie McIvey paying a call."

Barbara introduced herself and Shelley, and Erica said, "Let's go to the kitchen. I was just putting on the kettle to make a cup of tea. Would you like some?"

"That would be nice," Barbara said. Erica Castle was about her height and very handsome. Her hair was short and light brown with golden highlights, salon styled. Dressed in a simple black skirt and a heavy blue sweater, a single gold chain necklace, little makeup, she looked like an idealized elementary school teacher.

The house appeared to be almost spartan, as bare as her own apartment, Barbara thought, but scrupulously clean and neat. They walked through a hallway, past a staircase closed off with a door at the bottom and an open door to the living room on the left. Apparently the living room had only two easy chairs, a small rug before one of them, a television, an end table and lamp or two and a filled bookcase. The hall floor was bare polished wood.

"You might want to keep your coats on," Erica said as she led the way to the kitchen. "I just got home a few minutes ago and turned up the heat. It doesn't take long to warm up, but it's cool right now." A kitten bounded out to meet them, then raised its tail that puffed out like a bottle brush when it saw strangers. "That's Nappy," Erica said. "Todd's kitten. He hangs out down here when Todd's not around. You know about Todd?"

"Darren Halvord's son? Yes. Hi, Nappy." Barbara held out her hand for the kitten to sniff. It obliged, then raced away.

The kitchen was roomy with space for a table and three chairs, and abundant countertops. Erica picked up a coat from a chair near the back door, and her purse from the table. "Excuse me," she said. "I'll get rid of this stuff. Come on, Nappy. You, too." The kitten followed her.

Barbara walked to the back door and looked out

at a small porch, a flagstone terrace, a ragged lawn and beyond to a garage. On the porch was a miniature pagoda made of bamboo with a tiny tree in it.

Erica returned without the kitten. "Please have a seat. The kettle won't take a minute." She turned up a burner.

"You know who I am?" Barbara asked.

"Of course. Everyone at the clinic knows who you are and probably why you're around." She smiled. "I also suspect you've come to verify that I could see Darren leave that morning. Well, as you can see—" she waved toward the garage "—there's a door at the side of the garage, and that's how he gets his bike in and out, not by the overhead door at the rear. I saw him wheel it out and close the door, then get on and leave. At twenty minutes before eight."

"Good enough," Barbara said. "You can be sure about the time?"

"Absolutely. I had a book to deliver to a boy at the clinic, and I had thought Darren could take it as he went, but I hadn't finished dressing yet. I didn't have my shoes on, and he was already getting his bike out, so I missed him. I was afraid I'd be late, and I was paying attention to the time. Twenty minutes before eight. I left a few minutes after that."

The kettle began to whistle and she poured the boiling water into a teapot and brought it to the table, went back to a cabinet for cups, then sat down. "We'll give it a couple of minutes," she said. "It amazes me to see so many people riding bikes all winter. Believe me, you don't do that in Cleveland, where I come from. And Darren has a perfectly good truck in the garage. He says it would be insane to get it out to drive three and a half blocks to work."

She poured tea and Barbara sipped hers, then said, "I imagine that there are few secrets at the clinic. You probably have a more objective viewpoint than the others I've been talking to. What's it like working there? What did the others think of David McIvey? Would you mind giving your thoughts about all that? I'm trying to fill in background."

Erica hesitated, then said, "I've only been going over for a few months, and then only in the late afternoon to read to the patients. But, even so, I hear talk. As far as I could tell everyone disliked David McIvey. I think they hated him for being cruel to Annie. He was, you know. A real tyrant with her.... But it was more than just that. He was autocratic, a my-way-or-the-highway sort of personality, from what I heard. And they were all afraid that he was going to take over, turn it into a surgical facility. Most people would have been out if that had happened. I never met him, so I had no direct cause to like or dislike him, but I heard that he was out to get Darren, and that made people furious. They all love Darren, you see."

Barbara recalled what Annie had said, that everyone fell in love with Darren. "Why is that?" she asked. "What makes him so special?"

"If you ever saw him with a patient, or heard him talking to one, you'd understand," Erica said. A flush rose on her cheeks and she jumped up. "I'll put on more water."

When she hurried to the sink, Barbara and Shelley exchanged glances. Shelley nodded almost imperceptibly, as if to agree: *everyone* loved Darren.

When Erica took her seat again, Barbara said, "What about the patient who saw a demon or something? What do they say about her?"

"Oh, Mrs. Johnson. She's a dingbat. She likes to talk about her near-death experience and the various ghosts she's seen. She was in a car wreck and hurt her back pretty badly, I guess. She was there in the hospital for weeks, and still goes back to the clinic several times a weeks for therapy. No one pays much attention to what she says, of course."

A few minutes later Barbara asked, "Are the people at the clinic talking much about the murder?"

"Not as much as earlier, but sure. Now it's pretty much agreed that Darren is in the clear. If McIvey was killed a minute or two after seven-thirty, that lets Darren out of the running as a suspect, unless you can imagine David McIvey standing out in the rain waiting for him. From what they say about him, he waited for no one. Ever. Everyone's pretty relieved about that."

She looked at her cup, then at Barbara with a swift glance, then back at her cup. "I may be talking out of turn if Annie is your client," she said. "But you probably should know that they all seem to think she did it, and that he deserved it. They hope she gets away with it."

"Is that what you think?"

Erica shrugged. "I hardly know Annie, and I didn't know her the way others describe her, happy and laughing a lot, full of fun. I've never seen that side of her. As I said, I never even met David McIvey. I saw him around the clinic a time or two, and I must say he was extremely good-looking, movie-star handsome. But I have no idea why they got together or stayed together. He was a lot older than she. They say he got a servant out of the marriage, but what she got is a mystery. It seems that she could have walked away if it was a rotten marriage unless she thought it would pay off sooner or later, or else she is masochistic."

Barbara nodded. "Fair enough. Is there talk about Annie and Darren?"

"No." Erica looked at her watch. "I have to go in a few minutes. I didn't realize how late it was getting."

Barbara and Shelley stood up. "Of course," Barbara said. "Sorry to keep you so long. And you probably had a little rest in mind when you got home. Thanks for the tea and chat."

They walked back through the house, then, outside, Barbara turned at the front walk to go to the side of the house and look at the stairs going up to the apartment. They started six feet or a little more back from the porch.

"Okay," she said a minute later in the car. "Back to the office. What do you think? Would she lie for him?"

"Are you kidding?"

"Right. Shit." She turned on the ignition.

"It seems to me that everyone would lie for Darren," Shelley said. "I think we're right back where we started." Then she said, "Shit."

Barbara looked at her in surprise. Shelley never used language like that. She glanced at the yard with a six-foot high board fence and shrubs screening it from the neighbors. "More Bailey work," she said. "Ask around the neighborhood if anyone saw Darren leave that morning. Not that anyone would remember now, but give it a try." She started to drive and said, almost as an afterthought, "And ask if any of the neighbors think there's anything going on with Darren and Erica Castle." Shelley made a note.

15

"I'm stymied," Barbara said in her office the next morning. "And that's what I told them yesterday at the meeting. We have to wait for the cops to make their move."

Bailey was there awaiting marching orders for the day; Frank was there, as well as Shelley. Council of war, Barbara thought, but they didn't know who the enemy was, or where, or how to smoke anyone out.

"Seems to me that you might as well relax until there's an arrest," Frank said.

"I know. And if it weren't for those damn shares, and Dr. Kelso pushing, I'd sit back and just wait to see what next. But he's anxious, and when people like him get anxious, they sometimes behave in very foolish ways. I'm afraid that he'll push Sid Blankenship to go after probate for a decision, and that might provoke the district attorney to go ahead with an arrest. I'd hate to see Annie stuck in a cell for the next six months or longer."

"Be nice to know why they turned their sights on her so fast," Frank said. "I could make a better case for either of the Boardmans. Greg Boardman walked out with him and shot him, went back home and made coffee. Plenty of time to hide a gun. Or Naomi followed him out and same thing. Then she got the car out to account for being wet. Again, plenty of time to hide a gun. Or a transient looking for a quick buck. Why Annie?"

"You could go ask," Barbara said. "Speaking of making cases, how about Kelso? Who had more cause? His sacred clinic's at risk. He could have shot McIvey, and Boardman moved him. You can play that game with them all, as far as that goes."

Frank snorted.

"Okay, Bailey," Barbara said then. "That's it. See if anyone in the neighborhood saw Darren leave that morning. I'd like to have someone other than Erica Castle testify about the time. Poke around in her past. The police will be trying to find a way to discredit her statement. See if there's anything there for them to find. And after that—nada." She frowned. "Damn, it's that close range that's a stinker. Who would McIvey have been willing to share umbrella space with? Annie for sure, both Boardmans, probably. Kelso. A stranger? No way, from what I've heard about him. Darren? Never."

"Alex came up with an idea," Shelley said when Barbara leaned back in her chair. "If that patient saw someone, he thinks he knows how to find out what she saw. That could help, maybe."

This time Bailey snorted. "She's a nutcase," he said. "By now she might think she saw a flock of little devils with tridents."

"Tell," Barbara said to Shelley, ignoring Bailey.

"Last night at dinner we were talking about perception," Shelley said, blushing. She blushed a lot those days, especially when she started talking about Alex, about living with him, being with him. "He was saying how we try to make indistinct objects recognizable. You know, you see something from a distance and you think it's a tree, or a rock, or whatever, but when you get closer you see that it's really an elephant. But since you weren't expecting to see an elephant, you go through familiar things that it might be. If she saw something that she couldn't make out clearly, she might have called it something that made sense to her."

"Like a demon," Bailey said, deadpan.

"For her that might make sense," Shelley said earnestly.

"Okay. But then what?" Barbara asked.

"Well, Alex has this great drawing program that lets you manipulate objects every way imaginable. He said that if you show someone just the most basic shape that could be like what they saw, then you can manipulate it, change it, look at it from any angle, above or below, and gradually you can get pretty close to what they actually saw." She drew in a breath. "If you start with a dwarf dressed in black, for instance, and begin to manipulate it, you might end up with a close approximation of what was there."

"Could you do that?" Barbara asked.

"No, but Alex can."

"Would he be willing to do it?"

"He'd do anything for you, Barbara," Shelley said.

Barbara shook her head. Not for her, for Shelley. He would move the moon for Shelley. Grotesquely disfigured by a congenital birth defect, Alex Feldman had shunned the public, avoided people whenever possible and, until Shelley came along, had lived a hermitlike existence. This would be an ordeal for him, she knew. Was it even fair to ask him for help? When strangers first saw Alex, they drew back in revulsion or averted their eyes. His face was perfectly formed on one side, and hideous on the other, with a misplaced eye, too far to the side and too low, a little nose, lips dwindling to nothing and no chin. There were no muscles on that side of his face; it was frozen in a grimace.

"Barbara," Shelley said, "Alex owes you a lot, you know. Six months ago he was facing the death penalty, and now… He knows there's never going to be a way to repay you. Let him do something to start."

At three o'clock Barbara rang the bell at a duplex on South Seventeenth Avenue. Alex and Shelley were with her on the small porch. Dorothy Johnson promptly opened the door.

"Come in, come in," she said moving aside.

"Barbara Holloway, my associate Shelley McGinnis and our computer artist Alex Feldman," Barbara said entering. "Thanks for letting us invade you like this."

"Not at all, my pleasure," Mrs. Johnson said, then she stopped moving as she looked at Alex. With what appeared to be an involuntary motion, she reached out and put her hand on his arm. He held perfectly still. "You poor boy!" She closed her eyes, but continued to rest her hand on his arm for a moment. "You have a very powerful guardian angel, thank God. And are bathed in God's gift of love," she said softly, then opened her eyes and examined Shelley for a moment. She smiled and nodded. "We'll go to the dining room. I thought we might use the table there."

She was fifty-two years old, Barbara had learned, a widow for seven years. She worked in the financial affairs office at the university, and was now on sick leave. Her hair was dark brown streaked with gray, and she was a few pounds overweight. She leaned heavily on a crutch as she led the way through an L-shaped living room to a dining area.

The living room was bright and colorful: a blue sofa, yellow-and-red cushions, a flowered rug, bookshelves with a pair of matching frog bookends, their legs dangling over the edge. In the dining area a collapsible wheelchair was set against the wall, and a china cabinet was overfilled with figurines: fairies, elves, a giant or two, china angels, witches on brooms, porcelain birds, a cloisonné giraffe, a parade of frogs in diminishing sizes.

"Darren said I should use the chair when I get tired," Dorothy said. "I shouldn't punish myself and deny myself the relief of wheels. He said that you do more harm than good if you drive yourself to exhaustion, but every day I stay on my feet a little longer. Or at least I try to." She sank down into one of the dining chairs with a sigh of relief. "Will the table do for your computer?" she asked Alex.

"Perfect," he said, and proceeded to get the laptop set up. He had brought a surge protector with four outlets and a heavy extension cord, prepared for whatever was needed. It took him only a minute or two to get ready.

He and Dorothy sat side by side at the table. Barbara sat opposite them.

"Before you start, would you mind telling us what you did that morning, what you saw? Various people have reported different versions. I'd like to hear it from you."

"Of course," she said. "I know how that goes. I woke up a little after seven and debated if I should get up or wait for one of the nurses to come and help me, and decided to do it myself. I was still in pretty bad shape, you see, but I detest meals in bed, and they were all so busy in the morning, the night nurses leaving, day nurses coming in. It was a struggle to get out of bed, get my robe on and then maneuver myself into the wheelchair. But I did it and went to the bathroom. Then I had to go back to the bed to find the remote for the television, go around the bed to the other side where I could watch the news and reach the call button for the nurse to bring some coffee. Breakfast is at eight, but you can get coffee as soon as you want it, and I wanted it. I turned on the television when the commercials were starting at seven-thirty, and before I got the channel I wanted, I heard what I thought was a shot. I wheeled myself closer to the window where I could look out and that's when I saw it."

"You thought the noise was a shot? What made you think that?" Barbara asked.

"Before Ralph died—he was my husband, you know," Dorthy said, "we lived up near Junction City, on five acres, with a small orchard, big gardens and a nice pond that Ralph stocked with fish and lilies. It was so pretty, and we could even swim in it. Anyway, geese started coming in and messing up the pond something awful every fall and winter, and Ralph used to go out with a gun and shoot to scare them away. Not at them, but just shoot at the sky. Didn't do any good, and he gave it up after a while. You know the Canada geese winter over in the ponds and fields up that way? Messiest creatures on God's earth. But I got to know how a gunshot sounds when you're inside and it's not far away outside. And that's what I thought that morning—Dear God, Ralph is shooting to drive away the geese. You know about the little pond at the clinic garden? With koi? That was my first thought, that the geese were after the koi and Ralph was trying to drive them away."

That explained that, Barbara thought, but she didn't know if she should be relieved or not at the idea of Dorothy's dead husband out there shooting. "Well, let the show begin," she said. "I want to watch."

She and Shelley both moved to stand behind Alex and Dorothy, where they could see the monitor.

"One of the nurses said you saw a dwarf in a black shiny cape," Barbara said.

"I never said that. I said it was a dwarf in a black shiny carapace. That's what I thought at first, because of the short legs and the long torso."

"I thought that might be our starting place," Alex said. "A dwarf in a black cape." He loaded the image onto the screen.

"It wasn't anything like that," Dorothy said. She sounded disappointed.

"Wait a second. We have to shift the viewpoint, over by about five feet and then up about fifteen or sixteen feet." The figure began to change as the viewpoint changed. Dorothy leaned in closer.

"The head isn't right. All black and bigger than that. No face. I couldn't see a face. It was black all over—legs, head, feet, everything."

He made changes, and she said, "The carapace shouldn't flare out. It sort of curves inward a little, like a turtle shell or something."

Then: "The legs are too long. There. Stop there." The figure was becoming less and less human with each change. It was becoming buglike, Barbara thought with a shudder, recalling what Shelley had said earlier: A giant cockroach shot him. A cockroach with stubby legs.

"Remember," Dorothy said, "it was raining hard, and it was all wet and shiny, water running down it. It walked funny. I couldn't make out what it was doing, then I realized it was walking backward."

It got worse and worse, Barbara thought. This was one witness who never would be asked to testify.

"Then I think it sensed that someone was looking at it, and it turned around and took a couple of steps and I couldn't see it any more. That's how they do. They don't like to be seen. The nurse brought in coffee and asked what I was looking at and I told her a dwarf in a shiny black carapace. She laughed."

"Later you told someone else that it was a demon," Barbara said. "Is that right?"

"Yes. I kept thinking about it, and I realized it had to be a demon when I remembered that it had a tail. Like a short rat tail."

"Where?" Alex asked. He turned the figure around and waited.

"At the bottom of the carapace. Just a little black tail."

He added a short tail and Dorothy leaned back in her chair studying the image on the monitor. "I guess that's as good as you can get it," she said. "It's like drawing something you've never seen, going by someone else's description."

"What would you change?" Alex asked.

"I don't know. It just isn't quite right, but I don't know why. Too neat maybe. No rain. I don't know."

"I can make it rain," Alex said. He did.

"Oh, my!" Dorothy said. "You and God. But that's better, I guess. I only saw it for a few seconds, and I didn't know what I was looking at, what to look for. I don't know what I would change. That's pretty close, I think."

They all regarded the image on the monitor in silence. Then Dorothy said, "But who's going to believe me? I've seen the others all my life, you see, and no one ever believed me before. My father thought I was a nut, and my mother said just don't talk about it and it will be all right. I saw a doctor a few times, a psychiatrist, when I was thirteen or fourteen, and he decided I was a schizo, and my mother called him an ass and didn't take me back again. So I just didn't talk about it for the most part. I told Ralph before we got married, sort of as a warning, I guess, and he agreed with my mother. As long as I didn't talk about it, and I didn't feel threatened or have nightmares, anything like that, so what?"

"And it never frightened you, seeing things that no one else saw?" Barbara asked, studying Dorothy Johnson, who looked and talked as rationally as anyone she had ever known.

"Never. They don't do anything threatening. In fact, if they realize that I'm aware of them, they vanish. Usually it happens outside, when I'm being very still and no one else is around. I think I sense that someone is there, and I make certain not to move.

Often I get a glimpse, sometimes just out of the corner of my eye, but sometimes a full front and center sort of look. Little people mostly, now and then something else, a demon, like that or nearly like that." She pointed to the monitor. "Rarely it's a ghost of someone I've known. I used to see Ralph out in the garden now and then. He never spoke or seemed aware that I could see him. I hated to have to sell the farm, leave him there alone, but I couldn't manage it by myself."

She couldn't have been more matter-of-fact if she had been discussing the price of butter. Feeling almost helpless in the face of such certainty, Barbara walked around the table, then paused opposite Dorothy. "Can you estimate how long it was from when you heard the shot until you reached the window and looked out and saw whatever it was you saw?"

"Not very long. How long? Bring the chair over and I'll show you what I did."

Shelley, closer to the wheelchair, brought it to Dorothy's side.

"See, I was at the side of the bed," Dorothy said, getting to her feet laboriously, then reseating herself in the wheelchair. "Let's say the table here is the bed. The tray was here, where the chair is, and the window about where the china cabinet is. I was facing the television, away from the window. It was still muted. I heard the shot and sort of turned my head, maybe listening for a second one. Then I wheeled myself back a little to get room to turn around partway."

They watched her maneuver the chair away from

the table, turn and move to the china cabinet, then maneuver it again so that it was parallel to the cabinet. She pressed her forehead against the glass front, then drew back.

"That's just about how it was," she said. "I might have been a little slower that morning. I wasn't as strong as I am now and everything took a little longer than you'd think it should."

No more than a minute. Barbara nodded. "Mrs. Johnson, we won't impose on you any longer. I really appreciate your help. Thanks."

They got on their jackets and coats. Alex put the computer back in the case with the extension cords and surge protector, and in another minute or two, they left Dorothy Johnson, still in the wheelchair.

No one spoke for several blocks as Barbara headed back toward the office. Then Shelley said, "Well, it seemed like a good idea at the time." She sounded regretful.

"It was a good idea," Barbara said, surprised. "It worked extremely well. What do you think, Alex?"

"She saw something and interpreted it in a way that made sense to her," he said after a moment. "I'd say that what she saw is perfectly clear in her mind, and she did the best she could in correcting my version. It's probably pretty close to what it looked like. Would you call her as a witness?"

"I doubt it. But she did tell us something important. The shooter was dressed in black, probably a long black mackintosh or raincoat of some sort, and the shot was probably fired right after seven-thirty. And," she added, "I think it's safe to assume that the killer did not move the body. Damn! Why was the body moved at all?"

"Why do you say the killer didn't move him?" Shelley asked after a moment.

"The way I see it working," Barbara said, "McIvey is heading toward the clinic's side door, and someone perhaps calls to him, or is even waiting for him. The killer ducks under the umbrella and shoots. McIvey falls. The killer watches for a moment to make sure he isn't going to get up again and then begins to back up, still watching. He's backing up when Mrs. Johnson spots him, and keeps backing up a few more feet, then he turns and leaves the scene. No time to move the body before she sees him backing up, and to think he might have gone back to do it seems implausible. What for?"

"Everything keeps pointing back to the conspiracy theory," Shelley said.

"I know."

"Barbara, you realize that Mrs. Johnson didn't mention hands, feelers, tentacles, anything of the sort?" Alex asked then. "And she didn't mention a gun."

She nodded. "Right. But I believe she told us about everything she did see. Including a tail," she added morosely.

16

Barbara was at her desk brooding over the images on her monitor, going back and forth between the front and back views. Before leaving, Alex had downloaded them from his computer. She had sent Maria home, and Shelley had left at five. She wished that Shelley had not mentioned giant cockroaches, because the more she stared at the rain-shrouded image before her, the more it resembled a big black roach. Frank had left a message that he would drop in a little after five, and she was waiting for him, and building a case against Annie McIvey, she admitted to herself.

When the buzzer sounded, it was with a sense of relief that she got up to let Frank in. She helped him out of his coat and then, as they walked back to her office, she asked, "Do cockroaches have tails?"

"I'd say you've been out in the sun too much, except there hasn't been any sun to speak of for days on end. Drinking? Smoking an illegal substance? Overtired?"

"Have a look," she said motioning toward the laptop.

He crossed to the desk and gazed at the monitor for a time. "Maybe cockroaches do have tails," he said. "I give. What is it?"

She told him about the computer experiment, and he studied the image again, then nodded. "I'd say Mrs. Johnson had it right. It's a demon."

"Yep. Your turn. What brings you out this time of day? Why aren't you home feeding the worms, or peeling potatoes or something?"

"I've noticed that every time you get a little low," he said, "you bring up the subject of my worms, get in a little dig. No pun intended. They are God's perfect composting machine. Do you feel threatened by them?"

She laughed. "I'm going to sit on the sofa with my feet on the table and swill wine and wait for you to tell me why you're here. Would you care to join me?"

He would. Then, with chardonnay in hand, he sat in one of the comfortable chairs and began.

"While you were out playing with the children," he said, "I've been throwing my weight around at my office, which, you may recall, I am still helping to maintain financially, giving me every right to use its vast resources. Namely two of the young punks who sit around twiddling their thumbs most of the time."

And who, she thought, were probably scared to death of him. She did not say a word and suppressed a smile. She knew very well how much free time the young attorneys had; after putting in their seventy-hour weeks, they were as free as birds. Fresh out of law school, the bar exam challenge met and conquered, she had gone to work in the firm, and if it hadn't been for Frank and the few criminal cases he was still handling, she would have left within a week. Later, Sam Bixby, the other senior partner, had gathered a flock of tame junior partners around him and they had passed a resolution that the firm no longer would consider criminal cases—too unsavory, too disreputable, too publicity hungry. She had walked out.

"I wanted to learn the extent of David McIvey's estate and the terms of his will," Frank was saying. "It seems that he changed it immediately after his divorce years ago, cut out the first Mrs. McIvey altogether and left the bulk of his estate to his mother. A real spite will. There are other considerations— the education of his children, their maintenance until they reach college age, things of that sort—but that's the gist of it. Apparently he never had the will rewritten after his second marriage. And that presents a real can of worms now. The first Mrs. McIvey is claiming that since his mother predeceased him, his children should inherit everything. Sid Blankenship is claiming that the will is invalid since it predates his second marriage, and that he died intestate, since his situation had been changed by his remarriage. Therefore, his widow is his main beneficiary, the children secondary."

"If Annie's charged and found guilty, the kids get it all," Barbara said after a moment. "That's pretty much where we were before, isn't it?"

"It's slightly different. If Billy the Kid rose from his grave and claimed responsibility for the death of David McIvey, the estate would still be tied up, maybe for years. The estate comes to about two and a half million. We're talking about real money here, and the first Mrs. McIvey has become a player. She's been in conference several times with the police investigating the murder. I've no clue what they have to talk about, but there it is."

"Well," Barbara said after a moment, "it seems that Dr. Kelso was right all along. They need to settle the foundation scheme now, or it may never happen. I wonder how near death his wife actually is."

"If she's had Alzheimer's for ten years or so, she's damn near," Frank said. "Maybe overdue. You're right, though. No court would allow a change at the clinic until those shares are settled. They'll wait for the estate to be cleared and go on from there."

"I keep reminding myself that the clinic isn't my concern," Barbara said. "People should put their affairs in order before other people come along and start shooting guns." She drained her glass and set it down. "You up for some dinner?"

The next morning, after finishing a few routine chores, Barbara consulted with Shelley about two pending cases that Shelley was handling, then said, "Well, hold the fort. I'm off to see Dr. Kelso, and then lunch with Will. Back around two probably."

She was curious about the old man, she mused as she left. He was of her father's generation, but nothing like her father, who had slowed down but certainly had not stopped working. As far as she could tell Frank never intended to stop, no matter how often he said he was retiring. It could be harder for a doctor, she decided. You either doctored or you didn't, but probably you didn't do it part-time only when it suited you. With a dying wife, grown children who lived far away and no practice, it appeared that the clinic was the only real interest he had left.

It was a beautiful day with sunshine and the temperature edging up around sixty—a foretaste of spring. But it was a false spring that brought out crocuses and teased daffodils out of the ground, forced open the buds of daphne and swelled the buds of magnolias. Next week, or possibly before nightfall, the capricious god of weather might blow in a gale or sleet mixed with snow.

She was humming as she drove through town, then south on Jefferson. Even with their branches bare now, the trees were lovely, arching gracefully over the street—sweet gums, big leaf maples, an occasional oak and the ever present fir and spruce trees.

The neighborhood had been upscale decades before, probably when Kelso bought his house here, and although many of the gracious old homes had been turned into apartments, they were still fine. She parked at the curb, checked the number and walked to the front door. His house, pale green with russet trim, was well kept, the yard meticulous with pruned shrubs, colorful flower beds of primroses almost too garish in reds and yellows and a drift of deceptively delicate-looking pansies. Professional work, she decided, waiting for someone to come to the door.

Dr. Kelso opened the door himself. "Come in, Miss Holloway," he said. She entered a wide foyer with a staircase, an arched doorway to a room on one side, a closed door on the other. The runner on the floor was threadbare in spots. Oak-framed pictures of children were crowded on the wall.

"I thought we might use my study for our talk," Dr. Kelso said, leading the way down the hall to another closed door. Inside that room was a large desk with a clutter of objects, a cup of pencils and pens, several framed pictures, papers, a newspaper, lamp, telephone. A dark sofa with a worn leather cover was flanked by two matching chairs, tables, a magazine rack, bookshelves.... It was a well-used room, comfortable and bright with sun streaming in two windows.

A coffee table before the couch held several thick scrapbooks. Dr. Kelso motioned toward one of the chairs. Barbara took off her jacket and sat down.

Dr. Kelso was wearing a shapeless gray sweater, a blue-striped shirt without a tie and gray slacks. He kept his cap on.

"I've been thinking about the predicament we're facing," he said, his voice as raspy as ever, but forceful now. "And I wanted to talk to you alone, in confidence, not as part of a committee, so I'm grateful that you could come. Thank you." He cleared his throat; it didn't help his voice as he continued. "Sid tells me that you employ Bailey Novell as a private detective, and Sid has a very high opinion of him, as he does of you. Miss Holloway, I don't believe the police will solve the mystery of who killed David McIvey. We can rule out a passerby, a transient. Why would he kill him, move the body and then fail to take his wallet? And we can rule out David's office associates, since none of them is familiar with the routine at the clinic and none of them had any way of knowing that David would have gone through the garden to enter the clinic."

He was articulating the same reasoning that she had gone through days earlier. She nodded and did not comment.

"I think we all know that the killer was someone connected to the clinic," he said. "We won't bother with motives since likely everyone had one. And nearly everyone connected to the clinic would have known those things I mentioned before."

His eyes were sharp and steady as he regarded her. It was a strange combination, the furrowed, wrinkled face, the white cap and those steady keen eyes.

"I've been going through those scrapbooks," he said, motioning toward them. "Patients we treated at the clinic over the past fifty-two years. There have been thousands of them, Miss Holloway, successfully treated, restored to a tolerable or even a good state of health, a good life. Over a third of them would have received no treatment without us. In the vast scale of the universe, that's insignificant, I know, but to each of them—real people, children, women, men, old, young—to each and every one of them we made a difference."

He looked at the scrapbooks and said more softly, "We changed their lives. We made a difference. I know I appear to be obsessive about the clinic, about putting its future before all else. Frankly, Miss Holloway, that's because I do put it first. All else *is* secondary. I believe the police have stopped their real investigation because they're convinced that Annie killed David, with or without an accomplice, and that, as you surmised, they are waiting for a break. Waiting for someone to come forward with hard evidence, the gun, a raincoat, something conclusive. I understand that it often happens that way. In any event, the estate may be tied up in probate for a lengthy period because the first Mrs. McIvey has contested it. The only way to save the clinic is if we vote the fifty-five shares that we control to form a foundation. And we can't do that without Annie's cooperation."

Although Barbara had not intended to say a word yet, he held up his hand as if to forestall any comment.

"I know Sid and your father agree that she received good advice. I don't dispute that. But we can't let this drag out for six months or a year, possibly longer. Miss Holloway, I want to hire you and your detective to investigate David's murder, to find his killer and enough evidence to convince the police so that they will make an arrest, the case will be closed and we can move forward. I want to hire you, not as part of a committee, but as an individual, and in strict confidence. You will still have our previous agreement, and it will still be in effect if they arrest Annie or Darren and charge them with a collaborative murder. But I want you to find the real killer and prevent that arrest."

Barbara stared at him with surprise, then shook her head. "Dr. Kelso, I don't have the resources to do that. I have no access to whatever evidence the police collected."

"Sid has told me about some of the cases you've handled," he said. "I believe you do have the resources available to you. I'm not a wealthy man by today's standards, but I will pay whatever the charges are. Hire the people you need."

"It isn't that simple," she said. "Once an arrest is made, the defense attorney has access to the police evidence through a process called discovery. But until then, that evidence is locked away. I can't get at it. And I have no authority to start questioning people about statements they might have made." She shook her head again. "Even if I could make my own investigation, what if I learned that Annie did it? Or that she's involved with someone else who did it?"

"Then you report to me, and after that keep your

mouth shut," he said. He stood up. "I said the day we engaged you that I don't care who killed him. I don't, as long as it wasn't Annie. Darren, Greg, Naomi, anyone else, I don't care. Just not her. Everyone at the clinic will cooperate. They have orders to cooperate. And it was someone at the clinic."

Barbara rose from her chair. "Dr. Kelso, I believe that you understand very well that I can't agree to such a proposal. A serious conflict of interest would inevitably arise, to say nothing of the questionable ethics of such a dual role. I've been retained to defend both Annie and Darren if the need arises. I can't compromise that trust."

"You don't understand!" he cried. "Within a month of the death of my wife my kids will be looking for a buyer for their shares. There won't be a clinic after that. It will be in the courts for decades! And there won't be any money to pay your fees, Miss Holloway! Annie and Darren will be on their own, and they don't have money for their defense. Ethics and conflict of interest be damned! I'm trying to save something bigger here."

Color flared on his cheeks, then drained away swiftly, leaving him waxy looking, like old ivory. Barbara took a step toward him; he waved her away. "Get out, just get out," he said. "Think about it. Get back to me after you've thought about it."

In a booth at the Electric Station Restaurant, with a crab Louie salad in front of her, Barbara realized that she had been paying less than rapt attention to

Will Thaxton when he said, "What's wrong? Case gone sour on you?"

To her dismay she found that she couldn't tell him about her meeting with Dr. Kelso. Will talked about his clients and their problems without hesitation, with gleeful elation or even scorn at times, but she could not do that. "I hope not," she said. "Just thinking, and listening. I can also chew gum and walk at the same time."

"Have you a clue about what I've been telling you?"

"Of course. An Italian woman and an Englishman got married many years ago and there's a question of title to some property in England."

Will groaned. "I give you romance, intrigue, mystery, you give me Cliffs Notes. But that's the gist. Pay attention now. I'll be in Vancouver and then Victoria for about a week probably, and depending on what I find out, I may have to go to England and Italy. Do you want to go with me?"

"To Victoria?" She shook her head. "I'm up to here in work right now."

"Not to Victoria. To England and on to Italy. As my assistant. All expenses paid."

"You've got to be kidding. Your assistant? Come on."

"I'll need an assistant to help me resist those cool gray-eyed British beauties and those hot-eyed Italian women. I'll work a couple of hours a day, three, four days a week, then do a little sightseeing. I understand that to get to Italy from England, one must go through France, and we all know about those sultry-eyed French femmes fatales. I'll need a lot of assistance."

She laughed. "You'll need blinders and a chastity belt." Then sobering, she asked, "When will you go?"

"I won't even be sure I will go until I get back from Victoria next week. Is your passport in order, just in case? If it's on, will you go?"

"Oh, God, why didn't this come up two weeks ago? You know I've taken a new case. I don't know where it will be next week, or two weeks from now. Let me think about it while you go dodge the rain in Victoria and Vancouver." Then she added, "But I'll make sure my passport is up-to-date."

When she entered the office after lunch, Maria handed her a memo with several names—calls while she was out. "Mrs. McIvey sounded like she was crying," Maria said. "Really upset."

"Thanks," Barbara said, taking the memo. Bailey's name was on it, along with one or two others who could wait. She went to her own desk and called Annie.

She sounded as if she were still crying, her voice choked and thick. "I have to talk to you," she said.

"I'll come over," Barbara said. "Are you at the residence?" Annie said she was and Barbara told her to stay there. "Ten minutes," she said. "Hang on."

She called Bailey's number and got his answering machine. "I'm going out," she told it. "Be back around four-thirty."

It was almost two-thirty, and whatever was on Annie's mind wouldn't take more than two hours, she thought, hanging up. Bailey could call back, or drop in.

Spring had vanished, and winter was back with heavy gray skies and a cold wind. Rain, sleet, snow weather, probably all three, she thought, driving to the residence. Annie was waiting near the door apparently, for it opened even before Barbara could touch the bell.

Annie's eyes were puffy and red-rimmed, her cheeks blotchy from weeping although she was not weeping then. "No one else is here," she said. "Let's sit in the living room."

A fire was burning low in the grate, and as before the house felt almost too warm, but welcoming. Barbara pulled off her jacket, then warmed herself before the fire. "What happened?"

Annie sat on the sofa. "I used to keep a diary," she said, then stopped and shook her head. "The lawyer told me I should keep a journal. When I asked him about the prenuptial agreement, he said I should. So I'd have something to show, how life was with David, I mean."

It sounded incoherent, but Barbara didn't interrupt as Annie talked about writing down what was going on from day to day in the first years.

"I brought them here with me, three diaries, and I put them in a dresser drawer upstairs in my room. But I kept thinking I should get rid of them, burn them up. And today I decided I would. In case the police come back and search here, find them, or something."

She looked and sounded so miserable that Barbara had to resist the impulse to go over and pat her hand. She was afraid that the first show of sympathy might bring on another paroxysm of weeping.

"I brought them down when I came home for lunch," Annie said, her voice so low it was almost inaudible. "I just started opening one at random, not really reading or anything, I meant to tear out pages and start burning them, but I saw—" She wiped her eyes as tears filled them. Angrily then, she said, "Someone cut out pages. Someone read them and cut out pages."

She couldn't restrain the tears any longer, and weeping, she said, "Someone read them, all of them. He said, the lawyer said I should put them in a safe deposit box, but I didn't. And someone read them—" She couldn't go on.

Barbara walked to the kitchen, got a glass of water and took it back for Annie. She moved a box of tissues closer to the young woman and waited.

"I'm sorry," Annie said after another minute. She blew her nose and wiped her eyes, drank some of the water.

"Okay," Barbara said, sitting close to her. "Tell me about the diaries. Where are they now?"

Annie pointed to a tote bag, and Barbara reached in and pulled out three red-bound notebooks. "Is this all of them?"

"Yes."

"May I keep them for the time being?"

"Yes. I want you to take them with you."

"You understand that I'll read them?"

Annie nodded. "They aren't really like diaries," she said. "I mean, I didn't put down what I was thinking or feeling, things you expect in a diary. It's more like a record of our marriage, what he said, what I said, what he did. Not every day, just now and then." She drank more of the water. "I thought, from what the lawyer said, that I might have to show them to a divorce judge some day."

Barbara thought for a moment, then said, "Annie, you have to tell me the truth. I know you met Darren at his place at least once, but you denied it. Did you meet him more than that one time?"

Annie shook her head violently. "No. That wasn't what I thought you meant. I thought you meant romantic meetings, something like that. That night, I had to warn him that David was going to put some terrible things in his personnel file. Someone had to warn him so he could leave and not be forced out with that on file."

"Was that in a diary?"

"I wrote about our fight," she said, not looking at Barbara. "That was the last thing I wrote. That page is gone."

"Okay," Barbara said. "Who had access to them? You said you had them in a dresser drawer. No lock?"

"No. I never even thought of a lock. Not in this house."

"Is the house kept locked up during the day?"

"No. We're back and forth a lot. They never locked the back door."

"Where did you keep them before you came back here?"

"In my dresser. We had separate rooms. He—David—never even came into mine. I went to his when he...when we slept together."

"Annie, again, tell me the truth. Why did you stay with him?"

Annie seemed to shrink a little.

"You thought you could put up with a bad marriage for ten years and then collect a settlement, alimony, something like that?"

"Yes," she said faintly. "I thought of it as a bad job you had to endure for the pension, or like being an indentured servant for a certain length of time."

"Did you put anything like that in the diaries?"

"Not really. I put in the number of months or years remaining. No explanation, just the number." In a rush, she said, "I really wanted to drive up to Portland that day, just to think. I didn't play the radio, or a CD or anything. I kept thinking that he would wreck Greg and Naomi's lives, ruin Darren, ruin anyone who got in his way without a second thought. He hated the clinic and wanted to destroy it, make it into something else, something that would be his alone. He was jealous of it, said he'd played second fiddle to it all his life and was through doing that. I didn't think I could take it for five more years.

"I was trying to talk myself into leaving, then I

was trying to convince myself that I could stand it for five more years. Maybe go back to school, work in classes around his schedule. Make him pay dearly eventually. Then I knew I had to leave. It was like a loop, going around and around, getting nowhere. I wanted to vote for the foundation and I was afraid to. He knew how I felt about Naomi and Greg, and even Darren. He used that, used me, used everyone he could. I hated him so much! God, I hated him so much!"

Her voice was low and intense as the words rushed out. "He would do something particularly foul and later on he would take my hand and we'd go to his room and he'd undress me, and I'd forget. God, I'd forget. He could do that, make me forget the other times, and then I'd hate him even more, and hate myself for letting it happen like that. I started leaving mentally when he touched my hand, I felt like I was someone watching us from a distance. I think I must have been losing my mind, disassociating. I looked it up. It's a sign of mental illness."

Her voice dropped lower and lower until she was barely audible, as if she were thinking out loud. "He was killing me, I think. Then, when I saw that he would take the clinic for himself, drive Greg and Naomi away, ruin Darren, I knew it couldn't go on, but I didn't know what I should do. Around and around."

She was rambling, Barbara understood, voicing things she had never said before, perhaps things she had never thought before. Barbara waited her out, thinking hard. When Annie finally became still again, Barbara said, "Do you know what was on those missing pages?" Annie shook her head. "What we'll do is make a note of the last entry date before each one and the entry date that follows. Like this." She opened one of the diaries at random and found the cut edge of a page. "The date before this one is October four, and the next one is November nineteen. Over the next day or two, try to think if anything unusual happened during those periods. Use a calendar. Was it a weekend? Your birthday, his? There could be a reason why those particular pages were cut out. You and the person who stole them know what that reason is. You just have to work at remembering."

Carefully she went through the three notebooks. There were nine missing pages, cut out with a razor probably, so close to the center that it might have gone unnoticed for years. Annie's handwriting in the earliest entries was almost childish, the writing of a schoolgirl. The latest entries were written in a much bolder script, with more slant, less precision. Some looked as if they had been written in a rush of passion, of fury.

When they finished, Barbara put the diaries in her briefcase, pulled on her jacket and regarded Annie for a moment. "You have to live with it," she said. "Someone out there knows a lot about you and your marriage, and that's going to be hard to take. You have to put up a front, pretend you don't know anyone has tampered with your journals, that anyone is aware. If anyone noticed that I was here today and asks questions, tell them it was just more of the same. No more than that. No wandering about alone in the dark. Keep your door locked and put up a good front. And try hard to reconstruct what was on those missing pages. It could be important." Annie looked so wretched, pale and wan and frightened that Barbara said, "Hang in there, kid. I'm on your side."

Then, driving back to the office, she realized how much she meant that. She *was* on Annie's side.

17

Bailey was showing Maria a card trick when Barbara entered the office. He grinned at Barbara, then said to Maria, "Just put it on top of the stack." She put a card down, and he picked up a second stack and placed it on top of her card. "Now you see it, now you don't," he said. He picked up the entire pile and showed her the bottom card. "Four of clubs. Right?"

"How did you do that?"

"Recess is over, kiddies," Barbara said. "Maria, go on home when you're ready. Come on, Bailey. Work."

"Do you want coffee?" Maria asked.

"Just about a gallon," Barbara said, going past the reception desk to her own office. She tossed her jacket onto a chair and sank down into one of the comfortable chairs by the coffee table. "What do you have?"

Bailey slouched over to the bar cabinet, opened it and helped himself to Jack Daniel's. Barbara didn't say a word. He acted as if he truly believed it was his and there was nothing she could do to dissuade him. Months earlier she had promised to install a wet bar if and when he delivered, and there it was. Now and then she let the bar run dry just to get a rise from him.

"First," he said, settling down on the sofa. "More on Darren. You want the long version or the short?"

"Is the long version in there?" she asked, pointing to his old duffel bag.

"Sure is."

"Then wrap it up. Short version."

"Okay. His mom and dad split while he was out camping. Then twelve years ago, the dad was busted along with about a hundred other guys in the LAPD, just one of their regular house cleanings. He turned state's witness and got a suspended sentence and afterward dropped off the earth or something. Gone. Mom got a divorce and then married a farmer and is doing okay. Kid sister married Danny Canto, the original Teflon kid. Mucho arrests, nothing sticks, still out roaming and doing whatever it is that keeps him in chips and beer and convertibles. Four kids. Point is, that's an unsavory bunch, and a gun might be the easiest thing they could provide as a favor for a relative. Also, some of the kids who camped out with Darren have since returned to their evil ways and moved up in the world. Way I heard it is that the cops here are looking for a current connection."

Barbara scowled at him. "Okay. Next."

"Castle," he said. "The neighbors didn't want to talk about her at first, then they did. You know how that goes. The old lady was married to an associate professor, respectable folks, well liked, all that. The daughter Marion took off when she was about sixteen or seventeen. The old man died, Grandma lived alone for years, and then daughter Marion came home. She was a dopehead. The tenants upstairs moved out a few months later, too much noise, too many strange men coming and going, fights, just too much. So the old lady died and Marion was in charge of the house. She sold off everything worth a dime and hung out with the wrong crowd. Noisy parties, drugs, cops calling. Suspicions of drug dealing, no proof. And the place began to look like a slum. So Marion died of an overdose and Erica Castle came. Note the last name. No father listed anywhere, but there she was, and she dived in and started cleaning up the place. Darren came along, moved in upstairs and helped clean up. Nothing between them that the neighbors can see. And so far no one saw Darren leave that morning that they can recall."

He drained his glass and held it up in an inquiring sort of way. He never helped himself to more than one drink without asking permission. She nodded and he got up to refill his glass. "Anyway," Bailey said, "the neighbors are coming around to giving her the good housekeeping seal of approval. They were curious about where she goes every day after she gets home from school, but word got around, maybe through Darren, that she does volunteer work at the clinic, and they like that. She appears to be as clean as a whistle."

"So her word probably would hold up," Barbara said. "I wonder if something of her mother didn't rub off on her, though. Look into her background a little. Before she came to Eugene, I mean."

He nodded.

There was a tap on the door and when Barbara called come on in, Shelley entered carrying a tray with the coffee carafe and cups. "Maria said you were in conference. Anything for me?"

"In a minute. You're not in a hurry to get home or anything?"

"Nope." She sat down and poured coffee into two of the cups, handed one to Barbara.

"Anything else?" Barbara asked Bailey.

"I came across a book celebrating the fiftieth anniversary of the clinic. It's a pretty good history of the place. That's it." He began to root around in his duffel bag and brought out a thick folder and a glossy coffee table book.

Barbara nodded, opened her briefcase and pulled the three diaries out. Briefly she described her meeting with Annie, then, pointing to the books, she asked, "Can you lift prints from them? Annie's and mine will be there. Who else's?"

He eyed the books without touching them.

"Maybe. Got a big envelope? Don't want to handle them without gloves any more than I have to."

She got up to bring him a large envelope, and watched him pick up the books by the edges and place them inside. "That's first, by tomorrow if you can do it. I want to read through them, but not until you're done. Next. Lorraine McIvey, the first wife. She's put herself in the game and I want to find out something about her, what she's up to and why she's been talking to the police. All you can dig out—friends, boyfriends, pastimes, the works."

He raised his eyebrows, then shrugged. He rarely asked why verbally; his body language was enough.

She ignored the implied question. "And then, and this will take a little time—" she paused when he began to fish in his duffel bag and brought out a notebook "—I want as precise a timetable as we can get about the movements of everyone in that clinic the day of the murder, from the time they left home until they arrived and afterward until about eight in the morning. And an accurate layout of the clinic and garden, the residence and a map of the alley and surrounding streets. Someone besides Dorothy Johnson might have seen something, or possibly one of them should have seen something and didn't. I want to be able to place them all."

"And you want all this by tomorrow morning," he said.

"That's how it goes," she said.

"I'll need to bring in hired hands," he said.

She understood that it was a warning that it would

begin to get pricey. "Get them. That's it for now. The diaries first, as soon as possible. Okay?"

"Okeydokey."

After Bailey left, Barbara filled Shelley in with more details about her talk with Annie. "I know she lied to me before, but I don't think she was lying today," she said. "No one could fake the crying spasms. Naomi Boardman said that David humiliated Annie when he was alive, and then again after he died, and he's still doing it. She's suffering, knowing that now someone else is aware of how deep that humiliation really was."

"She stayed with him hoping to collect," Shelley said.

Barbara studied her for a moment, reflecting on the note of condemnation in the words and tone. "Yes," she said. "She was hoping that. She was crazy about him when they married, according to all accounts, truly infatuated. Think of her disillusionment when it became clear that he was simply using her, how hurt she must have been. She reacted the way a child might, vowing to get even, to get revenge, justifying herself by thinking of it as indentured servitude, to be endured for a limited time, and then retribution. I don't condone what she did, I'm just trying to understand her better. And she might not have told me the whole truth yet, I'm well aware. But let's leave that for now. I had another interesting conversation today. A busy day, all in all."

She told Shelley what Dr. Kelso had proposed, and before Shelley could comment, she said, "I don't want to discuss it right now. I want us both to think it over and talk about it tomorrow with Dad."

Shelley looked deeply troubled, but she nodded. "I don't understand how the first Mrs. McIvey has come into the picture," she said after a moment.

Barbara remembered that Shelley had not been present when Frank told her about Lorraine McIvey's contesting the will, and she repeated what he had said. "So she's been confabbing with the cops, and she's dealt herself in. And now you know as much as I do about everything."

Shelley grinned. "I doubt that. Anything you want me to do?"

"Not at the moment. Go home, give Alex a kiss for me. See you in the morning."

Alone in the office Barbara started making the many notes she always made after a day's work. She had put Bailey's reports and the clinic book in her briefcase—homework for later. Then she thought about what Annie had said: David McIvey had hated the clinic, resented it, was jealous of it. Had Kelso's children felt that kind of resentment? He claimed that if they inherited, they would sell their shares in a minute. No love lost there, she mused. Busy fathers, neglected children. It seemed very sad; so many children grateful for the attention they had received, the care they had been given at the clinic, while the children at home seethed with resentment.

She left her computer and got the book about the clinic from her briefcase, poured another cup of coffee and read, pausing at the many pictures of patients, of the two doctors who had founded the clinic and made it work, taking turns at being resident doctor, while keeping their own pediatric practices going for more than twenty-five years. Then they had bought the residence and brought in a full-time resident doctor.

Frank had said zealotry in a good cause was still zealotry, she thought, studying a photograph of David McIvey's father, a very handsome man back in the seventies. And David had been jealous because his father was caring for other people's kids, and not his own. Unloved? He must have felt unloved. Emotionally starved until he had become incapable of love? That was the picture she was getting of him.

He had charmed Annie, dazzled her, married her, and too late she had learned that sex and creature comforts without love were meaningless. And her love, when turned, became blinding hatred.

It was after eight and suddenly she felt ravenous; her stomach was making weird noises of protest and a headache was coming on. Hunger headache, she decided, thinking of the lamb shish kabob in her freezer—Frank's gift. As she started packing up things to take home, she remembered how it had been when she had been growing up and her father had worked the kind of hours she was keeping now.

Frank and Sam Bixby had started their two-office law firm at about the same time the two doctors opened their clinic, four young professionals determined to succeed. But Frank had always had time for her, she recalled, always. Or he had made time. She could remember clearly how he would put aside a paper he was reading and turn his full attention to her on occasion, never in any way suggesting that his work was anywhere near as important as she was. He had taken care of her, his kid, and he was still taking care of her, she thought, smiling slightly, thinking again of the leftovers in her freezer.

She locked her notes in the safe, checked the office and went home.

"Kelso's either as shrewd as Satan or he's a fool," Frank said the next morning when she told him about her meeting.

"Or maybe just desperate," Barbara said, turning to Shelley. "Well?"

"It seems that Dr. Kelso might actually think Annie killed McIvey, and he wants you to make certain that someone else is accused instead of her."

Barbara nodded. "I know," she said. "Shelley, how much of the work that you do here is for clients we get through Martin's Restaurant?"

"I don't know. I never thought of it that way. Some weeks it seems that's all I do. Twenty-five percent, thirty-five. I don't know."

Barbara turned an appraising gaze to Frank. "How about your prestigious firm? How many pro bono cases a year?"

"Make your point," he said sharply.

"I just did," she said. "That clinic will be up for grabs as soon as Mrs. Kelso kicks. Dr. Kelso knows that. I kept thinking of him and his partner working their butts off for half a century, scrounging for volunteer help, for donations, for grants, and all to be able to take in their thirty-five percent or more of nonpaying patients. I said before that the clinic isn't my concern. I was wrong. I find that the clinic has become my concern. I intend to save it if I can."

"Christ on a mountain!" Frank jumped up, glared at her and then around at the office, and abruptly sat down again. "What if you decide that Annie actually pulled the trigger? Or if Darren Halvord did? You can't play both sides."

"I was up pretty late last night thinking about this," she said. "You're right, I can't play both sides. I didn't agree to work for Kelso. I turned him down, remember. But I intend to try to find out the truth, and I don't intend to wait for the police to get their asses in motion. If it turns out to be Annie or Darren, or both, I'll have to decide at that time what next. Right now, I don't know what's next in that case."

"What do you mean?" Frank asked. "You mean foot the bills yourself?"

"Something like that," she admitted. "As long as I'm working solely on behalf of my clients, the board of directors will pony up expenses. I don't think I can bill them for expenses if I'm working for myself."

Frank eyed her narrowly. "You'll end up in the poorhouse yet."

"Sooner rather than later if Kelso's kids inherit and sell out," she said. "He told me outright that there would be no money for attorneys if that happens. Probably he nailed that one." She shrugged. "I figure I'll do a lot of the legwork," she said, "and take brown bag lunches. You know, peanut butter and jelly. It won't be too bad. And you," she said to Shelley, "may find yourself running the office quite a bit for a couple of weeks or so."

"I'm pretty good at legwork," Shelley said in a low voice. "And I don't eat a lot."

Looking at them, the little pink-and-gold fairy princess and his daughter, Frank thought that if Barbara said it was time to walk through the gates of hell, Shelley would run to her side to go in with her. His voice was gruff when he said, "It's going to be different without the benefit of discovery, you know. I can mosey down to the courthouse, maybe city hall, see some old friends, gossip a little."

Barbara closed her eyes hard for a second, and when she opened them, they were suspiciously moist. "Okay," she said rather too briskly, "let's move. I have a brochure you both should read, just to get a bit of history."

Frank looked at her thoughtfully. "I wonder who's the lead investigator. Any idea?"

"Nope. They haven't told anyone a thing."

He nodded. If she were a gambler, Barbara thought, she would put up money that he would find out before the day was over. He had a way of picking up a tidbit here, another there, almost as if the walls told him things as he passed by.

"I'll be on my way," Frank said. "Been out of

touch with old pals too long. Pays to keep in touch with old friends. Dinner, Bobby?"

"I'd love it," she said.

18

She had just hung up from speaking with Dr. Kelso when Bailey dropped in a little later. "I brought the diaries back," he said. "Nothing there. It looks like someone picked up one of them, saw what was inside, closed it and wiped it clean. Next time it was handled, he was wearing gloves. One wiped pretty clean, just Annie's prints and a couple of yours on that one. The others are smeared with her prints and some of yours over them. About what you'd expect."

"Thanks, I guess," she said. "What about that other stuff I asked for?"

"Barbara, take a hike. Be seeing you. Oh, by the way, that was not a marriage made in heaven. Later."

Shelley stuck her head inside the office as Bailey left. "Did you talk to Kelso? How did it go?"

"He's not surprised. Wonder what he'll try next." There was more, but she was uncertain what she meant by that. Dr. Kelso struck her as a desperate man.

"Maybe he'll confess that he did it."

Barbara grinned. "With a superhuman burst of strength that he didn't even know he possessed, he moved the body eight or ten feet, out of sight." She shrugged. "I can see him pulling the trigger easily enough. Get rid of his shares, make sure they're safe, then get rid of the nemesis. But moving the body is a pisser. Did you read Bailey's report? McIvey was lifted pretty much off the ground, hands under his armpits, like that. If they thought Annie could have done it, she'd be in the jug today."

"If Kelso confessed, do you really think they would question how he moved the body?" Shelley asked, starting back to her office again.

"I wouldn't," Barbara admitted. She picked up the nearest diary. It was not easy reading, no matter how legible the writing was. Again and again she stopped to look away, and she found herself thinking that if Annie killed him, it had been justified.

And now someone else had nine pages of what could be damning evidence to bolster exactly that accusation, not from outside observers, but directly from the prime suspect. And she thought of the note of condemnation in Shelley's voice and words; Annie had stayed with him hoping to collect. She had paid a very dear price, Barbara added, and she was still paying. If the police got their hands on those pages, and if they were as incriminating as the ones Barbara had read, the D.A. might decide that was enough even without a gun or a shiny black raincoat or an eyewitness. And he could be right, she added. He could be right.

That evening, nibbling on cheese and sipping wine, she told Frank about the diaries as he went about making dinner. She rarely tried to follow exactly what he did at the counter and stove. It was incomprehensible to her how anyone could take a few potatoes, onions, garlic and other common ingredients and turn them into delectable meals.

"Does she have any idea when they were taken?" he asked, pausing in whatever he was doing.

"Nope. She took them from the condo to the Boardmans' house when she moved back in, but she didn't open them until she decided to toss them on the fire. Anyone at the clinic could have done it. At least, David McIvey is ruled out. Why would he have bothered to wipe his prints?"

Frank nodded and started beating a piece of pork with a wooden mallet.

"I think it's already dead," she commented.

He didn't bother to respond.

With one exception, he had learned nothing that they hadn't already guessed or suspected: the police had sent detectives and a couple of their regular stoolies to the various transient camps trying to find someone wearing a new black raincoat with a hood, or anyone who had seen a silver Mercedes the morning of the killing. They were still waiting for the DNA test results from Darren's glove, boot and bicycle pedal, but no one doubted that it was David McIvey's blood. No one besides Erica Castle had seen Darren the morning of the murder until he showed up at the clinic at ten or twelve minutes before eight. The only thing gained, she thought, was that they knew that Milt Hoggarth was the lead detective, but what good that would do them was problematic. To all appearances the police were not doing a thing now, just waiting for a break, the tests or God's intervention. Frank had not learned what Lorraine McIvey was up to. She had talked with Hoggarth twice, even signed a statement, but then the curtain had closed.

He began to cut the flattened pork into narrow strips that he dropped into a marinade as he went. A pot was simmering with a spicy-smelling sauce; potato slices layered with onions, covered with milk, were in the oven.

He finished with the meat, washed his hands and turned toward her. "About all you can do now is wait for Bailey to do his work. The police have information that you don't have, but on the other hand, we have a little that they don't have—a possible motive for Erica Castle to lie about Darren, and the fact that someone took those diary pages. It sounds to me as if the killer was lying low, but you've stirred things up and maybe he, she or it will make that telling mistake. So be patient. You might want to look up the word in the dictionary."

"Right." And he was right, she thought. Dr. Kelso had made an impossible proposal; someone had stolen Annie's diary pages. Things had been quiet, and maybe a sense of security had set in, but now there was action, people asking questions, Bailey's crew all over the place putting together a timetable. Other people reacting? Perhaps. Be patient, she repeated to herself.

On Saturday Will Thaxton would come home, she reflected, and he would say whether his trip to England and Italy was on, and if it was, she had a decision to make. She had not mentioned the possible trip to anyone. It had been too iffy. She had not been able to decide when he asked, and she still couldn't decide. If nothing was happening with the McIvey murder, why not? If they arrested someone, the trial would not be for many months. Again, why not? Then, without warning, she was wondering if it was her work and the trip itself with so much time involved, or being with Will for several weeks that was confusing her.

Having the thought surface simply added to her confusion. She and Will had the ideal relationship; they didn't quarrel, he never criticized her or her work, but accepted her exactly as she was. They were good dancing together, or in bed together. Politically he was more conservative than she was, but in honesty she had to admit that most people were, and they seldom talked politics anyway. Neither one had ever suggested that they might take their relationship to the next level, a level that implied commitment, but was this his way of broaching that? And was she anywhere near considering a real commitment?

"Ahem," Frank said.

She looked at him in surprise. "Oh, right. Set the table."

"Well, you could do that, too, but that isn't what I asked. I asked if you warned Annie to take care, keep her door locked, not wander about the garden alone at night, and so on."

"Of course. I'll set the table."

His gaze on her was thoughtful, but he made no comment.

Friday morning Bailey brought in the timetable, a map of the premises and surrounding streets and the floor plan of the clinic. He didn't linger. A workaholic boss was cracking the whip, he complained before leaving. No time, no time.

Barbara studied the map and the floor plan, then put them both in an envelope and walked out to the reception room. "Going shopping," she told Maria. "I won't be long."

When she returned she had enlargements of the map and floor plan, two magnetic boards, a magnetic travel checkers game and a package of small round price tags. In her office again, on the price tags she wrote the initials of everyone at the clinic the morning of the murder and stuck them to the checkers; red for the girls, black for the boys, she thought as she worked. She taped the enlargements to the magnetic boards and stood them both on easels from her closet, then began placing the checkers on them.

Now and then she stopped to make a note: which way had Annie turned when she left the driveway? Had Bernie Zuckerman seen Annie's car leaving as she arrived? Had anyone seen the Mercedes that morning? Had Erica Castle passed Darren on his bike as they both headed to the clinic? Which streets had they used? She realized how very much she did not know about the movements of all those people on that particular morning.

She was still at it when Shelley dropped in to say she was off to court. She was wearing a simple dark skirt and jacket, low shoes, small gold earrings, no other jewelry. Shelley had a closet full of designer clothes and probably a safe full of costly jewelry, but always dressed down for her court appearances. Barbara always felt dressed up for hers. Whenever she had to put on a skirt she felt overdressed. Different strokes, she thought.

"It's a plea bargain," Shelley said. "It shouldn't take long. And I'll go to Martin's this afternoon. We don't really want a lot of work piling up next week, do we? If I go, I can guarantee we won't have it."

Barbara grinned. "Don't take it personally. I just spoiled them all."

Shelley was examining the layout of the clinic with the checker pieces here and there. "Does that help?"

"Not a lot. But it told me there's a lot I don't know. For instance, what kind of window covering is in the lounge? Open or closed drapes or blinds? If closed, who opened them, and when? Who saw whom that morning? Things like that. I think I'll bundle up all my toys and head over there and bring folks in one at a time to place their pieces. Dad says we've stirred them up and someone might make a wrong move. I think I'll stir the pot a little more."

"Maybe a hornet's nest," Shelley said. "See you later."

Barbara called Naomi to inform her that she would like to use the directors' room and interview people there, and Naomi said, "I was going to call you, Ms. Holloway. I want to talk to you." She sounded hostile, belligerent even.

Hornet's nest, Barbara thought when she hung up. Stir it up and watch them buzz.

Naomi Boardman was waiting for her by the reception desk. Her hair was sticking out in peculiar spikes and she looked mad as hell, Barbara thought. "I want a word with you before you begin anything," Naomi said.

Barbara put down the carrying case and laptop that she had brought in. "Good morning," she said to Naomi and Bernie. Bernie's eyes were bright with curiosity, as if restraining herself had raised her blood pressure. Barbara said to Naomi, "Fine, but I have a few more things to get. It won't take a minute." She turned and went back outside to her car for the easels and her briefcase. At the reception desk again she smiled at Naomi. "Want to bring that carrying case?" She led the way without waiting for a response.

Inside the directors' room she took off her jacket and then began to arrange the easels with the maps in place. She dumped the checkers onto the table and started to turn them right side up, all the while paying no attention to Naomi Boardman, who stood in tight-lipped silence.

After being ignored a few minutes, Naomi said, "Ms. Holloway, we retained you to defend Annie and Darren if the need arises. We did not hire you to harass, intimidate or frighten Annie. What did you say to her?"

Barbara looked at Naomi and raised her eyebrows. "No," she said. "You did not retain me. The board of directors did. And it was accepted that I would answer to no one except Annie and Darren. Ah, here you are." She picked up the checker with an N and B on it and placed it on the residence. "Did you happen to look out the window that morning?"

"No."

"Did you see your husband, speak to him before Carlos came?"

"No." A deep flush appeared on Naomi's cheeks. She wheeled about and strode to the door angrily, but she paused with her hand on the doorknob, then turned back and said, "I'm alarmed about Annie, Ms. Holloway. She is terrified. I believe she is ill, and it started after your last visit. If anything happens to that girl, I'll hold you responsible."

Barbara nodded. "All right. Today I intend to

bring in everyone who was here the morning of the murder between seven-fifteen and eight, one by one, and talk to them. Will you arrange it, or must I wander about searching for people? I have them listed in the order I'd like to see them." She picked up the list from the table and waited.

After an apparent struggle, and then moving stiffly, Naomi crossed back to her and took the list. "I'll see to it," she said.

"Thank you," Barbara said, as if unaware of the fury in the other woman's eyes and eloquent in her posture and attitude.

Dr. Boardman was first on her list. He entered and gazed curiously at the two easels, then nodded as he grasped what he was looking at. Barbara already had his checker out and ready, and she placed it on the residence as he approached the table.

"You can see what I'm doing," she said. "Just a couple of questions. Did you actually see Annie that morning?"

He shook his head. "I saw the car backing out, that's all. The headlights were on and I really couldn't see past them."

"Please sit down," she said. "I don't want to take too much of your time, but there are a few things I need to clarify." He seated himself and she sat across from him. "Did you see which way she turned at the street?"

"No. I didn't keep watching her. David was shaking his umbrella, and I stepped back, out of the way."

"Did you see your wife that morning or speak to her before Carlos came?"

"No. As I said, I made coffee and went into the study to watch the news and wait for David to finish up and leave. I heard her go out to the garage, but we didn't speak."

"Dr. Boardman, exactly how ill is Mrs. Kelso? People keep saying she's liable to die at any time. Is that how it is?"

He nodded. "I'm surprised that she's held on this long. Every day Thomas goes out to the nursing home and feeds her, but the day she refuses food, it means feeding tubes. And years ago she signed an advanced directive forbidding heroic measures." He shrugged. "That's how it is."

"I see. How ill is Dr. Kelso?"

He stiffened and his craggy face seemed to change, become masklike. "I'm afraid I can't discuss my patients with you."

"You could talk about her, but not him?"

"She isn't my patient."

"All right. Another topic. Could Darren be accepted at most clinics? I know his background, Dr. Boardman. He told me about it."

"Yes, he'd be accepted, and welcomed. He's had offers, in fact. He's known throughout the field and highly regarded. We made a couple of videos for the interns to watch, to see what he does, how he does it. Word got out, and now other clinics and schools use them. He gives them to anyone who asks, for the price of the cassette. He could work anywhere he chooses."

"But he chose to remain here," Barbara said, not

quite a question unless he responded to it. He simply nodded. "I'd like to see those videos. May I borrow them?"

"You should see them," he said.

"If the clinic were sold to a for-profit corporation, would you stay?"

He hesitated, then stood up and walked to the window overlooking the garden. He paused for a moment before turning back toward her. "Ms. Holloway, I honestly don't know. We've talked about it, Naomi and I, and we don't know. I don't believe investors should be enriched through the suffering of others, and I know for a fact that there are many people who would receive no treatment without a clinic like this one. I'm afraid I'm not a very good team player, and I am not at all sure a corporation would even hire me. Near retirement age, you understand. I'm fifty-nine, Naomi is sixty. I'm afraid our savings would dissipate fast if we had to live on that, and we're not due for Social Security for several years. We'd both have to work at something. Would it be better to retire early with good memories of the clinic, or watch it change into a grasping octopus and then be forced into retirement? I don't know. I can't answer that question. I just don't know."

"If David McIvey had turned it into a surgical facility, would you have stayed?"

"Not for a day," he said. "But there wouldn't have been any choice. I knew he would boot Naomi and me out the day he took over."

"One more thing," she said. "What kind of security do you have here? I keep hearing that the garden door is opened at seven-thirty. Who opens it then?"

"It's automatic," he said. "That door gets closed and locked at dusk by the volunteer at the reception desk, late in the summer, pretty early in the winter, and it doesn't get opened again until morning. Whoever is on duty sees to it that the front door gets locked at ten when the last visitor leaves, and that lock is put on the computer. When the shift changes at midnight, one of the nurses comes down to let the night nurses in. And that's how it works when the shift changes again at seven in the morning. At seven-thirty the computer turns off the other locks."

"So no one can get in before seven-thirty without ringing for someone to open the door?"

"That's right." He hesitated, then said, "Of course, I have keys for the doors, and so does Dr. Kelso. And we gave one to Stephanie Waters in the kitchen. She lets her helpers in."

"Okay," she said, standing up. "Thank you."

When he left she made a note by his name. Was the need for financial security motive enough to commit murder? Maybe, she decided. Maybe it was.

She looked up as Annie entered. She did look ill, pale and drawn, hollow-eyed, as if she had not slept since the last time Barbara saw her.

Annie sat down wearily and Barbara asked her the same question she intended to ask everyone: whom did you see that morning?

"I saw Greg at the door for just a second, then David moved in front of him. No one else."

"Which way did you turn at the street after backing out?"

Annie seemed to see the map for the first time. She pointed. "West, I guess. I was going to Delta Highway."

Barbara moved her checker away from the residence, out to the street, and west. "Did you turn at the intersection here?"

Annie shook her head. "No. Oaklawn Street goes to Country Club Road, and I went straight."

"Did you see any of the other staff members, or volunteers, anyone or any car that you recognized?"

She said no, and Barbara sat down opposite her. "Did you remember anything about those dates from your diaries?"

Annie nodded. "Three of them," she said in a low voice, looking away from Barbara. "That's all. Two were at the same time of year, May, my mother's birthday. He said I had to wait to go home until the weekend, he couldn't spare me during the week. I was pretty upset. I think I wrote quite a lot the first time it happened, maybe not as much the next year. It was...hard to take." She glanced at Barbara, then out the window at the garden. "Actually it had come up before, just a year after we married, and I thought that time it was because he couldn't stand being separated even for a few days. I really believed that." She shrugged, but kept her face turned away. "I was so thrilled and excited to think he couldn't bear letting me out of his sight for even a day."

"The third one?" Barbara asked after a moment. Then she said, "Annie, I had to read them, you know. I understand how it was."

Annie looked at her then, a quick glance, away again. "I'm so ashamed," she whispered. "It was degrading, and I went along with it. I felt almost as if I could stand back and watch us both, as if I was someone else." She shook herself. "The third one that I remembered was when we went to the resort, two years ago, in March. He took time off in March every year to go skiing. I don't ski. I stayed in the lodge and read while he did. There was a fatal accident while we were there, and they shut down everything for an investigation for a day. David was furious. He blamed the man for being stupid, for spoiling his vacation. He had no sense of pity or mercy. I wrote about it, that I wished it had been David, wished he was dead, things like that." She looked very young at that moment, almost childish, her head bowed, shoulders slumped. "It was the way a child might wish a tree would fall on a hated teacher, or that the schoolyard bully would get hit by a car, but the words themselves... I think they were pretty bad."

Her voice dropped to near inaudibility as she talked, and when she stopped, neither of them spoke for a time. That could be a big one, Barbara thought. Depending on how she had worded it, what she had written, it could be damning.

Stephanie Waters came in after Annie left, and Stephanie stated emphatically that she didn't have time for all this. "I have lunches to get ready," she said, perching on the edge of a chair.

"I won't keep you long," Barbara said. "I'm trying to find out exactly when people arrived on the morning of the murder. Coordinating movements in a way. Someone might have seen something significant without realizing it at the time."

"I got here before seven-thirty. I always get here before seven-thirty. A quarter after, twenty after. I put my stuff in my locker off the lounge and went straight to the kitchen and stayed there."

"Did you let yourself in?"

"Yes, I always do. And I switched the bell to ring in the kitchen so I'd hear my helpers when they came."

Barbara put her checker in the kitchen and made a note of the time. "Were the blinds open in the lounge?"

"No. And I didn't touch them."

Her two helpers, Lori Barlson and Thelma Perle, had come in together a minute or two after she got to the kitchen, Stephanie said, and they all had stayed there getting breakfasts ready. Barbara added their checkers to hers in the kitchen.

"Do you always work ten- or twelve-hour days?"

"I never do. I see to breakfast and then I leave for a couple of hours, come back around eleven to do the lunches, which I should be doing right now, and leave again in the afternoon. I don't clean up, I cook. I come back at about four and leave at about seven and that ends my day. On and off all day long."

Barbara nodded. "All right. So you saw Lori and Thelma. Who else?"

"Bernie. I don't know what time. Darren arrived as I was taking coffee to the lounge. I gave it to him and he carried it in for me. It was about ten minutes before eight. I always get the coffee in before eight." She glanced at the wall clock, then at her watch and her mouth tightened.

"How did he appear?"

"Wet. He appeared dripping wet. It's crazy to ride a bike in weather like that, but he did." She was sitting stiffly upright and she leaned forward. "I know that some people are speculating that Darren did it, but he never. If it had been Darren out there dead, I'd be just as certain David pulled the trigger as I'm sure Darren did not. He's incapable of hating anyone enough to kill."

"You knew David McIvey?"

"Yes, from years back. I worked for him and Lorraine fifteen years ago, as cook and housekeeper."

And no one had thought to mention this earlier, Barbara thought in surprise. "Is that generally known around here?"

"Of course not. Why would I talk about the past? David's mother and father knew. They might have mentioned it to the Kelsos. I don't know about that."

"And David McIvey? He must have known."

"I don't imagine he did. He never set foot in the kitchen here. And I doubt he would have remembered me if he had tripped over me. He never really saw people, not like most of us do."

She looked at her watch again and abruptly stood up. "I told you I have to see to lunches."

"All right, but I'll want to talk to you afterward, after you're done with the lunches."

Stephanie's mouth tightened again and she nodded. "At one, then. I'll come back at one." She walked out as stiffly as she had been sitting, like a windup soldier.

Barbara saw the two interns, who added nothing. They had arrived on the heels of Darren and had gone straight to the lounge to change their shoes—apparently everyone wore soft-soled shoes, walking shoes, court shoes, sneakers or the like at work. Others had been in the lounge, but they couldn't say for sure who they had been, except Darren. They thought the blinds were open when they went in, but they seemed uncertain. They had arrived together, and remained together until Tony Kranz had gone with Darren to his office at about eight.

Bernie Zuckerman came in hesitantly. "Naomi said I'm next," she said, "but I have a lunch date with a girlfriend, and it's going on twelve...."

Barbara waved her off. "Go on. I'll catch up with you later."

Then, alone in the directors' room, she felt she could place almost everyone who had been on hand that morning, and what it meant, she told herself, was that one of the Boardmans was the most likely candidate to have ducked out and committed a murder.

She thought of the motives for murder she had

discussed with Frank many times. He maintained that greed was the overriding one, followed closely by passion: love, hate or revenge. Zealotry in his litany came under passion. Passion for a cause or a belief. She could believe Dr. Kelso might kill to save his clinic, but Greg Boardman? If he was passionate about it, he managed to hide his emotion. Contented here, a believer in what they were doing, but passionate about it? He struck her as a go-along-get-along man, one who would not make waves. Even to ensure his next few years? Protect his security?

And Naomi? Barbara suspected that she was too self-reliant to be overly upset by any threat to her financial well-being. She would get by. Then she recalled the fury in Naomi's eyes when she thought Barbara had intimidated Annie. If she believed someone was really hurting Annie, damaging her… Maybe, Barbara thought. Maybe.

Then, moving slowly and deliberately, she picked up the checker with Annie's initials and placed it on a blank checker. Queen, she said under her breath, and put it back at the residence. She put David McIvey's checker there also. She moved his through the house, through the back garden, across the alley, onto the clinic walkway. At the same time, with her other hand, she moved Annie's doubled checker out through the driveway, turned east at the street, to the corner and around it to the entrance of the alley. She stopped it at the gravel turnoff for the gardener's truck and took off the top piece. She moved it onto the walkway in the garden, then back to the other checker and replaced it, and moved the queened piece out of the alley and onto the street.

"Why haven't they arrested her?" Darren said, from the door. She had not heard him enter.

"They don't know how she moved the body, or where she put the raincoat and gun," Barbara said, taking all the checkers off the map. "Some people knock before entering a room."

"And they miss a lot. I came by to tell you that I have a busy schedule this afternoon. Is there anything you want from me?"

"Are you on your lunch hour now?"

"Yes. I'll get a deli sandwich in a minute."

"Is there anything to add to what you already told me?"

He shook his head. "Nope. You have it all."

"Were the blinds open or closed when you went to the lounge?"

He glanced toward the wide windows with vertical blinds drawn all the way back, leaving a great expanse of glass exposed with a view of the garden beyond. "I think Winnie Bok had just finished opening them, like that, when I went in," he said. "Too late to see the killer and victim enact their little melodrama."

She nodded. "Too late. Did you see anyone else that morning before you entered the clinic? On the grounds, in the parking lot, on the street coming?"

He shook his head. "No."

"That's all I wanted to know. See you later." She had not made a token for Winnie Bok, who had arrived with her carpool companion at seven-forty-five.

He turned back to the door, paused, then looked at her. "Are you having lunch?"

"Eventually."

"I could bring you something. The deli is just a door or two down the street. Good sandwiches and salads."

She glanced at her watch. Twelve. Stephanie would come back at one, and until then no one. "I'll come with you," she said. "First, I'll lock up stuff in my car."

"Let's just lock this room," he said, taking a bunch of keys from his pocket.

She pulled on her jacket and they walked out. He locked the door and they left the clinic.

"By the end of the day the gossip will be all over the place," he said. "Darren and the lady lawyer had lunch together!" He laughed. "This way."

19

The deli was crowded and noisy, and although there were tables, Barbara and Darren opted to take sandwiches back to the directors' room. Walking back she asked, "What do you do when you're not working?"

"Bridge a couple of times a month, bicycle club, marathon rides now and then, a chess buddy I get together with occasionally. Read. What about you?"

"Long walks, hike a bit, movies, read, dance. Do you date?"

"Sometimes. Nothing serious. You?"

"The same. Nothing serious." Her answer had come without thought, and voicing it made her realize the truth of it. Nothing serious.

"You obviously do something to keep in shape.

You're a good walker," he said. "I set a pretty good clip and you didn't seem to notice."

She looked at him in surprise. She had not noticed.

He began to talk about his son, how they collected things like volcanoes, totem poles and, this coming year, trees. She recalled the miniature tree in its bamboo shelter on Erica Castle's back porch. Erica baby-sat Todd's cat and his tree? Apparently.

"Have you been to Kings Canyon?" he asked. "To see the giant sequoias?"

"A long time ago. There was snow on the ground and the tree trunks were like warm and furry walls, the cones so tiny I didn't believe those trees had produced them."

"They're on Todd's list," he said. "He's my advance researcher."

They had reached the clinic by then. They entered and he unlocked the directors' room and went to get coffee from the lounge for them both. Then, sitting by the windows overlooking the garden, they ate their lunch and talked. It occurred to her that he was drawing her out exactly the same way she was drawing him out, and she felt a touch of uneasiness at the thought.

It was getting close to one o'clock when she asked, "If the plan to turn the clinic into a nonprofit foundation fails, and it is acquired by a for-profit company, will you stay?"

He shook his head. "I told you I can get work anywhere. It's true. But I wouldn't stay. I can't work for just anyone. I can't take orders from incompetents who don't understand what I do and couldn't care less. There are other nonprofit clinics in the country or I could set up a tent somewhere. David McIvey suggested that I was qualified to practice in a tent revival." He regarded her for a moment, then said, "I'll tell you a secret, Barbara. I don't know what I do. I could never justify myself to a panel of insurance bean counters, or even a panel of doctors who demanded an explanation before proceeding. I don't have to explain anything to Greg. He's content to let me make my own decisions. He prefers it that way. He knows and I know that I run this clinic."

"I don't understand what you're telling me," she said. "You've had excellent training, good schools, clinical practice with experts in the field."

"I learned the jargon," he said. "I can bullshit with the best of them. The education means nothing to me. I went down that road because I was trying to understand what I had. I can tell the clavicle from the kneecap, sure. I know and can use all the standard techniques, but knowing what is accepted and standard has nothing to do with what my hands tell me. And that's what I can't explain."

He grinned suddenly. "There you have it. My innermost, darkest secret. Your turn. What's your darkest secret?"

She laughed, but it sounded false to her own ears. "You're out of your mind," she said. "I can't match that."

He stood up. "It's nearly one and I have a full

schedule. See you later. Thanks for the best lunch hour I've had in a very long time."

She remained seated at the window going over in her mind all the things Darren had said, trying to make sense of a physical therapist who apparently was really a faith healer. She was still there when Stephanie Waters came in.

"Do you want to sit over here by the windows?" Barbara asked, getting to her feet.

After an indifferent glance toward the garden, Stephanie pulled out a chair at the round table and sat down. "This will do," she said. "Look, Ms. Holloway, I know pretty much why you're asking about David and Lorraine. She's contesting his will, is what the rumor mill has churned out. That's why Annie's broke and staying with Naomi."

Barbara sat opposite her. "I keep hearing that there are no secrets in the clinic. I'm beginning to understand what that means. Right now I'm still trying to get some background on all these people. Okay?"

"Whatever. As I said, I worked for them. When I started, there was the little boy Aaron, still in diapers, and Lorraine was pregnant. They hired me to be a housekeeper and cook, and I ended up nursemaid, companion, cook, everything. Then Caitlin was born and the fuss and confusion got worse. David hated disorder and noise. Noisy kids especially. If he hadn't wanted them, he should have kept his zipper closed. But she wanted children. Round out the perfect family, cement the marriage, that sort of thing."

She grimaced. "Only the glue didn't hold. Anyway, I had tried cooking in a nice restaurant, and it didn't work out. Restaurant people are crazy. So I thought a private family might be better. Wrong. They were crazier. Lorraine was a beautiful woman. I had a terrible crush on her for a while." She paused and gazed steadily at Barbara. "I'm in a lesbian relationship, you understand. It's not a secret. We've been together for thirteen years, just another couple getting old and gray together. So I had a crush on Lorraine, and I tried to help her, but there was no pleasing that pig of a husband. I lost patience with her for putting up with him, for trying too hard to keep him satisfied, crying over him, for God's sake." She shrugged. "She was crazy about him in those days, just like Annie was when she married him. He must have been a hell of a lover."

She thought for a moment, then nodded. "That's enough of the background. It came to an end one day when they had a cocktail party, a catered affair that had nothing to do with me. It was the first party they'd had in ages. Caitlin was about three or four months old and colicky. She started to wail and, of course, big brother joined the chorus. Lorraine had given me a few of her cast-off dresses, and I was going to leave the house for the afternoon and evening, let the caterers earn their money. David saw me at the back door and he said something like, 'For God's sake, Lorraine, make those kids shut up or I will.' I turned around and he saw that it wasn't Lorraine, and he was furious. He said,

'What are you doing in her clothes? You've been stealing her clothes. Take off that dress.' So I did. Right there in the kitchen with the caterers standing around, and some of the guests watching, I took off the dress and let it fall to the floor. I went to my room and packed my gear and got the hell out of there. I could hear people laughing, and not at me. I thought David might have a heart attack. I hoped he would, to tell the truth. The next day his mother, Joyce McIvey, called me and asked if I wanted to work in the clinic kitchen, and I've been here ever since."

Barbara grinned, then she laughed out loud. "What a sight that must have been. Good for you."

Stephanie smiled and nodded; she even relaxed her rigid posture a little. "It worked out. He was like a slow poison, seductive and charming as hell at the beginning, handsome as the devil, but poison. Drip by drip he poisoned Lorraine, and then Annie. If he'd taken over running the clinic, he would have poisoned it, too."

"Would you have stayed?"

Stephanie hooted in derision. "The day he moved in, I would have been out. I'd begun looking around to see where I might go, in fact." She stood up. "I don't know who pulled the trigger. I wish I did, just so I could send a thank you card. And if I'd seen it with my own eyes, I'd deny it. That's just how it is. Are you done with me?"

"I think so. Thanks. You've been very helpful. I appreciate it."

* * *

Bernie Zuckerman was anticlimactic, Barbara thought a few minutes later when Bernie entered carrying a thermal mug that had a dragon coiled around it. She settled down into one of the window chairs, obviously prepared and eager to talk a while.

"I know what you're asking everyone," she said. "When did we come in and who did we see. Right? Well, I got here at twenty minutes before eight, the blinds were still closed in the lounge and I saw everyone," she said triumphantly. "It's my job to check them in. Just a check mark by their names so I'll know they're on hand when the patients start coming."

"Do they all come to the reception desk to get checked in?"

"No. No, they don't have to. I can keep an eye on the corridor from the staff door. They come in that way and go on to the lounge to change. If I see someone, I wave or something, and that's that. I have to listen to the messages, the voice mail, like that, and they just make sure that I've seen them. At eight the voice mail is off and I have to answer the phone after that."

"From your desk you can see the start of the corridor that leads to the garden door, can't you?"

"Sure. No one used it that morning until Carlos came in. The police asked me that."

"What about Stephanie Waters and her helpers? They get here so early. Do they come out of the kitchen to check in?"

"No. I stick my head in on my way through and make sure she's here, and someone's helping out. No problem."

"What if someone calls in and leaves a message on voice mail saying they can't make it, a flat tire, or something like that? Or if one of the volunteers doesn't show up?"

"I call Naomi right away and she gets on the phone and lines up someone else. No one did anything like that on that day."

Barbara looked at her thoughtfully, then stood up. "Let's go over to the map for a minute," she said. "I want to try something."

She found the checker with BZ on it and showed it to Bernie, who was studying the map and the floor plan with interest. "Your marker," she said, placing the checker on the map at the intersection of Country Club Road and Oaklawn. "You turned off Country Club Road here. Was there much traffic on Country Club Road that morning?"

"There always is in the morning."

"How about Oaklawn?"

Bernie shrugged. "Little, usually. Maybe none. I don't remember one way or the other for that day. Remember, it was raining to beat the band, and it was foggy to boot."

Barbara didn't move the checker, but put her finger on the floor plan of the clinic at the staff door. "So you parked and came to this door. Were you bundled up pretty much? Raincoat, boots, carrying an umbrella?"

Bernie nodded. "Yeah, it's about a ten-minute drive, and my car takes fifteen minutes to warm up. I was wrapped up. I stood under the overhang there," she said putting her finger next to Barbara's, outside the door. "I had to shake rain off the umbrella."

"Did you take it to the lounge with you?"

"No. There's a stand by the door there, for them to drip in. I put it in the stand and went on down the hall to the kitchen—" She stopped and her eyes narrowed. "I forgot this. I didn't just stick my head in. I went in to see if there was coffee. I was freezing."

Barbara nodded. "Good. Then what?"

"I got coffee," Bernie said. She looked from the floor plan to Barbara. "Maybe I said something or other to Stephanie. I probably did, just out of habit, but I didn't stay. They were busy getting breakfast."

"Did Stephanie stop what she was doing to get coffee for you?"

"She wouldn't stop for a train when she gets busy," Bernie said. "I helped myself, got my mug out of my bag and filled it, and then left." She patted the dragon affectionately.

Bit by bit with excruciating exactness Barbara had her reconstruct her movements that morning, and then she said, "So you must have actually arrived at the clinic at least five minutes before you sat at your desk. Is that about right?"

Bernie thought about it, then nodded. "I guess that's just about how long it all took. Getting the coffee, untying my boots, getting my shoes changed.

Then I had to wash my hands. It begins to add up, doesn't it? I should have thought of all that before."

"I think we all tend to forget how much time we spend at the most ordinary things that we do routinely. Well, let's back up a little, back to your car at the intersection. Why don't you move the checker down Oaklawn toward the parking lot?" she said. "I suppose you were driving pretty slowly on such a lousy morning, weren't you?"

Bernie had started to move the checker, then stopped and put it back at the intersection. "Real slow," she said, and started again, very slowly. "The windshield wipers could hardly keep up with the rain and all that fog—and it was a dark morning on top of it. It was slow."

"Right. I know those mornings. That's a long block, isn't it? Could you see to the end of it?"

"I don't guess so, but I don't really remember trying to see. I mean, if there had been headlights, I would have paid attention, I imagine, but I just don't know." She had moved the checker about a third of the way down the street and stopped. "There was a little bit of exhaust maybe. You know, like a car makes when it's cold outside? Maybe taillights, come to think of it."

"Where, Bernie? Where did you think you saw exhaust and taillights?"

Bernie shook her head. "Not right in front of my car. Down farther, like someone leaving the parking lot. One of the nurses maybe." She began to move again. "Or maybe I just thought I saw something like that. I can't be sure." She finished taking the checker to the parking lot and positioned it. "That's as close as I could get. The nurses and Stephanie and the others took the best places."

Barbara did not press the point. Instead, returning to her chair at the table, she asked, "If they turn the clinic over to a corporation or something, will you stay?"

"I don't know," Bernie said, sitting down. "It would be so different. I mean, like checking people in in the morning. We don't time anyone, keep track of every minute, make sure they earn what they make. And I guess a real company would change that. It wouldn't be the same. If some of my friends here left, I'd probably leave, too. Darren would leave. We all know that. And the volunteers. Why would they do volunteer work so shareholders in New York could make more money? We've been talking about what it would have meant. But it's a dead issue. Now that David McIvey's out of the picture, we've all relaxed a little. I don't think anyone would have stayed with him in charge."

Barbara encouraged Bernie to talk, to ramble actually, about the staff, the volunteers, whatever came to mind. What she learned was a mixed bag, she had to admit as Bernie veered from subject to subject, about people Barbara didn't know, and those she was interested in. Greg Boardman was a dear, sweet man, a wonderful doctor, but he couldn't make a decision if his life depended on it, unless it was about medicine. Naomi made the decisions in that family.

Stephanie's lover was a ceramicist who worked at
home while Stephanie ran the kitchen in the clinic
and moved back and forth from one to the other all
day. Darren had agreed with his ex that neither of
them would take Todd out of state to live, at least
until he was eighteen or in college. Darren was crazy
about Todd, and if he was aware that every woman
he met fell for him, he never let on. And he didn't
take advantage of that, either, she said emphatically.
Probably he didn't notice, just took it for granted, the
way he took it for granted that he was the best therapist in the West, maybe in the country. It just was.
David McIvey had used Annie as a doormat or something. His own personal slave. He couldn't stand
noise, loud music, anything alive.

Finally, when she hoped that all the irrelevancies
had eclipsed the one point she did not want Bernie
to toss into the gossip pool—the fact that she probably had seen the killer leaving the premises—Barbara looked at her watch.

"Good heavens. I had no idea it was getting so
late," she said. "And I've kept you far too long.
Thanks, Bernie. You've been very helpful in filling
in background for me."

Bernie beamed and stood up. "I enjoyed talking
to you. Back to the desk for me. Greg left a package
for you at the desk, by the way. I would have brought
it, but I forgot."

Driving a few minutes later, Barbara decided she
had to move, had to walk, to think. Accordingly she

turned toward the riverside park after crossing the bridge to downtown Eugene. Few people were out walking that afternoon. The sky had become overcast, the air quite cold and very still. The river looked like liquid pewter, as shiny as silver at the ripples, as dull as lead in other places. Suddenly she recalled a question she had asked Frank many years in the past: With all those rivers going into the ocean, why didn't it fill up? He had said something about evaporation, that as much water went into the air as flowed into the ocean, and without a clear idea of what that meant she had visualized a vast river out there somewhere, flowing up toward the sky in a steady stream, like a waterfall in reverse. She had added it to her wish list for when she grew up: go find the river that flowed into the sky.

She started walking at a brisk pace in order to keep warm, but after a few minutes she slowed down, and she was now considering the question Frank had posed. What would she do if she decided that one or both of her clients had collectively or singly murdered David McIvey? She had not known the answer when he asked, and she had no answer now. But her thoughts kept taking her back to the question. Before long she might have to come up with an answer. Bernie had seen someone drive away that morning, shortly after seven-thirty.

Bernie, she reflected then, was probably the only one of that whole crew who wouldn't lie about anything. What she knew she told, period. The Boardmans, no doubt, would readily lie for each other, and

Naomi certainly would lie for Annie, the girl she had taken to heart to replace her own dead daughters. Annie had lied, and for all Barbara knew, was still lying. Kelso? He would lie to God, she thought, if he believed it would help save his holy clinic. She grinned at the thought of Stephanie stripping off her dress before an audience. She'd lie for anyone who pulled the trigger. Erica would lie for Darren, she felt certain. And Darren? She didn't know. A physical therapist who apparently believed in magic, in faith healing or something. Was he really unaware of the effect he had on the others at the clinic? The near reverence they had for him? She didn't know that, either, she realized. He was an enigma, a puzzle she could not sort out. But if he had agreed with his ex-wife not to take their son from the state, it did limit his possibilities for another job comparable to the one he had. If even Portland was too far away for him to consider, then the threat of losing his place here could have become more daunting.

A pair of geese circled over the river ahead of her. She paused to watch them, but they didn't land. They liked still water, she thought; the Willamette River might appear too treacherous for them. Then she was thinking of Dorothy Johnson, who had half expected to see the ghost of her husband shooting to frighten geese away from the koi pond. She began to move again.

Her cell phone rang as she walked; Bailey wanted to know if she would be in the office at about four-thirty. He had stuff. She headed back.

20

"**G**ive," Barbara said in her office. Bailey was sprawled on the sofa with a glass of Jack Daniel's barely lightened with water.

"Long or short?"

"Short." She had a cup of coffee, more for the warmth it offered than because she wanted it. The temperature had dropped to forty and she had come in numb with cold.

"Okay. Erica Castle was involved in a shooting back in Cleveland."

Barbara nearly choked on a sip of coffee; Bailey grinned.

"That's a gotcha," he said. "Her old lady and her current boyfriend had a tussle. She hit him, he hit her, she hit him harder and someone pulled a handgun and shot a couple of times. Neighbors called the cops, and by the time they got there the boyfriend had skedaddled, Mom was nursing a black eye and didn't know what they were talking about, and Erica, age six, was hiding in a closet. End of episode. No more public notice for seven years. Then another boyfriend, another fight, more cops. Erica vamoosed to a neighbor's apartment and pretty much stayed there for the next few years. Worked her way through high school, community college, university, and began teaching. Clean as a whistle, Barbara, not even a parking ticket. Mucho credit card debt now, roof, furnace, things like that. She still owes school loans."

He took a long drink. "When the grandmother died, her will allowed Erica's mother to use the house, and she trashed it. Probably into prostitution, known as a dopehead, cited for disorderly conduct a couple of times. That's public stuff. How much private stuff do you want?"

Discouraged, she shrugged. "Leave it alone for now. What about the ex-Mrs. McIvey?"

"Lorraine McIvey is a case," he said. "She calls herself a publicist. A few artist clients, an actor or two. She arranges shows, gigs, whatever. A series of boyfriends over the years. The last one was Pier Longos, a two-bit artist. A couple of days after McIvey was shot, Lorraine turned up at a neighbor's house wanting to talk, which was weird, according to the neighbor, because Lorraine never had given her or any other neighbor the time of day before. But she needed to talk, she said. David had wanted to get back together with her, she said. He was fed up with the trophy wife, and was going to ditch her as soon as his private snoop got proof that she was having an affair. He said he knew it was true, but he needed proof. He wanted Lorraine to help run the clinic the way it should be run, not as a money-losing hobby, but as a real business. Lorraine had decided to give it a go when, bingo, he was shot dead."

"Right," Barbara said derisively. "Sure he wanted to get back with her."

"Well, she told the same story to her ex-boyfriend Pier, and McIvey took a cab up to her house one afternoon the week before he was shot. Told his office people to put patients on hold, there was an emergency, and he took off. The taxi driver waited twenty-five minutes for him and drove him back to the surgical office."

"Not even a he said-she said," Barbara muttered after a moment. "Just a she said." But it explained why the police had turned the spotlight on to Annie from day one, she thought, and why they appeared determined to make Darren an accomplice one way or another, either as the shooter or the hider of evidence.

Bailey held up his glass and she nodded absently. He ambled over to the bar and poured himself another drink. "I just bring in the dope," he said. "I don't interpret."

"Do you know where Lorraine was the morning of the murder?"

"Yes, indeed. Driving her daughter to school. The kid was cutting first period class—math—with some regularity, and the principal and Lorraine struck a deal to avoid expulsion, or horsewhipping, or whatever they do these days. She has to take the kid to school every morning and watch her go in. She did that morning. Got there at five minutes to eight. Won't work unless she took the kid with her and made her wait in the car while she popped the guy."

"Dead end," she said. "Okay. I'll try to think of something over the weekend. Maybe a fishing trip, or a hike on the coast, a trip to Mexico."

"Sounds good to me. See you Monday morning." He emptied his glass, set it down and hauled himself upright. Then he pulled on his yak coat and Barbara shuddered. "It's going to snow again," he said.

She did not dispute it. His batting average as a weather predictor was better than hers.

Shelley called a few minutes after Bailey left; she was in Cottage Grove, she said, excited. "Three clients today! Three, count 'em. I had to bring this woman down to the house on the hill, you know, the safe house in Cottage Grove? Martin carried her boyfriend out, literally picked him up and carried him out, and I took her to their place to pack a bag and brought her down here. It's snowing in the hills. I thought I might as well just go on home. You know how traffic is on I-5 this time of day—"

Smiling, Barbara cut in. "Go home, Shelley. Make a snowman with Alex. See you on Monday." Alex had bought seventy acres in the Coast Range hills. It probably was snowing up there already. She went to the window to peer out. Rain. Ah, well, she thought, and walked out to the reception room to send Maria home.

"Are you working late?" Maria asked.

"Nope. A few little things to wrap up and I'm out of here. Go boss your daughters around awhile."

"Hah! Be bossed by Mama, is more like it," Maria said, but she was cheerful about it. That was how life was. You bossed your kids, got bossed by your parents.

Half an hour later Barbara was ready to leave. She had the videos to watch, more notes to make, and she had to read Bailey's reports: homework. Her fellow tenant, Josh Mallory, was leaving at the same time, carrying a large plastic bag of trash out to the Dumpster. A CPA, he said he kept confidential stuff until Friday, when he shredded and tossed it.

"Hear the weather reports?" he asked. "Two, three inches by morning is what they're saying."

She laughed. "I'll believe it when I see it. Unless you mean two or three inches of rain."

"No. The white stuff that piles up and makes cars go zroom off the road," he said happily.

She pulled her hood up and started for her car; the rain felt like ice water. Josh went on toward the Dumpster. Suddenly, at her car door, with her key out, Barbara halted, watching him with his bag of trash.

"Oh, my God," she said under her breath. She got

in her car and sat there for several minutes waiting
for the windshield to clear, for the rear defroster to
fulfill its duty, thinking. Shop for dinner, buy milk.
She didn't know if she was out of milk, but when in
doubt, it was probably a good idea to buy some.
Often she had none at all, or as many as four quarts,
all out of date. Eggs. If it did snow, which she
doubted, it might be nice to have some food in the
apartment. She made her mental list, then drove to a
supermarket and promptly forgot most of what she
had decided to get. She bought large trash bags,
bread and a frozen lasagna.

That night she put the first video in the cassette
player and sat back to watch Darren Halvord at work.
There was introductory material—doctors talking
about a possible supranuclear palsy with subsequent
loss of proprioception—that she watched and listened to for a very short time before she hit fast forward.

Then Darren took over.

"See, Joey, you can't tell exactly where your
hands or feet are, and that makes walking, grasping,
holding a bottle of beer pretty hard. That's why you
lost your sense of balance."

"Bullshit," the patient said, slumped in a wheelchair. He was young, twenty-two, very muscular,
with a crooked nose, a wide mouth and close-set
eyes that regarded Darren with suspicion.

"Let me show you something," Darren said, at
ease, relaxed, unfazed by the belligerence in the
young man's attitude. "Close your eyes. Tighter.

Now put your right hand out at shoulder level, straight out, sideways from your body."

The hand shot out in a jerky motion, up, down, straight up. Darren caught it and held it. "Open your eyes and take a look," he said. He was holding the hand where he caught it, almost in front of the patient, low down.

"Try it again," the young man said in a harsh voice. He watched his hand and put it out to the side in a straight line with his shoulders. "See."

"Yep. Sure do," Darren said, holding the hand. "Now close your eyes, tight, like before. Okay. Touch your nose." He released the hand and again it jerked around in what appeared to be random movements until he caught it. "Enough," Darren said. "Have a look."

Joey looked near tears.

"What we're going to do," Darren said, "is teach your brain where your body parts are. It had a little bump and forgot, but it can learn again. Ever wonder why a little kid can't seem to walk, but goes racing all over the place? Instinct. Pure reflex. You lift one foot and all at once you're off balance. By reflex you put it down again slightly ahead of the other one, just to catch your balance. And it's easier to do it fast than to do it slowly. Reflexes work fast or not at all, you see. That's what you're doing. When you reach for something, reflex takes over and your hand stabs, jerks, moves too fast to control. We're going to get that control back."

Barbara watched without moving as the video

progressed and Joey undertook a series of exercises. He was holding on to a parallel bar, his knuckles white, sweat on his upper lip, on his forehead. "I can't," he whispered.

"Wanna bet?" Darren said. "I'm going to touch your foot. No, don't look, just feel the touch. Okay. Now bend the knee. Right. Up it goes."

Joey bent his knee without looking, grasping the bar desperately, until his leg made a right angle with his foot behind him. He held it until Darren told him to put his foot down again. Over and over.

The exercises got more complicated, harder, and throughout, Darren's voice was there, bantering, encouraging, supporting. The last segment was of them working together through the entire series without the parallel bars, Joey holding on to nothing, mimicking Darren's every movement.

Barbara watched it to the end, and then as the video rewound, she took a long breath, disturbed for a reason she could not identify. She put the second video into the machine, but did not start it immediately.

He seduced that kid, she thought suddenly, hypnotized him into believing, into doing things he thought he couldn't do. Joey had been malleable, helpless in the face of Darren's certitude; Joey had surrendered his will entirely. And it had worked. He had regained control of his limbs, his body, because Darren had insisted that he could, that he would. But it was even more complex than that, she thought. First Darren had taken control of Joey's body; Darren's will, his hands, his voice had dominated it, and then he had given that control to the boy. Too much power. That was too much power for one person to exert over another.

Darren's voice was the most seductive she had ever heard, she thought, and abruptly she stood up and went to the kitchen for a glass of water. When she returned to the living room she gazed at the television for a moment, then pulled the second cassette out and turned off the box. She felt she had seen enough of Darren at work to last for a long time.

Doing this, she heard her own voice in her head saying, "He is a dangerous man."

Will came home on Saturday and picked her up at six-thirty for an early dinner at The Chanterelle Restaurant. "We have extensive planning to take care of," he said after they ordered.

"Planning? For what?"

"Our trip. It's on. Friday. I figure a week in London, a few days in Bath and Oxford, then on to Paris. What about a week in Paris. Too short?"

"Hold it," she said. "What about your work? Aren't you planning a trip around work?"

He grinned. "I think I can stretch out the records search for about three weeks, maybe a little longer, and then I'll need at least a week of R and R. I have to be in London for a few days, a day or two in Bath and Oxford, Ravenna and Rome a couple days. That's it."

He was smiling widely. "I looked up the weather.

It shouldn't be any colder than it is here, and probably no rainier."

All day rain mixed with snow had fallen intermittently, with more forecast for the night and Sunday. If the temperature dropped just two degrees it would be snow, Barbara thought regretfully, but the thermometer seemed to be stuck at thirty-eight.

She sipped wine and looked away from Will. A month off, she was thinking, just fun and games for a whole month, museums, shopping, shows, sightseeing. Fine restaurants every day. Slowly she said, "I still don't know if I can leave right now."

"Not right now. Friday."

"That's like right now," she said, smiling slightly. "Depends on your frame of reference. Relativity or something."

"Put things on hold. Or let the peons carry the load for a while."

"Maybe. I'll know in a few days, I just don't know this minute."

"I'll make reservations," he said after a moment. "We can cancel yours later if we have to." Then he added, "We'd have a grand time, Barbara."

"I know."

His practice—trusts, wills, corporate matters—could all be put on hold, she thought then, and he could cheerfully turn his back on them and have fun. She almost envied him that luxury.

They lingered over dinner and afterward he took her home. He had been up at the crack of dawn in order to make his flight. "I'll call in a day or two," he said at her door. "Now I'm ready for a very long sleep."

Signs had been given, signals received and interpreted, body language had spoken, and she understood that he was waiting for her to make her decision, to leave her work in the office the way he did, or not. She could not tell how much he cared what that decision would be.

21

"Hi," Barbara said to Frank on Sunday afternoon. It was pouring rain at the moment, although half an hour earlier snow had been falling. She shook water off her umbrella at the front door, left it outside on the porch.

"What's all that?" he asked, reaching for her raincoat. She was carrying a shopping bag along with her purse and laptop.

"An experiment. I'll keep the coat on for a few minutes. Let's go to the kitchen, I'll tell you your part."

In the kitchen she fished in the shopping bag and brought out her digital camera. "Upstairs," she said then. She led the way to the bedroom that was always ready for her, with her old patchwork quilt in place, the Monet prints on the wall, her Raggedy Ann doll on the window seat. She went to the window and opened the drapes all the way, moved the sheer curtain to the side, peered out. The back garden was sodden, everything dripping. Thing One and Thing Two entered the bedroom and wrapped themselves around her legs, then forsook her and leaped onto the bed where they started to wrestle, tumbling over each other.

Ignoring them, looking as straight down as possible, Barbara could see the end of the back porch, and the pavement going to the garage. Just as she remembered, she thought in satisfaction.

"What I want you to do," she said, "is keep an eye out down there, and as soon as you see movement, start taking pictures."

"Pictures. Of rain. The porch railing. Give me a hint, Bobby. Pictures of what?"

"You'll know when you see it. Want to make sure the rail is in focus? I don't know if you should open the window or not. You decide. But don't lean out." She handed him the camera and went to the door.

Mystified, and a little annoyed, Frank peered through the viewfinder, and after a moment lowered the camera and opened the window, tried it again. A gust of wind blew icy rain into the room, but a little water was not going to hurt anything, he decided, and left the window open.

Then he drew in a sharp breath as a black figure moved into sight. Water poured off its shiny carapace, or whatever the hell it was, he thought, snapping a picture, another. Big head, shiny black outer cover of some sort, black feet—boots, he realized. The figure was moving awkwardly, walking backward. It turned and he sucked in another quick breath. There was the tail. He snapped two more pictures before the figure moved out of sight.

"Christ on a mountain," he muttered, lowering the camera. "She found the demon."

He closed the window and hurried downstairs to the kitchen. On the back porch Barbara was waiting for him, still in the shiny black thing. As he watched, she extended one gloved hand from a slit in the front of the covering, pointed her finger at him and said, "Bang, bang."

Trash bags, he realized. A large one covered her body, and a smaller one was over her head with part of it cut away leaving her face exposed. She extended a slit in the large one, reached up to pull the other one off her head, revealing her hood, and explaining the oversize head. She finished slitting the large bag to the bottom and pulled it away. Moving quickly she rolled it up into a compact ball, stuffed it inside the small bag and pulled a drawstring tight. Done.

A little later, sitting side by side before her laptop at the dinette table, they compared the pictures he had taken with the one that Alex had drawn and manipulated.

"Close," she said. "The drawstring is the tail. And remember, Dorothy Johnson was quite a bit higher than upstairs in this house. I bet if Alex manipulated this picture the same way he did his, it would be a very good match." She leaned back in her chair and said, "But even if we know without a doubt that's how it was done, so what? We knew it was premeditated, this just makes it more cold-blooded than simply pulling a gun and shooting."

"You could toss a trash bag into a ditch, on the side of the road, a Dumpster, who'd pay any attention?" Frank said. "And traces of gunpowder, blood, everything else forensics might search for also gone."

"What I was thinking last night while I was destroying plastic bags," she said, "is that there are too goddamn many saints mixed up in this murder. Saint Thomas Kelso devoted more than fifty years of his life to the clinic, probably alienating his own kids, but that's the price. Saint Greg Boardman, family doctor par excellence, father confessor. Saint Darren Halvord, whom everyone loves, gifted with magic hands, who can do no wrong. Saint Annie, living a life so virtuous it makes my teeth hurt. All those other saintly volunteers working hard to keep the clinic running. Think of Erica Castle, teaching kids all day, then reading to the patients every evening. She and Darren both hauled away at their bootstraps, rose above disastrous childhoods, avoided the usually inevitable, destructive behavior of everyone around them, achieved sainthood. Just one damn saint after another, all above reproach, all above suspicion."

"What about Erica Castle?" he asked.

He had not heard Bailey's report; she filled him in on Erica and Lorraine McIvey. "Now that one's no saint," she said. "Why make up such a story, that McIvey wanted them to get back together, wanted her to run the clinic as a profitable business? It must be to back up her claim that the children should inherit the whole kit and caboodle. Besides adding a real live motive for Annie to have pulled the trigger."

"I doubt her claim will hold up in probate, but the court won't be in a rush to decide, not until Annie is cleared, or found guilty, whichever comes first." After a moment he said, "You didn't mention that all those saints had a motive to kill McIvey, or else to lie about who did."

She nodded. "I know. I should talk to my clients with a truth serum in hand."

He looked at the images on her screen again, then, shaking his head, he moved away. "I thought Will was coming back yesterday. Change of plans?" It was a guarded question, the way he always approached the subject of Will Thaxton.

"He's home. We had dinner and called it a night pretty early and he went to his place to get some sleep." She shut down the computer and closed the top, then wandered to the door to look at the back garden. "He's going to Europe—England, France, Italy—for several weeks to do some work. He asked me to go with him. It's snowing again. I wish it would make up its mind."

"Unsettled," Frank said and realized he didn't mean just the weather.

Watching her, the back of her head when she pressed her forehead against the glass, he felt an ache that recurred with irritating regularity. He thought of articles he had read recently, how couples might soon be able to tailor-make their offspring, pick and choose among the genes for this or that quality. Given such a choice, would he have traded an iota of her mind for just a touch of… What? Domesticity? He shook his head impatiently. He knew people with less domestic calling than his daughter who still managed to have a fulfilled life beyond work. She needed someone as brilliant as she was, someone who would not interfere with her work, would give her room, not demand subservience in any manner, respect what she did, recognize that she was the best… A couple of times it had appeared that she had found such a man; one especially— Mike Dinesen—had been perfect, he had come to think. But Mike had died prematurely. Another one had turned out to be Mr. Wrong when the chips were down.

Will Thaxton was not even in the running. Although he would have cut out his tongue before voicing this, Frank knew that intellectually Will was a featherweight, and that he was just a little too dishonest, even for a corporate attorney. On the other hand, he thought then, maybe she didn't need any more mental stimulation than her work provided; maybe a lightweight at home would be even better, someone to play with, dance and have fun and relax with. And in that case Will would do. It occurred to him that she could be anxious to wrap up the McIvey business in order to go off to Europe with Will. He sighed deeply, and Barbara turned to regard him.

"Sorry," she said. "What?"

"Nothing. Just remembered I have to get something out from the freezer."

By the time Barbara left Frank's house, the weather had cleared up, and a few stars were visible. So much for snow, she thought, driving home. There, she read for a while, watched the nightly news, took a long fragrant bath and went to bed early. At this rate, she told herself, she'd run out of excuses not to go traveling with Will. Certainly work could not be used as an excuse. There was nothing for her to do until something broke; she had run out of ideas.

She backed up in her thoughts, troubled. Was she really looking for an excuse not to accompany her sometime lover on an odyssey to foreign lands? No excuse was called for, she told herself angrily. Strolls along the Thames, boat rides on the Seine? Not in the winter, for heaven's sake. Wrong time of year for a European vacation. She knew she was avoiding the real reason for her hesitation and finally admitted that it was more than just a little vacation that she was considering. Was she ready for the next step with Will? Although she couldn't think of any good reason not to take that step, on the other hand neither could she think of a good reason to go ahead. The status quo seemed ideal. Nothing was broken, nothing needed fixing, she told herself irritably. Why couldn't people just leave things alone?

She rolled over, determined to go to sleep, but she seemed stuck in a tape loop, around and around, until eventually, when she realized that her irritation was turning to anger, she got up to see if there was a late-night movie worth watching.

Glennis Colby liked her hours at the clinic, midnight until seven in the morning. She kissed her boyfriend good-night; he went to bed and she went to work. Overnight at the clinic was not a busy time; the patients slept like babies for the most part, and she read one mystery or romance novel after another. When she got home Phil usually had breakfast for two just about ready, then he took off for his job, and she went to bed. From a little after four in the afternoon when he returned they had until nearly midnight together, and that was fine, the best hours out of twenty-four. She was cheerful that Sunday night as she turned into the parking lot at the clinic at five minutes before twelve.

There were other cars in the lot. The evening shift had not left yet; they were waiting for their replacements. Another car pulled in close behind hers. She got out and waited to see who else was checking in, not really late yet, but close enough. It was Bev Werner. They started to walk to the door together, then Bev veered off to the side, murmuring, "That's strange. Isn't that Bernie's Corolla?"

Glennis didn't have a clue. She didn't know one

car from another. She joined Bev, and together they peered in through the windshield. Bev muttered something and went around to look in the driver's side window. Glennis followed and Bev stifled a scream.

Glennis pulled her back, took another look, then hauled Bev with her to the staff door and rang the bell. She did not remove her finger from the bell until the door opened and Stell Vogel said, "For heaven's sake! You want to wake up the dead?"

"Call the police," Glennis said. "Bernie Zuckerman's out there in her car. She's dead. Covered with blood."

The ringing of the phone jerked Barbara from a deep sleep. She pulled the cover higher, letting her answering machine take it, but after a moment, she stirred again and sat up. It was seven o'clock. No one in his right mind made a call at that hour. But a stab of fear made her first sit up, then get out of bed and pull on her robe to go listen to the message. It was unreasonable, she knew, to feel that jolt of fear when the phone rang at an unusual hour, but Frank had had a minor heart attack years earlier, and there was always the residual fear that he was in trouble. When she heard his voice on her machine, the fear flooded in.

"Bobby, there's been another shooting, Bernice Zuckerman's dead. It's in the newspaper, section B, page one. Call me when you wake up."

She turned on the radio in the kitchen, then hurried down the stairs to her front door to retrieve the newspaper. The news story was little more than Frank had said over the phone. Bernice Zuckerman had been shot dead in her car at the clinic sometime the previous evening. A recap of the death of David McIvey followed. After starting coffee, as the radio voice rattled on about everything except a shooting, she called Frank.

"There's been damn little released," he said. "Nothing on television yet. Just another murder. Shot in the head, close range. That's all I know about it. But we have to talk before the police come nosing around."

She nodded. Not her office, not yet. The cleaning crew might not even be finished. Certainly not his office where the idea of criminal law was anathema those days. And the police would be asking questions as soon as they learned how much time she had spent with Bernice Zuckerman on Friday. "Your place," she said. "Twenty minutes."

She hung up, thinking she should have told Bernie not to mention seeing a car leave on the day McIvey was killed. But even as she thought this, she knew it would have been futile. Bernie had been a talker; once she realized the importance of what she had seen, what she had said about it, she would have told anyone who would listen. But she should have warned her, Barbara thought miserably.

Driving to Frank's house, she heard a radio version of the story, tucked in between a weather report and some nonsense about high school sports. It was brief, no more informative than the newspaper article had been.

Frank was listening to the radio when the doorbell rang. A small TV on the counter was turned on to local news, but the sound was muted; they did not have a thing yet. He had stirred eggs, ready to scramble them, had sausages in the skillet browning, bread in the toaster ready to be started, and he was frowning fiercely at the inane chatter of news readers who seemed to think an early-morning audience wanted comedy.

"Why don't you use your key?" he demanded at the front door.

"Good morning to you, too," she said, giving him a quick peck on the cheek, then going on past to the kitchen. "Anything new?" She pointed to the radio.

"No. Just that she's dead, shot last night, found at about midnight."

Barbara took off her jacket and then helped herself to coffee.

"How much are you going to tell them?" Frank asked, going to the stove to finish making breakfast.

"I don't know. As little as possible."

"You know what they're going to claim, don't you? That she saw the killer leave that morning, and she had to be silenced. Also, that she told you what she saw."

Barbara nodded. She knew. "Well, we were all waiting for a break." It didn't sound as light as she had intended. In fact, it sounded harsh and grim and angry. And she was angry, both at herself for not warning Bernie, and at Bernie for talking too much.

"They'll go after Erica Castle," Frank said. "She's the only thing standing between Darren Halvord and jail, trial, the works. And they'll go after Annie. This will push them into action, and that's the only action anyone can see at this point. Including you, if you'll let yourself admit it. No one else was driving away from the clinic that morning. Just Annie."

She looked at him, his face fierce and set in determined lines. When he had something to say that she didn't want to hear, that's how he got, she well knew. "Finish it," she said when he paused.

"Castle lied about the time Darren Halvord left home that morning. Annie and Darren conspired to commit murder. She shot McIvey and took off and he moved the body out of sight and got rid of the evidence. He had fifteen minutes unaccounted for, plenty of time to clean up things before he entered the clinic. And now one of them has used the gun again. That's what they'll think, and it's just about the only scenario that works. And if it's true, that gun's still out there, and there's an opportunistic killer as ruthless as hell who probably thinks you know what it was that Bernice Zuckerman saw that morning."

She held up her hand for silence and in exasperation he turned back to the stove and moved sausages around while the news reader repeated the earlier story about the murder of Bernice Zuckerman.

"What I'm going to do," Barbara said when it became obvious that nothing new was being added, "is drop out of sight today. There's no going to the clinic, talking to people, anything like that, of course. And I'd really rather not talk to Milt Hoggarth too soon. I want thinking time. Sound reasonable?"

"No," he snapped. "It will just confirm that you know too much, to Milt, and to whoever keeps that gun in working order."

She nodded. "Exactly. Now that they know the gun wasn't tossed into the river, maybe they'll look harder for it. But where I can go is the question." After a moment she got up and went to the wall phone, called her office and left a message for Maria. "I'll be out of touch for the next few hours. Something came up. Hold the fort. I'll check in later on." Then, with her hand on the phone, she turned toward Frank. "Okay if I hang out here?"

"They'll send a cruiser around and spot your car," he said.

"But it won't be here," she said, and started to punch Bailey's number on the automatic dial. Halfway through, she stopped and disconnected. Not on this phone. If at some future date they demanded to see this phone record, let them see that she had been out of touch, using her cell phone all day. She pulled it from her purse and hit the number for Bailey. He answered when he heard her voice on his machine.

"Hi, it's me," she said. "Come around to Dad's place, will you? And bring someone to take my car somewhere for me." She listened, nodded, then said, "I know. I read the paper and I heard the news. We'll talk when you get here. But keep it under your hat, where you're heading."

Then, as she considered the coming day, Frank scrambled eggs, his scowl in place, his lips pressed tightly closed. He had said all that he intended. He knew there was no point in arguing with her, a lesson he had learned years ago. He didn't believe in starting arguments he knew he could not win, or at least draw, and she was as stubborn as anyone on God's little blue ball of a planet. She would talk to Milt when she was ready, and she would tell him exactly what she had decided upon in advance. And dodge a bullet? he asked himself silently and savagely.

She was thinking that she had her laptop, her briefcase and cell phone, and there was an upstairs room outfitted as an office, for her use, not his, just as the bedroom upstairs was hers when she wanted it.

"Let's eat," Frank said.

He was angry with her, she understood, and knew the reason: his fear for her safety. It occurred to her that it really wasn't fair to involve him in her cases the way she did. He had earned a life of comfort and ease, and she kept interrupting it with worry and danger. On the other hand, she told herself, he would be just as worried, but also bored, if left sitting on the sidelines, coddling old clients who wouldn't turn loose, having to listen to Sam Bixby talk about trust funds and estate planning and articles of incorporation. It was better if he knew what was going on. She was doing him a favor, keeping him young and active. The argument didn't ring true and impatiently she stopped it and said, "Someone has to look after the interests of our clients today. You or Shelley?"

"I'll go," he said.

"Great. When Milt shows up, rake in some of the chips he owes you, will you? Find out what happened at the clinic last night, why Bernie was there at night, what they have so far. You know."

Frank glared at her. They both knew that was exactly what he would do. At least she didn't tell him not to reveal her whereabouts, he thought angrily. That would have been the last straw.

"I won't go near your phone today," she said. "You have my cell phone number. And I won't answer a knock at the door, anything like that."

Bailey arrived while they were still at breakfast. Barbara gave him her car key.

"Where do you want my guy to take it?" he asked.

"I don't care. Just out of sight for a few hours."

He shrugged. "Right back." He left with the key and a minute later she watched through the window as her car backed out of the driveway and headed down the street. Bailey came back in. Then, finishing the eggs and sausage, he said he did not know a thing more than they did, just what was on the morning news.

"We don't know why she was there, what time she was killed, where anyone was. Nothing," Barbara said. "For all I know someone has confessed by now and is in the slammer. Fix that, Bailey. Whatever you can worm out of them at the clinic. Dad will be over there baby-sitting Annie and Darren and I'll be right here. Call my cell phone, not Dad's number."

"That thing's going to give you brain cancer," he said.

She rolled her eyes and poured more coffee for them all. Frank got up to make another pot, and she tried to think of what else she could do. The answer came out: nothing. She had to have more information, and until she got something to work with there wasn't a damn thing she could do.

22

After Frank left, Barbara put their dishes in the dishwasher, washed and dried the skillet, then took all her gear upstairs. She was missing something, she kept thinking, something that she had overlooked, or had not noticed to begin with. In the spare room, her office in this house, she started at the beginning of her notes. Pacing, reading notes, making new notes, studying the demon figure on her monitor, tripping over cats or nudging them out of the way now and then, she had to admit finally that whatever that something was, it continued to elude her.

The phone rang a few times; she ignored it. An unmarked car pulled into the driveway, a man got out, rang the doorbell, then wandered around the side of the house to the garage and peered in. She watched him from the upstairs window. He left again, and she resumed her pacing.

At the clinic Frank was walking from Naomi's office by Annie's side. "You did fine," he said. "Are you all right?"

She nodded, but she did not look all right. She was as white as a live person could get, he thought, and her eyes were so heavily shadowed it appeared that she had not slept for many nights. And now she had been questioned by two detectives for more than an hour. He patted her arm. "They won't bother you any more today. Why don't you go get some rest?"

She nodded again. "As soon as some of the others get back from lunch." Her lips felt stiff, she realized, and wondered how lips could become stiff.

"Mr. Holloway, can I have a word with you?" Darren Halvord met them outside the general office door. "Are you okay, Annie?" he asked, looking her over.

"I'm okay. Just tired. I'll see you later," she said through her stiff lips, and entered the office and went straight to her desk. Two of the other office workers were there talking but fell silent as she crossed the room. She could feel them watching her all the way, watching her back when she sat down. They thought she killed David. And now Bernie? Did they think she killed Bernie? The stiffness in her lips was spreading through her face, down her neck.

One of them could have stolen her diary pages. Maybe she was passing them around to everyone the

way they sometimes did with recipes or jokes. She
bowed her head and closed her eyes hard, then suddenly she was seeing another one of the missing
pages. She felt the earth dropping away from her.
She was floating and watching herself, watching
someone take her by the shoulders, listening to
someone say, put your head down, and it had nothing to do with her real self that was removed.

Then Naomi and Greg were there and he was acting like a doctor. Her other self came back in a rush.

"I'm all right," she said, but Naomi was wrapping
a coat around her, and Greg was holding her arm.
Then they all walked out, through the corridor,
through the garden to the residence.

Greg kept his arm around her shoulders when
they entered the kitchen. "I'll make you a cup of tea,"
Naomi said.

"No. I just want to lie down a little bit. I'm okay
now. I just felt dizzy for a second. All those questions…"

"I'll help you upstairs," Greg said in his doctor's
voice. He stayed at her side, kept holding her arm as
they went up the stairs and to her room.

She knew he was studying her, feeling her pulse,
looking for whatever doctors looked for with a dizzy
patient. She forced a smile and pulled away from
him. "I'll take a nap. We're all so tired, and scared."

He nodded. "I'll get you a mild tranquilizer,
something to help you relax. Sit down, let's get those
shoes off."

She shook her head. "Just a nap. I'll lock my

door so they won't barge in on me. Really, Greg, I'm okay now."

After a moment he nodded. "A nap would be good. Naomi's taking the rest of the day off. She'll be downstairs. And I'll bring something for you to take if you change your mind. You hop into bed and rest."

When he left, she pushed the doorknob in and turned it, locking her door. Then she stood with her forehead pressed against it. That look on his face. She never had seen that face before, watchful, appraising. Judging? If he or Naomi had taken the pages, they would have discussed them, burned them, not passed them around for others to see, and they would think what anyone would think who read them. Wearily she pushed herself away from the door and crossed the room to the window where she could gaze out at the backyard, beyond it to the clinic. She wished she had never seen it before, had never heard of it, had not seen the ad that brought her to it in the first place. She wished she was back home with her gentle father and mother.

The detective who had questioned her appeared at the gate and walked toward the residence. Panicked, she jerked away from the window. Of course, she thought, it would be all over the clinic by then, how she had nearly fainted, how Greg and Naomi had brought her home. Maybe he had come to arrest her.

The floor began to drop away, and she threw herself across the bed and pressed hard on it to hold it in place. If the police had the diary pages, would that be enough for them to arrest her? Keep her in jail for months, put her on trial, find her guilty? Execute her eventually?

In her mind's eye she could see a black basalt arm pitted with tide pools reaching out to sea, a thunderous wave crashing over it, sweeping it clean. And a lone figure at the end of the natural jetty, waiting, waiting.

Barbara had come to a stop in her pacing. There was something at the edge of her consciousness, she thought, something half glimpsed, half understood.... The two cats were on a chair, a great pile without definition, like Jason's golden fleece, when suddenly they both came wide-awake, their ears cocked; then they jumped up and ran out of the office and downstairs.

Frank's whistle, she realized. He had called the cats to warn her that he was coming, and that he wasn't alone. She went down the hall to the top of the stairs, but didn't turn the corner and stayed out of sight of anyone who might glance up the staircase.

There was a soft whistle, then Darren's voice.

"Wow! They're beauties. What are they, coon cats?"

"Yep. This way to the kitchen. I said we'd go have a bite to eat. This is the place. You're not a vegetarian, are you?"

Darren laughed. "No. I tried it a few years ago, but it didn't take. I kept dreaming of steaks, barbecued ribs and fish."

Frank was giving her the opportunity to stay in hiding, Barbara realized as the voices grew fainter. She hesitated only a second or two, then went down to join her father and his guest for lunch.

Frank was at the sink washing his hands when she reached the kitchen door. He glanced at her and nodded. "He said he has to talk to you," he said, inclining his head toward Darren, who was standing at the door, gazing out. He swung around to look at her as she entered.

"Right," she said. "And I have to talk to you. Or listen is more like what I intend to do. I suggest it's time to back up and undo some statements. You first."

"It's time," he said. He glanced at Frank, then at the kitchen table. "Here?"

"Here," Barbara said, pulling out a chair. He pulled out another one and turned it around to straddle it, his forearms on the chair back. Now, with the light behind him, his eyes appeared black and fathomless.

"I told you that Thomas Kelso saved my life," he said. "He did. My sister had married a gangster, Dad was on the run somewhere, my mother remarried…and I was on the down slope gaining speed fast, ready to start hanging out with my sister and her husband, take whatever came along. Then Kelso called me for an interview. He tossed me a life preserver that day." He glanced again at Frank, who was busy assembling sandwiches. "Mixed metaphor," Darren said, "but you get the picture.

"Okay, to bring it to the present. That morning in November, I rode my bike, just as I said. When I turned into the alley, I saw a car leaving at the other end. I could see the brake lights, the exhaust, then it was gone. Okay. Then I saw the umbrella, just like I said before. I went into the garden, and McIvey was there on the main path, dead. I went to the side door to call the police, call someone, but I realized what I had seen, what it meant, and I went back to him. I moved him out of sight and closed the umbrella, and the rest is exactly what I told you."

"Fill in the one detail," Barbara said in a low furious voice. "You saw a car leave. Whose car?"

"Kelso's."

"Why did you move the body?"

"To give him time to get away from there, to get home. To toss him a life preserver."

"You damn fool! Don't you know the police don't believe a word of your story? You had to have been there within seconds of the murder to account for blood on your boot! The way it was raining that morning, not enough blood would have been on that path for you to pick up and track to your bike ten or fifteen minutes after he was shot. They're waiting for DNA test results, and they're looking for a link between you and Annie, searching for the gun, drawing the net tighter. And now you'd bring in that old man to counter anything that Bernie said. It won't wash! You can't start squirming out of it this way now."

He nodded. "I've been a fool, all right. But I

would do it again. He's dying, Barbara. The hope of saving his clinic is all that's keeping him alive. I didn't blame him for taking McIvey out. I was sorry I didn't pull that trigger instead of him, in fact."

Across the kitchen Frank made a throat-clearing noise and Barbara bit back her furious response and took a deep breath. She couldn't account for her anger, she realized. Darren was voicing exactly the scenario she had outlined earlier.

"And now that Bernie's dead and can't contradict your story, you've decided to come clean," she said with bitter sarcasm.

Darren shook his head. "It's not just like that. Because she's dead, and unless there are two killers running around out there at the clinic, I knew I'd made a mistake. Kelso would not have harmed Bernie."

"Not even to save his clinic?" Barbara demanded.

"That's beside the point. She was no threat to the clinic. McIvey was. And Kelso wouldn't have hurt her to save himself. What for? He's dying. He gave away his shares, maneuvered McIvey into getting rid of a few shares, did everything he could think of to make sure the clinic survived. McIvey was the only threat he saw. That's what it amounts to, Barbara."

"What's wrong with him?"

"I don't know."

"You just know he's dying. You put your hand on his fevered brow and knew he was doomed. Is that how it goes with you?"

He shrugged. "Something like that."

"Sweet Jesus," she muttered and jumped up to walk to the door and back. "How much of this have you told the cops?"

"Not a word yet. That's why I told your dad I had to talk to you."

"Why did you think it was his car, seeing it from such a distance, with the rain and fog on a dark morning like that?"

"The pattern of brake lights," he said. "Wide spaced, no light in the rear window like Annie's car, like most cars ever since about 1985. It wasn't Annie's Mercedes, if that's what you're getting at."

"Does your truck have a brake light in the back window?"

He shook his head.

Barbara swung around toward Frank. "What happened last night?" He stopped cutting sandwiches, put the knife down and wiped his hands before he answered.

"Zuckerman got a phone call at about seven-thirty, didn't say who called, just that there was an emergency at the clinic and she had to go over there for a few hours. From all appearances, when she arrived in the parking lot, someone approached her car. She rolled down her window and was shot in the head. If that's how it went, she was probably killed shortly before eight, allowing fifteen minutes or a little longer to drive over. Two nurses reporting for duty at midnight found her body in the car."

"Where were you from seven-thirty on?" Barbara asked Darren in a harsh voice.

His voice was almost as edgy as hers when he answered. "I took Todd home by seven, over in Springfield. Our agreement is for me to get him home by seven. Then I drove to the Amazon Center, got there at seven-thirty probably. The bridge group meets there every other Sunday night. But I didn't go in. I sat in the truck thinking for a while, not in the mood for cards. I decided not to play and drove home again. I don't know what time I got back. An alibi wasn't on my mind."

"You never seem to know what time you did anything, but you'd better pray that someone saw you out there thinking," Barbara said. "Not only that, but that someone can pinpoint the exact time you were communing with nature."

Frank had the sandwiches on plates by then, and placed one of them on the table. They all stiffened and grew silent when the doorbell sounded. Frank thrust a plate at Barbara and nodded toward the hall and the stairs to the upper floor.

"Don't you breathe a word about Kelso's car," she snapped, then hurried from the kitchen and to the stairs as Frank went to the door. On the stairs she paused long enough to hear him say, "Milt, just in time for some lunch. Come on in." She ran up the rest of the stairs and around the banister at the top, out of sight from below, where she could still hear voices from the hall.

"God almighty! I forgot that you keep mountain lions as pets," Milt Hoggarth said.

"Now, Milt, I told you they're coon cats. We're eating in the kitchen. This way."

Of course, Frank thought a second later, Milt had assumed that when he said we he had meant himself and Barbara. In the kitchen, he watched Milt's glance take in the two sandwiches, two coffee cups. "I believe you and Mr. Halvord have met," he said. Both men nodded.

"I want a word with you," Milt said. "Your study?"

"All right. Don't wait for me," Frank said to Darren. "And don't let one of those monsters get to my lunch. I'll be back directly."

He led the way through the hall to his study and seated himself behind his ancient desk as Milt settled in the equally ancient arm chair that seriously needed recovering.

"We go back a ways," Milt said. "You and me. Sometimes pulling together, sometimes crossing swords. You know I'm as straight as I can be, and I know you don't bullshit any more than you have to. So we both know where we stand."

Frank nodded. "Seems I knew you when you had hair all over your head."

Milt grimaced. "Rub it in. Rub it in." His once-red hair was now a fading gray tonsure, his scalp gleaming pink above it as if the color had fled hair to take up residence in skin.

He leaned forward and said, "The D.A. wants an arrest, and he wants it yesterday or last week. He wanted it six weeks ago and I held off. Let's build a decent case first, I said. DNA labs are so backed up, it takes three months or longer to get results. No gun, no raincoat, no forensics. No case, not yet. I have a thousand pieces but I don't have the linchpin, I said. I still don't have it, but your daughter does. And I want it. It's all over the clinic, how Zuckerman saw the killer leave back in November, and she told Barbara. Zuckerman's dead and Barbara can't be found. The D.A. said maybe she's in a ditch with a bullet in her head, and I said, no way. With you and Bailey out there carrying out marching orders, there's no way you don't know where she is or how to get in touch. The D.A.'s talking about obstruction of justice, material witness, bench warrant, serious stuff like that, and I'm talking about having your kid in the crosshairs of a gun with a determined shooter holding it. I want her, Frank. I want to talk to her really bad."

He drew in a long breath. "Anyone can see that Annie McIvey's ready to crack wide-open. We get what we need to tie things up, McIvey breaks, we can have a wrap overnight nice and neat. Your daughter still has her defendants to see through the process. And no more shootings." He stood up and went to the study door, where he paused with his hand on the knob.

"The D.A. also said that if it turns out that she's holding out on us, he'll get a judge to heave her out on her can. She won't represent Halvord or McIvey or anyone else from the clinic. He says a judge can do that. You know better than I do if he's right. Pass it on, Frank." He looked almost embarrassed then when he said, "We're getting a search warrant to go through Halvord's apartment and garage. I expect you or Barbara will want to be there."

Frank shook his head. "Now you're bullshitting. You know and I know that whoever used that gun didn't tuck it away under a pillow for safekeeping. Was it the same weapon?"

Milt shrugged. "No exit wound. Probably." He looked at his watch. "A couple of guys will be at Halvord's place in about an hour. Give Barbara my message."

After seeing Milt out, Frank headed upstairs. Barbara was standing in her old room looking out the window. "He wants to talk to you," Frank said. She nodded. "And they're sending people to search Halvord's apartment and garage." She nodded again without turning toward him. "Barbara, come on down and eat your lunch."

"In a minute," she said. She faced him, but with such an abstracted expression, he doubted that she even saw him. "Go on, I'll be down in a minute or two. There's something I have to do first." She was dialing her cell phone as he left the room, taking her untouched sandwich with him.

Five minutes passed before she appeared in the kitchen, with her coat over her arm, and carrying her briefcase, laptop and purse.

"What are you up to?" Frank demanded.

"Waiting for a call," she said and picked up her sandwich, took a bite. She had just begun to chew when her cell phone rang. With her mouth full she said, "It's me. Hold on a second." Waving to Darren and Frank, she left the kitchen, went into his study and closed the door.

Disgruntled, Frank finished eating and drank his coffee. "Five minutes," he said, "and we have to go. Don't want them to have a search party without us."

Darren had already finished and began to gather their dishes to take them to the sink. They both looked around when Barbara hurried back to the kitchen and grabbed her coat. "I'm leaving," she said, putting it on. "Perfect deniability, Dad. When they ask you where I am you won't even have to cross your fingers when you say you don't know. I'll be in touch later." She rushed out before he could say a word.

Watching her, Frank took a deep breath, exhaled softly. Christ on a mountain, he thought, she's got it.

A laptop was a wonderful invention, Barbara thought a little later; portable, more computing power than the machines that had launched the moon landing, fairly user-friendly, but with a curious ability to grow heavier and heavier minute by minute. Her arm was starting to feel stretched out of shape. She switched hands, but even her briefcase seemed inordinately heavy by then. She felt too conspicuous walking by the street that ran through the park at the base of Skinner's Butte with the river off to her right, an occasional car passing very close on her left. Not now, she kept thinking. Don't let one of Milt Hoggarth's flunkies spot me now. It was not cold, and not raining, for which she was grateful. She would have needed a hat with an umbrella attached.

She crossed the train tracks, went under the Jefferson Bridge and through the park, where teenagers were tossing a basketball back and forth, through hoops, this way and that in what seemed random movements to her, although the kids apparently knew what they were doing. Everything was green: grass that needed mowing, bay laurel trees, holly trees, all the conifers. Brown leaves clung with tenacity to the oak trees, and crocuses were in bloom, backed by daffodils that would open their buds within a week.

By the time Barbara reached Martin's Restaurant, she had worked up a sweat, and her legs and arms were throbbing. She had not run, but neither had she dallied. The door opened before she reached it, and Martin moved aside for her to enter.

"Shelley said you were on the lam," he said gravely, taking her laptop, "and I said you could hide out here until dark and we'll smuggle you out by way of our secret tunnel."

"And sneak me crusts of bread from the kitchen from time to time," she said, equally grave.

He nodded. "Whatever it takes."

"Meanwhile," she said, heading for the booth farthest from the front door, "I expect Bailey to show up in a few minutes. I told him to use the back door. Okay with you?"

"Sure. The cops were by earlier. Asked me very nicely to give them a call if you showed up. I said I would do that."

"They may drop in again," she said. "Maybe just for today when Shelley turns up you could keep the door locked, open it if a client comes by. Give me time to crawl under a table or something."

He grinned, and she settled into the booth and opened her laptop. Five minutes later Bailey eased himself into the seat opposite her.

"Turn yourself in," he said, "face the music, you're only making things worse by running and hiding. Anything to drink?"

"Coffee," she said pointing to the carafe Martin had provided, along with two mugs.

"Better than nothing." He helped himself, added too much cream and sugar, tasted it and made a face.

"Tell me about last night," she said. "Where was everyone?"

"Not much to tell. Not an alibi worth a penny anywhere. Naomi Boardman alone in her office preparing schedules. Dr. Boardman in his study, doing some paperwork. Annie McIvey in her room reading. Darren Halvord and his kid had dinner with Erica Castle, and after that he was running around in his truck. Dr. Kelso at home alone. Stephanie Waters left a few minutes after seven and went home. The girlfriend was out somewhere and got home at about nine. It's like that." He added more sugar to his coffee. "Zuckerman got a call at seven-thirty. Her old man and kid were in the garage working on a junker. She yelled out to them that she had to go to the clinic, and took off a minute or two later. Hoggarth left me a message to get in touch if I hear from you."

She looked at her watch. One-thirty. "Okay. Find out where Erica Castle is teaching today and waylay her and bring her over here the minute she gets out. Probably two-thirty or three."

"Bring her or send her?"

"Bring her. I have to talk to her before she goes home. The D.A. is coming on like a hotshot, sending a couple of suits over to toss Darren Halvord's apartment and garage. I don't want her to walk in on that scene."

He jerked his thumb toward the back door. "Come in that way again?"

"You got it. I'm in hiding, remember? Don't bring anyone else with you."

He finished the coffee and shook his head. "That'll take the hair off your chest. See you." He started to amble toward the door, then paused and looked back at her doubtfully. "Or is it put hair on your chest?"

She laughed. "That's the kind of philosophical puzzle to worry with at three in the morning when you can't sleep."

23

Shelley, clad in a bright-blue raincoat, arrived by way of the front door as Bailey was leaving through the rear. The bluebird of happiness, Barbara thought with a grin; Shelley was brimful to overflowing with happiness that she could not have concealed any more than Martin could have concealed his blackness. Martin admitted her, smiling hugely, hung the Shelley Is In sign and locked the door behind her. Barbara waved her to the booth.

"Lieutenant Hoggarth is looking for you," Shelley said. "I'm supposed to call him when you check in."

"I know. I'm in hiding. Have a look at this." She turned her laptop so that Shelley could see the image of the thing that might have been an over-size cockroach.

Shelley gasped, then turned a wide-eyed gaze back to Barbara. "What is it?"

"Me. Two trash bags, one with an opening for my head, down over my shoulders to my boots, a smaller one to cover my head. What I'd like you to do is get that over to Alex and have him position it exactly the same way he did the one he and Dorothy Johnson worked on. Same distance, same height, everything, and after he's done, take it over to Johnson and see if it's like what she saw. Can do?"

"Sure. What about people here?"

"You've been complaining that no one shows up. Let's hope today is like that. Otherwise, after an hour, you just have to take off. Bailey's bringing Erica Castle over for a talk, and I don't want your clients and her to see each other. So plan to leave by two-thirty. The cops might drop in, by the way. But I don't think they expect to find me here."

Shelley nodded.

"And after that, one other little thing—" The doorbell interrupted her. "Better get to the usual table and spread your stuff around. I believe you have a customer."

Actually Shelley had two clients that afternoon, but by two-thirty she was finished. She ushered the second woman to the door and took down the sign, then hurried to the back booth.

"I e-mailed Alex," she said. "He's waiting at the

office. It'll save time, instead of going all the way out there and back. And I'll call Johnson and make sure she'll be available. What else?"

Barbara explained what she needed and Shelley didn't ask a question, simply nodded, as if Barbara asked her to shop for a wig routinely. "And the thing they put them on, ball, mold, stand, whatever."

"No problem. Are you going to hang out here the rest of the afternoon?"

"No. After I talk to Erica I'll find a new hiding place. She might let it slip that I'm here. Call my cell phone. I'll let you know where I'll be."

When Bailey returned with Erica in tow, Barbara met them at the rear door. "Give us half an hour or so," she said to Bailey.

He saluted and left again.

"Thanks for agreeing to this," Barbara said to Erica, after glancing up and down the alley behind the restaurant as Bailey got into his old Dodge and took off. It was raining again, not hard yet. "It's pretty irregular, but necessary," she said turning to Erica. "Let's sit in the booth back there."

"It's true? Bernie?"

"True."

Erica hugged her raincoat tighter around herself. She was pale and looked very frightened. "I called the clinic, but they had voice mail on, and no one came. Oh, God! Bernie!"

"I'll get us some coffee. Would you rather have tea?"

Erica shook her head. "I don't care. Anything hot. Bernie!" Then she looked around at the restaurant, back at Barbara. "What is this place? Why here?"

"In a second," Barbara said. She went to the kitchen door and asked Martin for coffee, then returned. "Okay, this is my office away from the office," she said, seating herself opposite Erica. "I work out of here a couple of days a week. And today I'm here because I'm staying out of sight of the police while I see to a few things. I really wanted to catch you before they do. So, Bailey. He'll take you back to school for your car when we're done here."

"It's true that Bernie told you she saw the killer leave that morning?" Erica's eyes widened. "You haven't told the police? Is that why you're keeping out of sight?"

Barbara shrugged. "Let's just say I had too much to do today to be tied up with the district attorney for hours. Ah, coffee. Thanks, Martin."

He put a tray down, took away the old carafe and cups, and withdrew.

"What do you want from me?" Erica asked, leaning forward.

Barbara poured coffee and slid a mug across the table to Erica. "I really just wanted to prepare you for what's coming your way. I'm afraid it's going to be something of an ordeal."

"Why? What does that mean?"

"Look, it's no secret that I've been retained to defend both Darren and Annie, and it looks like the police are homing in on them. You're the main reason they haven't arrested Darren yet. No doubt they're investigating you from the day you were born until this morning, looking for a chink in your armor, so to speak."

Erica looked more frightened than before. "What do you mean? Why me? I don't have anything for them."

"You provide Darren with an alibi for the morning David McIvey was killed," Barbara said. "You're a respectable schoolteacher, involved in volunteer work, a homeowner, taxpayer, not a drug user or candidate for AA. In other words, your word in court will carry weight. You provide the reasonable doubt a jury needs in order to acquit. If you say Darren left that morning at twenty to eight, that's hard to argue with. Unless they can find a way to discredit your testimony, discredit you personally. And they'll try to do that."

"There isn't anything for them to find," Erica said in a low voice. "I haven't done anything to be ashamed of."

"Good. How about your family? Mother? Father? Brothers, sisters?"

Erica moistened her lips and picked up her coffee, put it down untasted. "They'll look into my family history?"

"Sure they will. They probably already know all about the house you inherited, your grandparents. They've questioned neighbors, looked into public records. Tell me what they've been finding, will you? Let's go over it and see how damaging anything might be."

Erica began to talk haltingly about her mother, about her death from an overdose, the neighbors' complaints about noise and fights, the shape the house had been in when she arrived. Barbara didn't interrupt to ask any questions; all this she already knew. When Erica stopped speaking, she gazed at her sadly.

"It's going to be bad," she murmured. "Was your mother into prostitution? That's almost guaranteed if she was a longtime addict, you understand. The police will assume that."

"She had a lot of different boyfriends," Erica said dully.

"Did any of them molest you? Or threaten you? Beat you? That's almost always a given, also."

Erica drew back, her cheeks turned crimson, then white. "My mother always protected me! She wouldn't let any of those creeps touch me! They can't make assumptions like that without a shred of proof."

"They'll look into the records in Cleveland, search for proof," Barbara said. "Erica, listen to me. Don't get angry with me, or turn me off. This is what they'll put you through on the stand. They'll paint a picture of a neglected child, possibly molested, certainly mistreated, growing up in a violent household in a violent atmosphere. They'll point out that you never married, and suggest that you're probably repressed sexually, that you've found a piece of respectability and stability in your life and you'll fight like a cornered cat to protect it. They may bring in a psychiatrist to support a diagnosis like that. They'll paint a picture of you that you'd never recognize, and then tell the jury your word has been tainted by your past and must be regarded with grave suspicion. If they catch you in even one tiny lie or mistake, they'll impeach you, discredit everything you say and the judge will go along with that. One lie and everything is suspect."

Erica was pale down to her lips. "That's rotten," she whispered. "That isn't fair or decent."

"Or," Barbara said, "they'll say that you were simply mistaken in the time, but that you can't be trusted to recant your story because you can't afford to lose the rent money that's much of your support now. Or that you fell in love with Darren and will do anything to protect him. There are a number of different paths they might take to make the point that your alibi for him is either deliberately false or innocently mistaken."

"You sound as if you want me to change my story," Erica said. Her fingers holding the tabletop were as white as bones, her eyes wide with horror, or disbelief.

"I'm telling you how it is with witnesses who get in the way of the verdict they want," Barbara said harshly. "I want to know where I stand in this case. If they break you and you change that story, or if they can cast enough doubt on your story to sway a jury, I have to be prepared. If I build a defense based on the fact that he didn't leave until twenty minutes before eight, I don't want to have to backpedal down the line and find a new approach. And I want you to be prepared for what they might insinuate, or even come right out and state as fact. I know I've shocked and alarmed you, but now they won't shock and alarm you quite so much. It's better to hear things like this in advance, in private, rather than in a courtroom full of strangers and a jury watching your every expression."

Erica slumped in silence for several minutes. Barbara waited, sipping her coffee. Finally Erica straightened and raised her head defiantly. "I won't change a word," she said. "I know what time it was when he left. I looked at the clock. I didn't have my shoes on yet or I would have gone out to call him. I'm not responsible for anything my mother did, I hadn't even seen or heard from her for more than ten years when she died. And I have no reason to lie for Darren. I had only known him for a few weeks before that day, and I could have rented out the apartment to anyone within days of getting it ready. I was engaged for six years and finally broke it off and came out here when my fiancé kept delaying a wedding. We were lovers for those years and I wanted to get married and start a family. I am certainly not repressed sexually or any other way."

"Okay," Barbara said. "You've covered the bases. Did Darren have women visit in the apartment? Annie, in particular?"

Erica shook her head. "Never. I would have heard them, and I didn't."

"What about last night? Can you vouch for him? Was he home? Did he appear upset or anxious?"

"No. He was perfectly normal. He, Todd and I spent a couple hours planning a garden for next summer. We ate pizza. He took Todd home before seven, and then had his usual bridge club meeting. I had a little shopping to do, and later I was up and down in the basement doing laundry. I don't know what time he came back home, but it's usually about eleven when they play bridge."

"Ah, yes," Barbara said. "The plight of us working women, do the shopping, catch up with laundry on Sunday night." She stood up. "Boy, I wish Darren had played bridge last night instead of driving around alone. Well, I've kept you too long. I just felt I had to warn you before… I'll see if Bailey's back yet."

He was in the alley, the hood of his car open, with him peering inside as if he knew what he was doing. It looked good, she thought; the old Dodge in fact might well have been on its last legs or rolling over its last mile. If she hadn't known that every other year he traded in a shiny SUV for a new one, she might even have felt sorry for Bailey. When she opened the restaurant door, he slammed the hood, nodded at her nod, got inside the car and started the engine. He had fixed it.

"Come back for me after you take her to her car," Barbara said, and he nodded again.

After Erica left with Bailey, Barbara checked her cell phone and found a message from her father: "Done here. I'll be in the office. Boardman wants to talk to you. He says it's urgent."

She reread the message, walked to the kitchen door, back to the booth, did it again, then she called Greg Boardman's number.

"Barbara Holloway," she said when he answered his phone.

"Ms. Holloway, we have to see you. No one could find you all day, and I have to see you. Annie has to talk to you. She's... I'm very concerned about her, Ms. Holloway. She's desperate. She wants to go to the coast, to her parents' house, and as a physician I can support that. She has to get away from this madness. Can you arrange something like that?" He sounded as desperate as he said Annie was.

"What's wrong with her, Dr. Boardman? What is she saying?"

"She won't talk to anyone. Not me, not Naomi. No one. She says she has to see you. She's locked in her room. Naomi's over at the house, but Annie won't talk to her."

"What's the residence number?"

"Not on the phone. She won't talk over the phone. She wants to see you in person."

"Just tell me the damn number."

He gave her the number and when she called it, Naomi answered on the first ring.

"Holloway," Barbara said. "What happened to Annie?"

"She was working in the office. I wasn't there, but one of the girls said she turned as white as snow and looked ready to faint. They got her seated with her head down, and someone called Greg and me. We brought her home and she locked herself in her room. She said she has to see you, no one else, just you, and she hasn't said another word."

"Okay. Tell her I'm on the line and want to speak with her."

"She said in person."

"Do what I said. Tell her I have a message. Instructions."

Annie's voice was nearly inaudible when she whispered hello.

"Don't say a word until I'm done," Barbara said. "You know the detective I work with, Bailey Novell. I'm sending him to pick you up and bring you to where I am. I don't want others to know where that is, so don't say anything to anyone until he shows up, and then say you're following my instructions. Nothing else. Until he gets there, just stay in your room with the door locked. Got that?"

"Yes," Annie said after a slight hesitation. "I'll wait here."

"Good. It shouldn't be too long. See you soon."

"Do you want to speak to Naomi again?"

"No. Hang in there, Annie."

Martin appeared bearing a tray as she pushed the automatic dial for Frank's direct line at the office. "I insist that you try this pinot gris," Martin said. "And Binnie said you probably skipped lunch and you shouldn't drink on an empty stomach, so she sent these." He uncovered a plate stacked with steaming savory pastries, each the size and color of a walnut.

He popped one into his mouth and grinned. "Not bad at all."

She picked up the wine, then heard Frank on the phone. "It's me, Dad," she said. "Martin's plying me with food and drink, and when we're done with this wanton abandonment, dare I show my face at your office?"

"I pay my share of the rent and slave wages," he said in a growly voice. "You don't need permission."

"I want to meet Shelley there, and Bailey's bringing a guest. Annie McIvey. Still okay?"

"Oh, for Pete's sake. Should I send out invitations? Bring an army."

"See you," she said, and hung up. Then she tried the wine and ate a pastry and groaned with pleasure.

"Why don't you hire a taxi driver and car for the day?" Bailey said in the Dodge on the way to Frank's office. "Or you could rent a car and drive it yourself. Or buy a new car. Or let my guy return yours."

"Any of the above would be cheaper than your rates," Barbara said, "but I like to hear you bitch. You should get the windshield wipers fixed, or toss them and start over." They squeaked and left streaks on the glass.

Her cell phone rang. "Yes?" she said. "I'm here."

In a nearly breathless voice, Shelley said, "Dorothy Johnson says you caught the demon and you'd better turn it loose, and don't let it know you have its picture."

"Great. What about that other little task? Gone shopping yet?"

"On my way now."

"Okay, swing by Dad's office when you're done. The crew will be there waiting."

As Bailey drew near Frank's office building, in bumper-to-bumper traffic at that time of day, she said, "Just tell Naomi that Annie has an appointment with me, and that I'll give her some dinner and bring her back to the residence afterward."

"You'll take her back? Not me?"

"I'm not sure who. But I'll need you later on. For a couple of hours."

"Do I get a dinner out of this?"

"Ah, and it's a hard deal you cut, laddie. We'll see what we can work in."

He stopped the car; she got out, waved, and entered the building as he drove off again. She was thinking that it would take Bailey about half an hour to go collect Annie, and by then Shelley might put in an appearance. Half an hour: enough time for her to tell Frank what she was up to, and too little time for him to throw a humdinger of a hissy fit.

24

Bailey was philosophical about traffic: sometimes you get the breaks, sometimes you don't. To Barbara's relief this was one of the better days and he arrived with Annie before Frank could launch his tirade. She knew it was going to be a tirade when he left the comfortable chair by the round table to seat himself at his desk. It was a handsome desk, lovely old walnut so polished it could have been metal. The entire office was like that, old, established so long ago that it looked lifted out of a history book or the setting for a period movie. Fine bookcases with glass fronts, the seating arrangement by the coffee table, his desk, all rich, cared for, demanding decorum. His desk was practically bare, no papers cluttering it, no jar of pens and pencils, just a telephone and double silver-framed studio portraits of Barbara and her mother.

"I'll go get them," Barbara said when the receptionist called to announce the arrival of Bailey and Annie. "And maybe you and Bailey could leave us alone. Just a hunch that she'll be happier without much of an audience." She did not wait for his response.

When Barbara returned, Frank was as gracious a host as always, but he did not extend his warmth to Barbara. "Would you like coffee, tea, a little wine perhaps?" he asked Annie, taking her hand, leading her to the coffee table.

She shook her head. "No, thanks."

He helped her off with her coat and, carrying it over his arm, said, "Bailey, there's something I want to go over with you. Excuse us, please."

Annie looked relieved and sat down, and Barbara sat opposite her. As soon as the door closed behind the two men, Barbara said, "Okay, give. What happened today?"

"I was in the office wondering if people were reading the pages from my diary, passing them around, everyone seemed so suspicious, or scared. Then I remembered something that happened a couple of years ago." She swallowed hard, but her voice was steady, and there was a glint in her eyes that Barbara had not seen before. "It hit me hard," Annie said. "And I knew why someone cut out some of those diary pages, that one in particular. It's practically a confession, a blueprint for murder. They must not have given it to the police yet or they would have arrested me by now, but it's out there. Someone has it and is waiting for the right time, something like that. Maybe to sneak it into my room for when the police search again, and they will. They went over Darren's place and they'll be back. They'll find it and that will be the end." Her words were coming faster and faster, and getting more incoherent. "Someone is planning to frame me with my own words taken from my diary."

Barbara drew in a breath and said, "Annie, calm down and start earlier. What happened a couple of years ago? Start there."

"I was visiting David's mother. She had the flu and David really never liked to be around sick people. Ironic, isn't it? A doctor who can't stand illness? It scared him, I think. He liked things he could fix with his scalpel, nothing chronic, nothing mundane." She shivered, then shook herself. "We watched a movie, Joyce and I, a murder mystery that was pretty dumb. Then she said she could plot a perfect murder and never even be suspected, and so could I, or anyone else with a decent brain. It was a game. A diversion for her. On a Saturday. Then David called and I had to leave, but I told her I'd be back on Sunday, and she said I should have my plot ready and so would she. There were conditions. The victim couldn't be a random stranger, for instance. A few others. I don't remember now what they were." She stopped and closed her eyes hard.

Dismayed, Barbara understood what was coming.

She didn't press Annie to continue, but let her think through the rest of it.

"I didn't give it another thought until that night," Annie said, looking down at her hands. "Then I remembered and started to think about it, and I wanted to make a few notes. If I write things down, I remember them better. But I didn't have any paper in my room and David was in the study and I didn't want to go there, so I jotted some things down in the diary." She looked up at Barbara, her face so white it looked like marble, her eyes wide and luminous, bright with tears. Tears of anger or fear?

"I plotted a murder," Annie said in a low voice, hardly above a whisper. "It started with something like *Plan ahead.* Then, *Steal a gun.*" She stopped again, then said, "I can't even remember what I wrote, but it was all like that, shorthand, notes. I never gave it another thought. David went with me on Sunday for a short visit, and Joyce didn't mention the game. Neither did I."

Barbara stood up and went to the bookcase that concealed Frank's bar, which she opened. She poured two glasses of wine without paying any attention to what kind it was. It was something to do, something for Annie to do with her hands. There wouldn't have been an explanation, of course. What for? You don't explain your shorthand notes, and Joyce, the only person besides Annie who had known what they were for, was dead.

She handed one of the glasses to Annie, who sipped it as obediently as a child, then put it down.

"Okay," Barbara said. "I get the point. What to do about it is the problem now. Not your problem, mine."

"Mine," Annie said in a small voice. "There's something else." She groped in her purse and pulled out an envelope and handed it to Barbara. "I have to know if this is enough, if it's legal." She looked at her wine as Barbara opened the envelope and took out a sheet of paper and started to read.

It was short, reading it took only a minute, but then she read it again, slower, to give herself a moment to think. Finally she looked up and said, "It's valid. Handwritten, dated today, signed, it's legal. Why, Annie?"

Annie continued to gaze at her wine, as if she had glimpsed something swimming, vanishing, appearing. "I thought what if a truck hit my car, killed me, or a giant wave crashed ashore and carried me out to sea. It happens every year. You read about it every year."

Barbara nodded. "Why now?"

"I want to go home, spend a little time with my parents. Did you know I have two sets of parents? Funny isn't it? But I do. They'd get over a tragic accidental death. People get over it eventually—act of God, nature's little practical joke, whatever. They get over it in time. But if I'm arrested, convicted…you know. That would be harder. And they shouldn't have to hassle with the mess the clinic's in. They don't know anything about it. And Naomi should be a shareholder, not me. Just in case that truck driver loses control, or the big wave…"

Barbara regarded her soberly, but Annie did not look up, and finally Barbara said, "I'll keep it for you. It's perfectly valid."

Annie had written a will, leaving everything she owned to her parents with the exception of the five shares of the clinic, which were to go to Naomi. She put the paper back in the envelope and it inside her purse, then stood up, thinking hard.

She looked at her watch. Five after five already. Maria, she thought then, and went to Frank's desk to call her own office. Maria answered on the first ring. As expected, she had delayed leaving, hoping to hear from Barbara before the day ended. "Hang on a minute," Barbara said. She put the phone down and returned to the coffee table. "Annie, I'm sending you home with my secretary, Maria Velazques. You met her at the office. She and her mother and her two daughters will be delighted to have you as a guest for dinner. Mama might try to adopt you, in fact. And she'll certainly try to fatten you up. Be on guard. Okay?"

"Why?"

"Well, I sent word to Naomi that I'd give you dinner before you returned, and I have too many things to do to make good on that. Mama's cooking is wonderful. You'll love it, and her and the two kids."

"I don't want to eat."

"I know. But there's another reason to get you out of the snake pit for a few hours. To remind you of other kinds of life. I'll tell Maria to swing by and pick you up."

Annie seemed to have no more resistance, and
simply shrugged. "Whatever you say."

Barbara went back to the phone and asked Maria
if Mama was up for a dinner guest. She knew the answer, and looking at Annie across the room, she
could imagine what kind of fuss Maria's family
would make over her, their own live Barbie doll for
the evening.

"Come on," she said to Annie after hanging up.
"It won't take Maria more than five minutes to get
here. I'll walk down with you, make sure you get in
the right car."

In the conference room on the way out, she
stopped to greet Shelley and retrieve Annie's coat.
Shelley's sky-blue raincoat and Annie's dark-red
coat were both on a chair. She picked up the blue
one, saying to Frank, "Annie's going home with
Maria for dinner. I'll wait with her. You want to
make that call? Make sure it's on for seven-thirty?"

He scowled at her, the face that sent the junior attorneys into a panic. She smiled sweetly and said,
"I'll be up as soon as Maria gets here."

In the lobby she handed the coat to Annie, who
looked at it and shook her head. "That isn't mine."

"Oh? I must have picked up Shelley's coat by
mistake. She'll probably be the one to collect you
later, you can switch then. Okay?"

Annie shrugged and put on the coat. They waited
near the outside door where they could see the traffic. "For the next few hours, try to relax," Barbara
said. "If Mama thinks you haven't eaten enough,

she'll try to sneak tidbits into your pockets or purse for you to snack on later."

"Greg agrees that I should go home, over to the coast for a few days. Will they let me do that?"

"I'll see what I can work out," Barbara said. "Are you comfortable in your parents' home? Some adults are, some aren't."

"I am," Annie said. "I love it over there, and you make Mama sound a lot like my mother."

"Ah, there's Maria now. No parking or stopping either is allowed there. Let's go before someone starts honking a horn."

When she returned to Frank's office, Shelley asked, "What's happening? What's going on?"

"In a minute," Barbara said. "Did you get the wig?" She went to Frank's desk, sat down and pulled the phone around. She was already dialing when Shelley brought the wig out of a shopping bag. "Perfect," Barbara said, listening to the ringing phone. The wig was a near match to Shelley's own hair, and it was perfect. Then Naomi was on the line.

"Kelso-McIvey Rehabilitation Clinic."

"Mrs. Boardman, this is Barbara Holloway. I have to speak with Darren. Is he still there?"

"Yes. I think he's just getting ready to leave. Just a second…"

Barbara listened to her voice calling Darren, a pause, then her voice again. "It's Barbara Holloway. She said she has to speak with you." To Barbara, she said, "He's coming."

"Thanks. And after I talk with him a minute, I have to speak with you. Don't leave. Okay?"

"Of course. Where's Annie? Is she all right?"

"She's a nervous wreck, as you know. I'll tell you after I talk to Darren."

When he came on, he sounded amused. "Are you still dodging the cops?"

"You'd better believe it. Look, I have to talk to you in private, not at the clinic, not at a restaurant. Your place. Are you going to be home tonight?"

"Sure. I was just on my way."

"Wait for me. I can't get there before six-thirty or even a few minutes later. Just wait for me, will you?"

"I'll be there," he said, no longer sounding lazy and amused.

"Good. Put Naomi back on."

She didn't give Naomi time to speak. "I have to call a meeting of the board of directors and you for tonight," she said. "It's important. I'm sorry about the short notice, but it has to be done. Seven-thirty in the directors' room. Will you see to it? Maybe you could ask your cook to provide coffee. The meeting might take a while. And tell Dr. Kelso. We'll go ahead without him if he can't make it, but if it's possible I want him there, too. I'll fill you in at the meeting."

When Naomi started to say something, Barbara interrupted her. "I can't talk right now. I have to go. Seven-thirty." She disconnected.

From across the room Frank's scowl was enough to curl her hair as he muttered, "Christ on a mountain."

"Did you make your call?" she asked him.

"Yes." It was not quite a snarl, but close enough.

"The snowball is starting down the hill," she said. "No stopping it now."

25

The expected wave of hard rain had blown in by the time Barbara climbed the stairs to Darren's apartment. She ducked her head and drew her hood down lower against a gust of wind, glad that Darren didn't keep her waiting when she knocked at his door.

"Come on in," he said. "Welcome to chaos."

She glanced around. Books lay on the floor by the cases, cushions were off the sofa, nothing unexpected. A partly opened door afforded a glimpse of his bedroom—mattress askew, bedding in a heap on it. She could imagine what the rest looked like. "It would have been worse if Dad hadn't kept them civilized," she said. Inwardly she was seething. They had him down as an ex-con; they didn't have to be polite, not even in the presence of a respected attorney.

"Yeah, I know. Take your coat?"

"I'll keep it. This isn't going to take very long."

He had started to move toward her, but at her sharp words, he stopped. "Why do I get the impression that you come with bad news?" He moved back into the room and sat on the arm of the sofa, watching her.

"Because you're perceptive, I imagine. You don't miss a trick, do you?" She walked through the living room to glance into the kitchen. Apparently he had put things more or less back in order there; at least the signs of a search were not instantly noticeable. "Did they do Todd's room?"

"Yep. Can't tell much difference between before and after, though." He nodded toward a closed door. "Have a look."

She shook her head and went to stand near the outside door again, next to another closed door with a chair in front of it. "At our first meeting you asked me if I still wanted you as my client. Remember? At the time, I said yes. I'm rescinding that now, Darren. I'm quitting on you."

He regarded her steadily for a moment, his expression revealing nothing. "Throwing me to the wolves?"

"I think that just about sums it up. It was a mistake for me to take on two clients who might end up presenting an insoluble conflict of interest. I have to abandon one or the court might force me to leave both and I'm not willing to do that. If you had stopped with McIvey, I probably could have gotten you off, cast enough doubt to convince a jury that the case was not proved. Not the best way to save a client's neck, but you take what you can get." She shrugged. Darren had not moved from the arm of the sofa, and she could not tell from watching him if he had heard what she said, or realized what she meant.

"I've arranged for a meeting with the directors for seven-thirty to inform them of my decision, but I wanted to tell you first, not wait and hit you with this at that time."

He nodded. "So that's what it's about. Everyone knows you called for a meeting. Bernie talks to you and babbles afterward. Bernie gets killed and you hide out all day. From the police, or the killer? It's a toss-up which it is. What else do you suppose they're talking about over there? Are you going to tell me why?" he asked. "Or is that the cliff-hanger, to make sure I'll attend, see the next chapter in your melodrama?" He sounded interested, the way a child might be interested in something found crawling under a rock, or in retelling a B-movie plot, distant and not personally involved. He sounded the way he did when talking to a patient.

That was the key to him, she thought suddenly. He had learned how to hide behind a facade of amusement, even indifference. He had to be anxious; he knew better than she did what awaited him if he was charged and found guilty of anything at all. Not a juvenile prison ranch this time, but hard time. And he had learned how to control his fear and put on a mask of absolute confidence. She thought of how he had talked about his imprisonment, how he had spoken to his patient on the video she had watched, how relaxed he had appeared. Now he seemed totally relaxed, and no more than mildly interested—no clenched hands with white knuckles, no facial tic, no blanching or blushing. At ease, comfortable. Sure of himself.

"I'll tell you why," she said, making no effort to hide her sudden fury with him. "Darren and David, David and Darren, two sides of the same coin. Equally arrogant, equally egocentric, equally determined. David never hid his disdain, contempt even, viewing everyone as if he stood on Mount Olympus and belonged there, while you were in a place where you had to hide. You learned your lesson well, but you're up there, viewing the world from Olympus, gazing down on poor humanity below. Both the best in the field, magic in their hands, power of life and death at their disposal, but there's only room for one god. How it must have stung when he snatched Annie out from under your nose. No one does that to Darren, do they? Everyone loves Darren, but David McIvey didn't. First Annie, and then he was going to take the clinic away, too. You lied about that. A whiff of suspicion of drugs in your résumé, in your personnel file, death to a career, back to the gutter. You said it, you run the clinic. It's yours to run, no questions asked, your fiefdom, everyone agrees about that, and you weren't going to stand aside and let him take it away, and destroy you."

She drew in a breath and Darren stood up, backed

away from her a step or two, then stood leaning against the wall. "This is what they've been saying from day one," he said. "No proof, remember? Speculation. Suspicion. No case. What changed?"

"I talked to Bernie," she said. "You know what she saw, and you made up that cock-and-bull story to try to cover it. It won't work. Today I had a long talk with Erica Castle. She won't change her story under pressure, and she'll be a credible witness for your defense. Actually, she's the only thing standing between you and a cell at this moment, but she didn't see everything that happened that morning, did she?

"You left in your truck early and got to the garden before David showed up, let yourself in and waited for him. You're one of the select circle with a key to the garden gate. You knew what his schedule would be, everyone at the clinic knew. You waited for him and killed him and moved his body out of sight. Then you got in your truck and left again, and Bernie saw brake lights as she arrived. Your brake lights. You drove the truck back to the garage and got out your bike and made sure that Erica saw you leaving at twenty minutes to eight. But Bernie talked too much and you had to tell a new story to cover hers, and you had to kill her. Your usual bridge game had to be missed—no time for fun and games. There was work to be done before Bernie had time to make a statement to the police. You'll go down for it, Darren, but I won't let you take Annie with you."

"Isn't it a little foolish for you to come here alone and say these things to me?" he said in a low voice.

"Don't be an idiot. I didn't come alone. Bailey's waiting for me, probably just outside that door, and Dad and Shelley both know everything I know."

"I didn't kill anyone, Barbara."

"Save it for your defense attorney. I called that meeting for seven-thirty. Shelley and Dad will take Annie back home and put her to bed, tranquilized to her eyeballs. I told her what this is all about and there's no need for her to attend. She's in no shape to attend anything, to tell the truth. She's heading for a nervous breakdown if she doesn't get relief from the pressure she's under. Tomorrow morning Shelley will pick her up and take her to her parents' farm where maybe she'll get some rest for the next few months. And tomorrow morning I have a date with the lead detective. I'm through dodging the cops. I told you I'm an officer of the court, sworn to uphold the law, give them relevant information. Everything you've said to me up to now is privileged. I don't have to reveal a word, but from here on out, nothing is. Be warned."

She turned toward the door. "You can come to the meeting or not. Get in your truck and take off or not. Frankly, Darren, I couldn't care less what you do from this point on."

"I wouldn't miss this meeting for the world," Darren said. He smiled. "Be careful on those stairs, they get slippery when it rains. It would really look bad for you to have an accident on my doorstep."

* * *

At 7:25 Frank pulled into the driveway of the residence. He glanced at Shelley and Barbara in the
back seat and shook his head. Barbara looked ridicu-
lous in a blond wig. "Action," he said. He got out and
hurried to the front door of the house. Greg Boardman opened it.

"Now," Barbara said. She got out and opened an
umbrella, reached inside as if to help Shelley out.
Shelley, in Annie's red raincoat, looked fine. Barbara
pulled the hood of her mackintosh over her head,
then, ducking their heads low, they hurried through
the rain to the porch.

"Can I have a word with you and Mrs. Boardman?" Frank said to Greg Boardman, gently herd-
ing him away from the door as the two women
entered the house and went straight up the stairs.
"Shelley's going to help Annie get settled," Frank
said. "We're running a little late for the meeting,
I'm afraid."

"Where's Annie?" Naomi Boardman said, entering the hall from the living room.

"Going to her room," Frank said. "Shelley's with
her. Mrs. Boardman, Annie's in a pretty bad way. She
saw Shelley's doctor and he gave her a tranquilizer.
We agree with your husband that she should go to her
folks' house on the coast, get away from all this for
a time. Shelley will take her over in the morning."

Naomi's lips tightened and she pushed past Frank
and started up the stairs.

In Annie's room, Barbara quickly took off the

mackintosh and Shelley the raincoat. Shelley put on the mackintosh, and Barbara went into the bathroom, closed and locked the door just as Naomi knocked on the bedroom door.

Shelley opened the door. "Oh, Mrs. Boardman, Annie asked me to tell you that she doesn't feel up to a meeting. She wants to lie down and rest for a while. She said maybe you could tell her what it was about when it's over." She held up the raincoat. "I don't know what to do with this, it's a little wet to hang in her closet, I think." Naomi took it.

They heard the toilet flush, and after a moment tap water running.

"I'll just help her get settled down, and then Mr. Holloway and I will join the rest of you," Shelley said. "She's really all right, just very tired. And she wants to talk to you later, after the meeting."

Naomi hesitated a second or two, then turned and walked away stiffly. In the downstairs hall she said, "Annie isn't coming. She needs a little rest. Thomas is waiting. Let's go and get this over with."

"As soon as Shelley comes down I'll bring her over," Frank said. "I'll move the car around to the clinic. No need to bother you folks after we're done over there. It shouldn't be more than a minute or two."

Naomi hung up Annie's coat and put on her own, then she and Greg left by the back door. Upstairs, Shelley closed the drapes in Annie's room while Barbara arranged the bed, put the wig form in place on the pillow and the wig on it. It looked phoney as hell, she thought, but with the lights off, a dim night-light on in the hall… It would do. It would have to do.

"Go," she said to Shelley and waited until she was at the door, then switched off the light. She followed Shelley down the stairs. Frank turned off the hall light and the porch light, nodded to Shelley and opened the door. He opened the umbrella, and a figure in black slipped onto the porch and took it from him—Bailey playing his part. With the umbrella low over them, he and Shelley hurried out to the car, and two other dark figures eased into the residence—Milt Hoggarth and one of his detectives, Sergeant Larkins. Light from the living room was enough to reveal Milt's mouth set in a tight, thin-lipped grimace.

"If this doesn't work, Holloway," he muttered, "you're dead in the water from here on out."

"This way," Barbara said, going up the stairs again.

In Annie's room Milt used a penlight to look the situation over. The closet had bifold doors; Frank and Barbara could duck in there, he said. He would take the bathroom. There was no good place for the sergeant to hide. Barbara pushed clothes out of the way in the closet, making room, while Milt and the sergeant went out to the hall, down to Naomi and Greg's room. The sergeant would have to stay there, and if anyone entered Annie's room, follow him.

"He'll probably leave the door open," Milt said,

"to get the light from the hall. Just keep out of sight until he makes a move. That's it."

Back in Annie's room he said to Barbara, "Your dad's pulled some fast ones in his time, but he never turned on a client as far as I know. If your guy doesn't show tonight, I'm taking him in the morning. Just to tell you."

"I didn't say anything was guaranteed," she said. "I said there was a good chance to nab the killer with the gun. That's all. And I have one client, Annie McIvey, who is right now eating tortillas and fried plantains and mango salsa..." Her stomach growled and she stopped her recitation of the probable menu at Mama's house. She was watching her cell phone. It was muted, but the caller ID came on after another minute and she said, "That's Shelley's signal. The stage is set at the clinic."

Barbara and Frank were sitting on the bed, Milt in a chair, and as far as she knew the sergeant had stretched out and gone to sleep on Naomi and Greg's bed. There had not been a sound from him. The wait was interminable, and she was thinking that Frank had no business here at his age. This was really too much. He had insisted; if he couldn't be in on the end, he wouldn't play at all, and he had meant every word. So stubborn, she thought. He could teach a mule.

Finally Milt said, "My beeper just buzzed me. Someone's coming through the backyard." He got up and closed the hall door; the dim lighting instantly turned into stygian darkness.

They took their places in the closet and the bathroom. A hanger made a startlingly loud sound; Barbara pushed the clothes back farther. And they waited again.

She couldn't hold her breath and survive, Barbara thought, and she let it out slowly, but if she breathed it sounded like a pneumatic pump of some sort. Beside her, Frank made not a sound. What if her stomach began to growl again? She ordered herself not to think of food, not to think of her stomach, not to think of the noise her heart made. Then the bedroom door opened and the dim light was back in the room. The door was opened wider. She caught in her breath and held it as a demon walked into the bedroom.

Black, shiny, wet, reflecting light eerily from the hall, black from head to foot, it moved to the bed and stood there for a second. It was doing something, the black skein of plastic, reflecting light, revealed movement, but she could not see what it was doing.

The world exploded into thunder and light, and Sergeant Larkins lunged simultaneously. The shot echoed and reechoed in the room, and the light was blinding. Larkins seemed to swoop across the room to knock the demon onto the bed, facedown, and bat away the gun all in a single leap from the doorway.

Milt ran to the bed and jerked the top plastic bag off, and then he stared, openmouthed. Joining him, Barbara said, "It's over, Erica."

Erica twisted in Larkin's grasp and looked at Barbara with hatred. "You're too late!" she cried. "Too late. If I can't have him, neither can she!"

Barbara pulled the covers back and picked up the wig. Erica screamed and would have fallen without Larkin's grip on her arm.

26

"You let me think we'd nab Darren Halvord," Milt Hoggarth said bitterly. They were in Naomi's office at the clinic with Shelley and Frank, waiting for Bailey to deliver Annie before Barbara faced the directors with her message that Erica Castle had been arrested.

"I was afraid you'd back out if I told you I expected Erica," Barbara said. "You've had your cap set for Darren and Annie from the beginning."

"We knew from the start that it had to be someone connected to the clinic," Milt said, not quite defensive, but not yielding much either.

"And I doubted that from the start," Barbara said with a shrug. "They all act as if the clinic is a holy shrine. I didn't believe any of the regulars would desecrate it with an act of violence, have cops swarm all over the place, bad publicity, frightened patients and volunteers. Any one of them could have found a way to lure McIvey to some other place and pull the trigger. He jogged on the Amazon Trail on Saturday mornings, for heaven's sake. How many people are out there at eight-thirty on Saturday morning? Erica couldn't have known that, although the regulars probably did. The clinic meant nothing to her, just a means to an end, and she had never even met McIvey. That made it harder. It had to be someplace where she could find him alone, and she had no way of learning his routine, except from scuttlebutt in the clinic. It was known that Annie would drop him and take off that morning, that Naomi would wait at the house, and that Greg Boardman and other staff would not go to the clinic much before eight. In other words, that morning was the one and only time she could count on McIvey's being alone, and it was a morning made for murder. She seized the moment."

"That's it? That's what you were counting on?" the lieutenant asked in disbelief.

"Not exactly. I talked to her. She was in love with Darren, that was apparent, and she set out to get him, reel him in when the time was right. And get rid of Annie in the process, either by framing her for murder, or…well you saw what she intended tonight. Everyone at the clinic knew that McIvey intended to drive Darren out, and she was determined not to let that happen. Erica told me she had been engaged for six years, then broke it off to come west. A woman who really wants that picket fence and a couple of kids does not hang in there for six years when the clock is ticking faster and faster and the big forty is coming up. She had choices when she was engaged: insist on marriage, get pregnant, get out. She got out and headed west, a new start, a house to sell, a bit of money in the bank, and then Darren came into sight. She marked him as hers and went on from there. When you're forty and fall in love, maybe for the first time, you tend to act a little crazy."

"Guesswork," Hoggarth said in disgust.

Barbara shrugged. "Check out the old boyfriend. Bet you a buck he's a dud, a shoe salesman, something safe like that." At his continuing skepticism, she said patiently, "Look, Hoggarth, she is the polar opposite of her mother. Her mother was a teenage dropout, addict, prostitute, single parent, no father in sight, that whole route. Erica is squeaky-clean, worked her way through school, keeps her house as clean as a convent, impeccable reputation. She would not have become engaged to anyone who was not as straight as a ruler, and it was a dead-end relationship. Also safe, up to a point. Then she had a chance at a different life, and she ditched him."

She felt a wave of sadness, of compassion for Erica, who had worked so hard to remake herself into an image of respectability, of middle-class virtue, only to see her story-book ending threatened by David McIvey. You can't really leave the past behind, she thought. It has molded you, shaped you, and will assert itself if aroused because it is part of you, slumbering deep within your cells.

She shook herself. "Anyway, moving on. You talked to Dorothy Johnson and dismissed her story of the demon out of hand. I listened to her and tried to make sense of what she had seen beyond the fact that the murder took place at seven-thirty or a minute later. Someone in disguise, maybe. Or someone who wanted to be seen bone-dry within minutes of the murder. Annie? No. She's not the brightest light on the tree, but she has enough sense to have chosen a better and more convenient time and place if she had murder on her mind. And she didn't turn up dry within a few minutes. She wasn't seen again for hours. The other person who turned up bone-dry in the right time frame was Erica.

"She gave a patient a cheap paperback book early on, no big deal. But then she gave a twenty-six-dollar book to another patient the morning of the murder. Why? She was in debt big time, no steady job, scraping pennies and getting in deeper day by day. But someone might have seen her old station wagon near the clinic that morning. She needed a reason to be there. So she alibied Darren, and herself, in a way that would be remembered. Why so precise about the time she claimed he left? How did she know what time would be meaningful? The time of death was not part of any news story that day, but she knew when Darren had to leave to be in the clear. He said from the start that he didn't know what time he left that morning. She couldn't have seen him leave. She wasn't even at home when he left. She was busy shooting McIvey."

She narrowed her eyes and said, "Picture it, Hoggarth. She was there, parked and waiting, in her demon suit probably, and McIvey came from the residence and unlocked the gate, went into the garden. She followed. Maybe she called to him to wait for her, let her go in when he did. However that went, she got close enough to shoot him through the heart. Back to her station wagon, off with the trash bags, off with the Totes boots, everything shoved into one of the bags, and then she drove around to the front of the clinic. Maybe she sat out there a minute or two to calm down, maybe not. Deliver the book, make sure Bernie noted that she was dry, and what time it was, then off to teach her class. Neat, tidy, no loose ends. No blood, no trace evidence, hair, fibers, anything. It's all in the trash bag. Toss the bag into a Dumpster somewhere, take the gun home and hide it again, and that's that."

"This is even lousier than the case we had against Halvord," Milt said after a moment. "What if this? What if that? Maybe something else."

"I know that," Barbara said, exasperated. "There wasn't a shred of tangible evidence. That's why I wanted her to show up with the gun and the demon suit. What more do you need?"

"What about Zuckerman? What exactly did she tell you?"

"Exactly that maybe she saw car lights leaving the

parking lot or the alley that morning. Maybe. From a block away. So I stayed out of sight and let Erica stew about what she had said."

"And got Zuckerman killed," Milt said. He was frowning at her in a way that suggested he wanted to bring charges, if he could think of anything that would stick.

Slowly Barbara nodded. "Yes. But even if I had broadcast what Bernie told me, I doubt Erica would have been swayed. She must have gone through one scenario after another in her mind. What if you guys reenacted that morning, let Bernie watch car after car leave the alley in near dark, with fog and rain? Rule out one car after another, including Annie's Mercedes, with the distinctive three brake lights. What if someone tried an old station wagon? Bingo? Maybe. I think as soon as she knew Bernie had seen something, Bernie was targeted. And she timed it for Darren's bridge club meeting. Another alibi with irrefutable witnesses. Except he didn't go that night. So I set the stage and gave directions for her to follow, and called you. And it worked. What more do you need? You have her, the latex gloves, her demon suit, the gun and an eye-witnessed attempted murder."

He was not happy. He chewed his lip, frowning at her almost absently now. "How did you know she'd overhear you talking to Halvord?"

"I thought it very likely. I had been in her half of the house. I knew about the inside stairs. Your guys must have known about them, the way they tossed

Darren's apartment. I knew she would hear me arrive. She heard me the first time I went to the house, and she had been in the kitchen that time. I didn't think she could resist sneaking up those stairs and putting her ear against the door, and I stayed close to the door and spoke quite clearly. If we had been face-to-face, I couldn't have made it plainer that Darren would be arrested in the morning, Annie spirited out of town, case closed. I talked to her this afternoon and let it slip that Darren had no alibi for Bernie's death. That was a shock for her. And I gave her a preview of what to expect from an eager-beaver assistant D.A. determined to break her alibi for Darren last November."

Hoggarth's face darkened and she said, "Oh, come on. You know as well as I do how that plays in court. I made sure that she understood that her testimony would have been discredited one way or another. Tonight was going to be her only chance to get rid of Annie and clear Darren. I arranged the meeting so the coast would be clear for her. She had to act now or it would all have been for nothing."

She stood up and stretched. "This is pure speculation, understand, but I think she intended to try to make Annie's murder look like suicide. Shelley gave the signal that Darren was in the directors' room with the others, and she asked him to close the blinds, so that if Erica was watching, she would know that he was covered this time. Your guy said she came from the garden to the residence. No doubt she had been watching and was reassured on

that point. She believed Annie was heavily tranquilized—if not asleep, then too dopey to be a
problem. Shoot her at close range, get her finger-
prints on the gun and leave it with her." She regarded him thoughtfully. "And you would have
bought a suicide, wouldn't you? A confessional
suicide."

"Maybe," he said. They both knew he meant yes.
Clearly he was not satisfied, but before he could
raise another objection or ask another question, Barbara said, "When Erica was a little girl there was a
shooting in her mother's apartment. You might check
the records, see what kind of gun was used then, if
it was her mother's. I suspect that Erica got her hands
on it years ago and has held on to it ever since.
Maybe her mother gave it to her and told her to use
it if one of her johns got too familiar. Maybe it's on
record in Cleveland."

There was a tap on the door and Shelley hurried
to open it and slip out. She reappeared almost instantly. "Annie and Bailey are here," she said.

"Tell them to go to the directors' room. I'll be
along in a second." She looked at Hoggarth. "Was
there anything else?"

"After I talk to Castle," he said. "I'll want to see
you after I get a statement from her."

"I'm not going anywhere," she said. "You know
where to find me."

"Sometimes," he said. "Sometimes." He went to
the door, glowered at her another second and left.

When the door closed behind him, Frank said, "I

believe he thinks you might be holding out a thing or two."

She shrugged. "He has all he needs. Ready? Let's get this over with."

While Milt and Sergeant Larkins had struggled with Erica, getting her out of the demon suit, Barbara had picked up the diary pages from the bedside table where Erica had put them. Frank, who missed very little, had seen her do it. He didn't say a word, simply followed her out and to the directors' room.

Naomi and Annie both wept when Barbara told them it was over. She kept the report short, with few details. Greg Boardman looked disbelieving and then bewildered. "Why? What for?" he asked no one in particular. And Thomas Kelso said in his terrible rasp, "Who the hell is Erica Castle?"

"She must have been crazy," Naomi said. She was holding Annie in her arms. "She said she wanted to apply for Bernie's job and I said it was hers if she was sure. She must have been insane."

Darren sat as silent and unmoving as a carving, his gaze intent on Barbara. She ignored him. "We may never know why she did it," she said. "Maybe all killers are insane. Tonight she went to the residence with the gun and shot a dummy in Annie's bed, thinking it was Annie asleep there. If the gun checks out with ballistics, that's all they'll need to charge her and bring her to trial."

Thomas Kelso said, "You should have taken me up on my offer. Since you won't be needed to defend anyone, no clients, I think your payment for tonight's entertainment will be scant."

Greg Boardman stood up. "I think the whole board of directors will determine that, Thomas."

Kelso looked at him in surprise and then nodded. "Call that meeting sooner rather than later." He turned back to Barbara. "I knew you could do it, you understand. Now I'm going home."

Before they disbanded, Barbara took Annie aside and gave her the diary pages. "I'll get the diaries over to you tomorrow. Might be a good idea to make sure they all get burned this time."

"I will," Annie said with elaborate emphasis. "It's really over? No one suspects me anymore?"

"It's over. You're above suspicion again," Barbara said with a smile. "You realize the estate might still be held up while they deal with the first Mrs. McIvey's claim."

"I don't care about that. Can I tell Greg and Naomi that we can go ahead with the foundation? Would that be okay now?"

"You can go ahead."

Annie flung her arms around Barbara and hugged her hard. "Thanks. Thank you more than I can say." She left with Naomi and Greg.

For just an instant Barbara had the impression that Annie's feet were not touching the floor. She shook her head and closed her eyes hard, then opened them and held up her car keys, delivered by Bailey, who had informed her that the car was in the front parking lot. "I'm out of here," she said.

"Bobby, have you had anything to eat today?" Frank asked.

She didn't even have to pause to think about it before she realized her stomach was making express train noises again. Then, from the doorway, Darren said, "Want some dinner?"

Frank looked from her to Darren, then back, recalling her words to Hoggarth: I'm not going anywhere. He said, "Come on, Shelley. I'll take you over to pick up your car. Bailey, you want some dinner?"

"Any place in particular in mind?" Barbara asked, at the wheel of her car with Darren in the passenger seat.

He named an Italian restaurant in the south end of town and she began to drive.

"No one asked me about Kelso's car," he said later, breaking a long silence.

"Unless you mentioned it to the police, they have no reason to ask," she said. "I told you that everything you said to me until this evening was privileged. I haven't mentioned it. I didn't mention it in your apartment where Erica could overhear. You didn't see Kelso's car, you saw Erica's old station wagon. A block away, rain, fog, dark, not expecting to see it, you interpreted it in a way that made sense. I didn't mention that you saw anything that morning, by the way."

"What made you suspect her in the first place?" he asked after a moment.

"You did. In Dad's kitchen when you said you saw car lights leaving. McIvey couldn't have been dead for longer than a minute or two if you saw the killer leave and got blood on your boot. It meant that you didn't leave that morning when Erica said you did. She was lying about it. I had suspected that from the beginning, but I hadn't taken it to the next step. Giving you that alibi gave her one, too. No one ever suspected her of murder, just of lying to save you."

"Won't they have the same problem with her moving the body that they had with Annie?"

"Of course. The prosecutor will say she could have done it. Her defense attorney will say she couldn't. She'll probably deny everything, or else go for insanity. The devil made her do it. What would be really insane would be for her to admit to anything at all, and then deny moving him. As for the prosecution, when you can bring a charge of murder one, you don't worry too much about obstruction of justice or interfering with a crime scene. What they needed from day one was the gun, and now they have it."

There was a lengthy silence. "That was an impressive charade you put on in my apartment," he said in a lazy-sounding voice, as she drew near the restaurant. "You stung me more than once. The whole thing was for her benefit, wasn't it? Goad her into taking action again, come out with the gun in hand."

She nodded, pulled into the parking lot, stopped and opened her door.

"Why did she do it?" he asked.

"Because she was seduced, she was in love with you, and meant to have you at any cost." She got out and walked to the restaurant door. He was at her heels.

A waiter met them, guided them to a booth, placed menus before them and left, all in silence.

"I've never seduced anyone in my life," Darren said. "You're playing a hunch for all it's worth. You suspected her and you're twisting everything to make your hunch work."

"Not a hunch. Who knew David McIvey was planning a surgery at the clinic? He told Kelso and Annie. Kelso told the Boardmans and Annie told you. Who told Erica? No one else at the clinic knew. His ex-wife didn't know. They all thought he meant to continue it as a profit-making rehab clinic, but Erica knew. She has good ears. She heard me drive up to the house when she was in the kitchen. She heard Annie arrive the night she turned up there. She must have listened at the door to the stairs, but why? And why take action like that? She had her own game plan and it didn't include seeing you driven away, maybe ruined professionally."

She opened her menu. He ignored his. The waiter returned with dipping olive oil and crusty bread. "The seafood lasagna and house salad," she said, closing the menu. "House Soave."

Darren held up his hand. "Two." The waiter left.

As if there had been no interruption, Barbara picked up where she had left off. "Erica came to

Eugene with every intention of selling that house and she changed her mind after she met you. She stretched out her volunteer work to five days a week. And you heard Naomi tonight, she applied for Bernie's job. She made up to your son, bought him that bonsai. Didn't she? Wasn't that from her?"

He nodded.

"Forty bucks," Barbara said. "And she was penniless, living on plastic practically. It all begins to add up. Not just a hunch."

The waiter brought a decanter of chilled wine and poured two glasses. Barbara waved him away, and from across the room, he glanced back at them and sighed. They were both leaning forward, ignoring the wine, ignoring the oil and bread, and he was very afraid that when he served their dinners, they would ignore them as well.

"I never gave her any reason to believe I was interested," Darren said. "And I sure did not seduce her, or even try to seduce her."

"You seduce everyone in your path. You do it automatically, without noticing what effect you're having."

He looked startled and drew back. "Earlier, when you were riding me in my apartment," he said, no longer lazy sounding, or drawling either. His words were clipped. "I kept thinking, does she realize she's talking about herself? Describing herself? Arrogant. Sure of herself. Sweeping aside opposition. Take charge and keep it."

"Oh, that got to you, didn't it? I meant every word."

"The night you first came to the meeting," he said, "you took the ball away from Thomas Kelso and put it in your pocket, and it's been there ever since. Your game, your rules, your way. You know what I told myself that night? You'll never guess. I told myself that you're the most dangerous woman I've ever seen. I would not want to get in your way."

"The difference between us is that I can admit I'm fallible. I make mistakes. I can't be sure of myself, not the way you claim to be. I'm not afraid to admit that up front."

"That's arrogance hiding behind fake humility. And you know it. You couldn't work for anyone any more than I can. You'd set up a tent first. You talked about Mount Olympus. You claimed that mountaintop a long time ago and you won't let anyone else near it. You run your office to suit yourself, your way, and you do exactly what I do. You get a hunch, make an intuitive leap and find the evidence to support it. You don't let the evidence take you to a conclusion. You force it, following what you believe, what you know, is the truth."

"Now you're talking about yourself," she said furiously. "Your magic hands tell you things and you follow where they lead without question. I don't pretend to have magic. Logic and reason, cause and effect, watching people's actions and reactions, sizing up evidence, there's nothing mystical or magical about it. It's simple hard work."

"If you really believe that's how you operate, and I doubt it, you're delusional."

Across the room the waiter rolled his eyes. It looked like a long night shaping up.

* * * * *

Attorney Barbara Holloway has been called "dynamic," "complex," "brilliant" and "maddeningly flawed." Join her in her next case, as she defends a young woman accused of murder, never anticipating the bizarre twists waiting ahead, or that much more than a verdict will rely on the stunning discovery of…

THE UNBIDDEN TRUTH
by
Kate Wilhelm

Available in hardcover from MIRA Books
September 2004

Please turn the page for an exciting preview.

1

It was a lazy Friday afternoon, the kind of day that leads thoughts to hammocks and shade trees. Barbara Holloway stifled a yawn as she escorted her last client of the day at Martin's Restaurant to the door. August was always slow, and she had taken notes of four clients' complaints about neighbors, evil debt collectors, recalcitrant landlords. She had caught up with Internet news, had her terrorist anxiety renewed, answered e-mails and was wishing that she had a shade tree and a hammock. She was looking forward to a dinner with friends and then a movie.

Now it was time to take down her Barbara Is In sign. "Don't worry," she said. "Guys like that turn into pussycats when authority hits them in the head. Sometimes the law can carry more punch than a bat." Her client, a thin young woman of twenty-one, with a three-year-old child and a one-year old, looked relieved.

When Barbara opened the door she was surprised to see another woman standing by the steps. And she was not the sort of client who usually turned up at Martin's. Her hair was gray and beautifully styled, short with a bit of wave; her skin was lovely and unwrinkled. About sixty, trim, and well-dressed in a cream-colored linen skirt and silk shirt, wearing a gold chain and small gold earrings, she looked as if she could be the owner of the black Saab parked at the curb. It was as out of place here as she was. Martin had renovated a simple house, had torn down interior walls to make a dining room with six tables and six booths, and he cooked some of the best food to be found in Eugene, but Barbara doubted that the woman on the doorstep had ever driven through this neighborhood, much less considered eating here.

"Ms. Holloway, may I have a few minutes?" the woman asked.

It was ten minutes before five, and at five-thirty Martin liked to have the restaurant empty, in order for him and his wife Binnie to set the tables.

"Of course," Barbara said, moving aside. She took down her sign and motioned toward her table where Martin was picking up the carafe and cups. He paused a moment.

"Can I bring you something? Coffee, wine?"

Martin was big enough to fill a doorway and as black as night. A white beret was striking in contrast;

it seemed to glow. And he never offered wine to her clients. He had sized up this woman as rapidly as Barbara had done.

"No, thanks," the woman said, seating herself.

Then, as Martin walked back to the kitchen, she turned to Barbara. "I know it's late and I'll be as succinct as I can. My name is Louise Braniff. I'm in the music department at the U of O, and I give private piano lessons to a few students. Also, I'm a member of a society of women. We call ourselves the Crones' Club, but officially we're the Benevolent Ladies Club. We sponsor various causes that we consider worthy. Sometimes surgery, sometimes a scholarship, or helping someone get a start in business, various things. All directed at girls or women. We want to retain you."

"To do what?"

"Defend Carol Frederick, who is accused of murdering Joe Wenzel."

Barbara studied her more closely. "Murder suspect comes under your definition of worthy cause? I think you'd better start a bit further back."

"Of course. How we choose our recipients is a starting place, I imagine. When one of us learns of a particular instance where a gift of cash would change a life, we meet and discuss it and investigate the person we're considering, and if we all agree, then one of us is chosen to make the proper arrangements. In this instance we decided that I should approach you, since I was the one who proposed helping Carol Frederick originally."

She paused and gazed past Barbara as if gathering her thoughts, then continued. "One of my associates at the university told me about a young woman who was playing piano at a lounge here in town and insisted that I go hear her. Another member of our group and I went together. We had dinner in the adjoining restaurant and then sat in the lounge for most of one evening listening. She is a first-class pianist, gifted but untutored. She needs a bit of technical help. We took it up at our meeting and the other members arranged to go hear her play, and then we voted to assist her. What we proposed was to make it possible for her to go to Hamburg and study under the tutelage of Gustav Bremer. He is the master, and after a year under his guidance she could become a world-class pianist. I am convinced of that. I was chosen to make the arrangements, but before anything could be done, someone killed Joe Wenzel, and the following week, last week, she was arrested."

"Do you know her, anything about her? Or him? Wenzel?"

"No. None of us know her. Apparently she has been here in Eugene for no more than five or six weeks. I don't think any of our group ever met Joe Wenzel. I don't know whether she killed him, but that's beside the point. She needs the best defense possible and we agreed that you could provide it, not a public defender, who is overworked and understaffed. She, of course, has no money."

As Barbara continued to regard her thoughtfully, Louise Braniff opened her purse, withdrew a check and placed it on the table. "If you agree, there are certain conditions," she said.

"I thought there might be."

Louise Braniff nodded. "First, you won't try to find out who else is in our club. We prefer to remain anonymous. For tax purposes you are to give the Benevolent Ladies Club as the payer for your services. I am the only one you will ever contact, and then only if the retainer is not sufficient to cover your expenses and your fee. We understand that if she accepts a plea bargain, the expenses will be minimal, but if she continues to plead innocent and there is a full trial, the expenses will be much higher. In that case you will notify me and I will provide another cashier's check for whatever amount you name. And finally, Carol Frederick must never be told who her benefactors were, only that a group of people put together a defense fund for her."

"I see," Barbara said, although she didn't. "Why the secrecy? Why did you come here instead of using my real office? I assume you investigated me and know that I have an office."

"Yes, we know about your office. And some of us have followed your career for the past few years. We know about you. But my name is never to be associated with this any more than the names of any other members of our group. Not in your records, not in your files, nowhere. The only client you will have is Carol Frederick, and the Benevolent Ladies Club will be financially responsible. You won't report to me or anyone else except your client. We shall follow the case as it is reported in the newspapers, that's all."

Barbara glanced at the check then. Twenty-five thousand dollars. "I have to think about this," she said. "You must know how irregular it is, and for all I know you killed Joe Wenzel yourself, and in a fit of conscience you're trying to make amends to a wrongly accused woman." She spread her hands. "You do see my point."

"I do." Louise Braniff smiled. "And it's well taken. I have permission to give you one name for reference. Judge Barry Longner. But I warn you, that's all he will admit. We exist, and we help girls and women. You'll want my card, my address and phone number so you can verify my identity." She took a card from her purse and put it on the check.

"It will be her decision," Barbara said. "If she says no thanks, then what?"

"Send the check to that address, registered mail. That's all. If it isn't returned, we'll assume you've accepted our proposal and that you're working on this." She pushed back her chair. "But first, your word that you accept the conditions I outlined."

"No written receipt? No lawyer-client agreement? Not even made out to the Benevolent Ladies Club?"

"Just your word," Louise Braniff said. Her expression had remained almost bland, neutral, as if she were interested but not involved in the matter and now, for the first time, she leaned forward and watched Barbara intently.

After a moment Barbara nodded. "If she agrees and becomes my client, I'll honor your conditions."

Louise Braniff stood up, her expression once more that of an interested bystander. "Thank you, Ms. Holloway. Don't bother to see me out." She turned and walked to the door and left as Barbara remained by the table watching her.

Barbara sat down again wondering what Louise Braniff's stake in this case could possibly be when Martin came from the kitchen carrying two glasses of pale wine.

Barbara stirred herself. "Thanks, Martin, but she's gone."

"I know. I saw her leave. That's one classy lady. This is for you, and this one's for me. You look like you've walked into quicksand and haven't got a clue about how to get out."

Barbara took the glass he offered and sipped a very good chardonnay. "Martin, you're not only the world's greatest chef, you're also a very perceptive mind reader. That's exactly how I feel, as if I've blundered into quicksand."

**In a matter of seconds everything can go wrong...
And then there's no turning back.**

ALEX KAVA

**A line has been crossed.
Suddenly there's nothing left to lose.**

Melanie Starks and her seventeen-year-old son, Charlie, have been running
one con job or another for as long as she can remember. But Melanie is
getting sick of that life and wants out.

Then her brother, Jared, reappears in her life. There's something different
about Jared since his release from a life sentence for murder—a new,
dangerous edge. He has the perfect plan for a big score and he needs
Melanie's and Charlie's help. Deciding this will be the last job she ever
pulls, Melanie agrees to Jared's plan to rob a local Nebraska bank.

But then everything goes terribly wrong....

ONE FALSE MOVE

Available in August 2004 wherever books are sold.

**From the *USA TODAY* bestselling
author of *Getting Lucky***

Susan
Andersen

Were things getting
too hot to handle...?

When Victoria Hamilton's "no strings, no last names" vacation
fling resulted in a baby, she knew she had to begin a new life
far from her family's corrupting influence. Now her father has
been murdered, her half brother, Jared, is the prime suspect
and Tori has no choice but to return to Colorado Springs with
her six-year-old daughter. She'll do anything to prove Jared's
innocence. But confronting her past when she opens the door
to her new private investigator and comes face-to-face with
John "Rocket" Miglionni—the former marine who rocked her
world six years ago—sure isn't what she had in mind....

hot

& bothered

If you enjoyed what you just read,
then we've got an offer you can't resist!

Take 2 bestselling novels FREE!
Plus get a FREE surprise gift!

Clip this page and mail it to MIRA®

IN U.S.A.
3010 Walden Ave.
P.O. Box 1867
Buffalo, N.Y. 14240-1867

IN CANADA
P.O. Box 609
Fort Erie, Ontario
L2A 5X3

YES! Please send me 2 free MIRA® novels and my free surprise gift. After receiving them, if I don't wish to receive anymore, I can return the shipping statement marked cancel. If I don't cancel, I will receive 4 brand-new novels every month, before they're available in stores! In the U.S.A., bill me at the bargain price of $4.99 plus 25¢ shipping and handling per book and applicable sales tax, if any*. In Canada, bill me at the bargain price of $5.49 plus 25¢ shipping and handling per book and applicable taxes**. That's the complete price and a savings of over 20% off the cover prices—what a great deal! I understand that accepting the 2 free books and gift places me under no obligation ever to buy any books. I can always return a shipment and cancel at any time. Even if I never buy another The Best of the Best™ book, the 2 free books and gift are mine to keep forever.

185 MDN DZ7J
385 MDN DZ7K

Name	(PLEASE PRINT)	
Address	Apt.#	
City	State/Prov.	Zip/Postal Code

Not valid to current The Best of the Best™, Mira®, suspense and romance subscribers.

Want to try two free books from another series?
Call 1-800-873-8635 or visit www.morefreebooks.com.

* Terms and prices subject to change without notice. Sales tax applicable in N.Y.
** Canadian residents will be charged applicable provincial taxes and GST.
All orders subject to approval. Offer limited to one per household.
® and ™are registered trademarks owned and used by the trademark owner and or its licensee.

BOB04R   ©2004 Harlequin Enterprises Limited

MIRABooks.com

We've got the lowdown on your favorite author!

☆ Read an excerpt of your favorite author's newest book

☆ Check out her bio

☆ Talk to her in our Discussion Forums

☆ Read interviews, diaries, and more

☆ Find her current bestseller, and even her backlist titles

All this and more available at

www.MiraBooks.com

KATE WILHELM

66872	DEATH QUALIFIED	___ $5.99 U.S.	___ $6.99 CAN.
66846	THE DEEPEST WATER	___ $6.50 U.S.	___ $7.99 CAN.
66785	NO DEFENSE	___ $5.99 U.S.	___ $6.99 CAN.
66749	SKELETONS	___ $6.50 U.S.	___ $7.99 CAN.
66628	DEFENSE FOR THE DEVIL	___ $5.99 U.S.	___ $6.99 CAN.

(limited quantities available)

TOTAL AMOUNT	$_____
POSTAGE & HANDLING	$_____
($1.00 for one book; 50¢ for each additional)	
APPLICABLE TAXES*	$_____
TOTAL PAYABLE	$_____
(check or money order—please do not send cash)	

To order, complete this form and send it, along with a check or money order for the total above, payable to MIRA Books, to: **In the U.S.:** 3010 Walden Avenue, P.O. Box 9077, Buffalo, NY 14269-9077; **In Canada:** P.O. Box 636, Fort Erie, Ontario, L2A 5X3.

Name:_____
Address:_____ City:_____
State/Prov.:_____ Zip/Postal Code:_____
Account Number (if applicable):_____
075 CSAS

*New York residents remit applicable sales taxes.
Canadian residents remit applicable GST
and provincial taxes.

MIRA®

MKW0804BL